Praise for Judy Fong Bates and *Midnight at the Dragon Café*:

"Judy Fong Bates has created a novel that does what the very best fiction can do — take us into a world we could not have otherwise entered; put us among people we could not otherwise know."

— Shyam Selvadurai, author of *Cinnamon Gardens*

"An engaging contribution to our rich literature of immigrants."

—*The Toronto Star*

"Her prose is unornamented and exact, sometimes catching the light, other times transparent as glass to let us see into the Dragon Café . . . Her attention to physical detail is matched by compassionate understanding, which gives real weight to the telling of the submerged, drowning passion hidden in this household."

—*The National Post*

"A terrific page-turner of a first novel."

—*The Quill and Quire*

"Such a writing style, free of gilded and glorified language but full of the symbolism of action."

—*The Globe and Mail*

"That a writer of Judy Fong Bates's compassionate talent will add her voice to be heard, and will tell her stories with such insight and frankness, will add to our perceptions of what it is to be human."

—Wayson Choy, author of *Paper Shadows: A Memoir of a Past Lost and Found*

MIDNIGHT AT THE DRAGON CAFÉ

Also by Judy Fong Bates

China Dog: And Other Tales from a Chinese Laundry

MIDNIGHT AT THE DRAGON CAFÉ

JUDY FONG BATES

COUNTERPOINT
A MEMBER OF THE PERSEUS BOOKS GROUP

Published by Counterpoint,
A Member of the Perseus Books Group

Counterpoint books are available at special discounts for bulk purchases in the
United States by corporations, institutions, and other organizations.
For more information, please contact the Special Markets Department at the
Perseus Books Group, 11 Cambridge Center, Cambridge MA 02142,
or call (617) 252-5298 or (800) 255-1514, or e-mail
special.markets@perseusbooks.com.

First published in Canada by Mclelland & Stewart Ltd.
Canadian ISBN 0-7710-1098-2

First published in the United States by Counterpoint,
A Member of Perseus Books Group.
ISBN 1-58243-189-2 (pbk.)

Cataloging-in-publication data is available from the Library of Congress.

05 06 / 10 9 8 7 6 5 4 3 2 1

For
Michael

MIDNIGHT AT THE DRAGON CAFÉ

I HAVE KEPT ONLY three possessions from my childhood. Each one is a book. The first is a coil-bound sketch pad with a cover made of heavy cardboard, a muted olive green. The pages are filled with drawings – of trees and flowers, of animals and soft nudes, but also of fantastic creatures, some beautiful, some hideous, entwined and growing out of one another, out of eyes, bellies, tongues, mouths. As a child I found the drawings magical, yet they unsettled me, pulling me into a world I did not understand. When I look at them now, many years later, they disturb me in a different way; I am left feeling hollow and haunted.

The other two books are from China, handwritten with red cloth covers, bound with red string. One book is thick with pages of line drawings of Buddha-shaped faces, dotted with moles. A mole in a certain place on a cheek might be lucky, my mother once told me, but in the same place on the other cheek could spell a life of tragedy and pain. In the rows of faces, the noses, eyes, lips, and ears are drawn in different shapes. Long, fleshy earlobes mean longevity and wealth; thin lips mean poverty. Whenever Chinese visitors came to our restaurant, I would catch my mother secretly studying their faces. Once, there was a Chinese man who passed through our town and had supper with us. He kept trying to engage my mother in conversation, but she took an instant dislike to him. Afterwards she said, "*Syah how, sei gnun,* that's what he is. A serpent head with dung-filled eyes." His narrow eyes were shaped in an evil way, she told me, a bad person, not to be trusted. Later we found out the man was a notorious gambler and womanizer in Chinatown in Toronto. Sometimes her face readings were more direct. "That man, he has ears that are too small and thin. No matter how hard he works, he won't amount to anything." She once said to me about my grown-up brother, "The shape of his face and nose are strong. He will eventually be rich, but he will always have to work hard. His mouth is too full. He wants so much, yet nothing in the first half of his life will be easy."

The second book from China, though it looks similar on the outside, holds other secrets. It holds the story of my life, my destiny. Before leaving Hong Kong, my mother took me to a fortune teller to have my *I Ching* read and my fate revealed. I have no memory of what the fortune teller looked like, only of watching his long, slender hands lay out narrow sticks of different lengths. The smell of incense had filled the air. My mother paid a handsome price for the book. Each page was filled with black hand-brushed characters, on the front was a single column of elegant black calligraphy. The characters held such power and mystery, all the more so because I could not read them. When I touch the pages, I can almost sense the heat of the fortune teller's hand moving down the rice paper with the bamboo-handled brush in his fingers. As a child, I often found myself with the book upside down, turning the pages backwards; I had to remind myself to open it left to right, opposite to the way I opened books at school.

Whenever I asked my mother what was written inside, she seemed to hesitate. Her unwillingness made me uneasy. She told me that I would live in more than one country. She told me that until the age of thirteen, water would be my danger sign, that I was never to trust it. I would beg her for greater details about my future, but she would only shake her head and say there was nothing else in the book that mattered.

1957

Several months before my mother and I came to Canada, my father, Hing-Wun Chou, and his oldest friend, Doon-Yat Lim, bought the Dragon Café in the town of Irvine, not far from Toronto. They considered it a good buy, as it was already a Chinese restaurant, with woks in the kitchen and a rectangular sign with gold Chinese-style script above the front window. But most important for them, an enterprise in a town the size of Irvine cost less money than one in a bigger place. At the time I didn't realize that my father's business was typical of so many Chinese restaurants in small towns across Canada, often known as the local greasy spoon, every one of them a lonely family business isolated from the community it served.

While my mother and I were still in Hong Kong, we visited a tailor; he made each of us a woollen coat and several cotton dresses. But for my mother he also made a dark green travelling suit and a beautiful rose-coloured cheongsam. She packed our new clothes in a large brown leather suitcase, smoothing them carefully around bolts of material, folded sweaters, packages of medicinal herbs, small gifts for family, and our few personal belongings.

As I stood beside her in a long line to board the airplane, it was hard to believe that the beautiful woman in the *lo fon*–style suit and black high-heeled shoes was my mother. Until then, I had only seen her in cotton pyjama suits that fastened up the side or a light dress with a loose skirt. She had told me that we were going to a country called *Gun-ah-dye,* a land that was cold and covered with snow, a place where *lo fons* lived, a place where only English was spoken. She had pointed them out to me in the streets of Hong Kong. "They don't speak Chinese," she had said. "But soon you will learn English, and talk just like the *lo fons*. I am too old to learn, but you, Su-Jen, you will be just like them." I wondered what English sounded like. I didn't understand why it would be easy for me but difficult for my mother.

In the weeks before we left, she didn't seem excited about going to this new place, yet she took care to show me how to print the letters of the English alphabet, combining circles and sticks and half-circles. I traced the letters on the window of the airplane and remembered what she had told me about the missionaries, that when she was a child, they had taught her how to write the ABC's but not to read the words.

Whenever I looked out I saw clouds above and below and wondered if we were really moving through the sky. It seemed that our journey would never end.

My mother said that we were lucky my father already lived in Canada, otherwise the Communists would never have allowed us to leave China. She said that we were going to Canada because of me. There I would have a better life, I could go to school and our family would be together. But I knew if she had her way we would stay in China despite her fear of the Communists. Whenever I asked my mother who the Communists were, she was unable to explain in a way I understood; I only knew that in Canada, we would be safe from them.

The only thing about Canada that my mother seemed to look forward to was reuniting with Aunt Hai-Lan, her mother's youngest sister. Before the war, Hai-Lan had married Uncle Jong, who was from my father's village in Hoi Ping County. They had two sons before Jong returned to Canada. When the Japanese attacked, she and the other villagers fled and hid in the hills. My mother told me that she and Hai-Lan and Hai-Lan's sons were the only ones in her family who had survived the war. When it was over, they had found each other, and Hai-Lan had taken her in and cared for her. When my father returned to the village from Canada, she introduced him to my mother, and then left for Canada herself soon after my parents were married.

I stayed close to my mother after the airplane landed in Toronto, fearful of being lost in this crowd of strangers. We stood in a long line and waited for a *lo fon* man in a dark uniform to look at some papers that my mother thrust at him. She seemed nervous, even when the man smiled at me. The man finally gave back her papers and my mother quickly grabbed my hand and followed the crowd into another room. She was busy struggling with our bags when I saw a man and a woman rush toward us. They were a funny-looking couple – he was short and round while she was tall and thin with a head full of tight black curls. My mother looked up from her bags and held out her arms toward Aunt Hai-Lan. They embraced each other, laughing and crying at the same time. Afterwards Aunt Hai-Lan bent down and pressed me to her chest, speaking in our Four Counties dialect. Uncle Jong smiled and told me how grown up I looked for a six-year-old. He picked up our large brown suitcase, while Aunt Hai-Lan took the smaller one, chattering and hugging my mother with one arm. We walked through a large bluish-green room with narrow wooden benches. I saw a *lo fon* man pushing a broom and some *lo fon* women working behind a counter.

There were many *lo fon* men and women outside the building, waving and shouting in their strange language, some of them getting into cars lined along the road. My cheeks tingled with the cold. Uncle Jong led us to a taxi and spoke easily in English to the driver. I sat in the back seat, squeezed between my mother and her aunt; I leaned against my mother's arm. When I peeked up at the window, I saw only darkness.

Aunt Hai-Lan and Uncle Jong lived on D'Arcy Street in Chinatown, in the centre of Toronto. The first things Aunt Hai-Lan showed my mother were her refrigerator and electric stove. I didn't know anyone else who owned such luxuries, but Aunt Hai-Lan told us that in Canada all the *lo fons* had them in their homes and that most of them even owned cars. When I asked my mother if my father had a car, Uncle Jong laughed and said, "Only *lo fons.* We Chinese are too busy saving every penny we make. Your father would never spend that kind of money on himself. He's the only person who could make a monk look like a spendthrift. But now that you and your mother are here, Su-Jen, maybe things will be different."

While the adults sat in the kitchen and talked late into the night, I went to sleep in the sitting room on the couch that Aunt Hai-Lan folded down and covered with sheets and blankets. It wasn't quite flat, and when my mother came to bed, I kept rolling into her, into the long crease where the back and the seat of the sofa met. She tossed and turned for most of the night. At one point, I woke up and found myself alone on the couch. My mother was standing by the front window, gazing into the street below. I got up and stood beside her. She put her arm around me and together we looked at the strange landscape. The solid row of houses across the road was dark and there was not a person in sight. The street was coated with white. I had never seen snow before. It looked so smooth and even that I wanted to run out and touch it with my hands. I wondered if something was wrong with the trees, all those bony-looking branches without leaves. Everything was so still except for

Uncle Jong snoring in the next room on the other side of a heavy cloth curtain.

In the morning my mother put on one of her new dresses. Uncle Jong and Aunt Hai-Lan took us for dim sum at a restaurant down the street. The yards in front of the houses were still white, covered with snow. I bent over and scooped some up in my hand. It was cold and light. I tossed it in the air, surprised by the way it fell apart and fluttered to the ground.

Although the walk from their house was only a few blocks, my mother and I shivered in our thin wool coats in spite of the extra sweaters we wore underneath. She looked around at the grey sidewalks and the piles of snow. "It's so cold, how can you stand it?" she asked.

"I felt the same way," said Uncle Jong. "*Ay see gun*, it takes time, but you get used to it."

She pursed her lips. "I suppose you're right," she said, then added, "It's so quiet here. So few people on the street compared to Hong Kong." In Hong Kong my mother had always held my hand in a tight grip whenever we walked down the street. People pressed in so closely that we were both afraid of losing sight of each other and being separated.

"It gets more busy in the centre of Chinatown. But the cities in Canada are never as crowded as the ones back home," said Uncle Jong. "Here, there's plenty of space and room to breathe. Wait until you get to the small town, it's even quieter and not many people or stores. It's more like the village back in China, except much more modern, of course."

"And it's safe here," said Aunt Hai-Lan. "Not like in China, where we worried about bandits in the country and pickpockets in the city. Here, there are no bandits, not even beggars. *Eeii-yah!* Those ones in Hong Kong, with the gouged-out eyes and the bad smell. Makes me queasy just thinking about them."

I thought of the men we used to see, in their filthy, ragged clothing, some with missing limbs, and I was glad to be far away.

"*Mo sow,* you don't need to worry about beggars here, Su-Jen," said Uncle Jong. "There are no beggars in Canada. This is a safe country and a good place to grow up. When I came I was sixteen, too old to go to school, but not too old to learn English. You, though, are especially lucky to arrive so young."

The restaurant was on the second floor, above a Chinese grocery store. We followed Aunt Hai-Lan up the steps, with Uncle Jong coming behind. It seemed like a fancy place with tablecloths and Chinese waiters in jackets. The tables were filled with Chinese customers, and the air was loud with Chinese voices. I didn't see any *lo fons* in the restaurant, though I had seen some on the street, along with lots of Chinese people. Maybe my mother was wrong, maybe Canada wasn't full of *lo fons.*

Uncle Jong joked with the waiter and told him that my mother and I had just arrived from China. He ordered a lunch with food not unlike the sort of food we ate in Hong Kong, but my mother didn't seem hungry; she ate a shrimp and then a pork dumpling and sipped a few mouthfuls of tea. I looked around the restaurant, and it seemed to me that *Gun-ah-dye* wasn't all that different from Hong Kong, where my mother had wanted so badly to stay.

Before leaving on the train to Irvine, my mother changed back into her dark green suit. She gave Uncle Jong and Aunt Hai-Lan a package of ginseng and a set of ivory mah-jong tiles. "Lai-Jing," Aunt Hai-Lan said to her in a pleading voice, "you must not think so much about China. We couldn't have stayed, China is no longer the country we knew. Life here really is better. You must concentrate on Su-Jen. Give yourself some time, and soon things will improve. Now come and visit, don't spend all your time hiding in the small town."

Smiling with her lips together and a sad look in her eyes, my mother nodded and said, "I have to visit. You have the mah-jong set." They both laughed and Aunt Hai-Lan hugged her goodbye.

During the trip my mother barely spoke to me. I watched her play with the top button of her coat and thought about the man I was about to meet, my father, whose face I knew only from a small black-and-white photograph. At last my mother pulled me close to her and I nestled into her softness and warmth. I started to fall asleep, feeling her finger lightly circle the whorl of my ear.

My mother had shown the conductor a white envelope on which Uncle Jong had written the name of our town. When we left Toronto the sun was low on the horizon and the city's buildings had towered into the sky, but when we arrived in Irvine, it seemed the empty darkness would swallow us. My mother remarked to herself how quickly the day had become night. The conductor gestured to us and pointed at the door; my mother and I followed behind, hesitating at the steps. He took our suitcases off the train and placed them on the long platform that ran in front of a low-roofed, wooden building. Then he scooped me up and carried me down from the train. I started to laugh but stopped when I saw the anxious look on my mother's face.

In the dim light of the overhang, I saw an old man running toward us, his woollen peak cap pulled over his forehead, his brown, loose-fitting coat flopping up and down with each step. He stopped as he drew near, huffing out of breath. I noticed how the sleeves of the coat covered his hands. He touched my mother lightly on the arm and spoke in our dialect, "Lai-Jing, you are here, at last."

"Yes, Hing-Wun, we are here," she said, nodding and holding his gaze for a moment. "This is Su-Jen." Gently easing me from her side, she looked down at me, "Su-Jen, this is your *ba ba*."

My father knelt down and lifted me into his arms. I peeked over his shoulder and saw my mother staring at us, her face without expression, her eyes wet with tears. I looked up and saw stars against a dark, deep sky. Small puffs of mist escaped from my mouth. With his hand against my head, my father gently pressed my face against his shoulder. I felt the rough texture of wool chafing my cheek and breathed in the faint scent of cooking oil. The memory has remained as crisp as the air that night. Over time, my life in Hong Kong and in our village in China became distant, almost forgotten, with only flashes of clarity, rare memories of sleeping on a straw mat in the humid summer, or watching my mother close the wrought-iron accordion gates in front of our home.

My father carried our suitcases and we followed him onto the empty street to a taxi parked in front of the station. The light from the street lamps reflected off the snow. Everything around us was still and quiet.

My mother sniffed. "What is that strange smell?" she asked. There was a sour odour in the air.

"It must be the tanning factory," said my father, "where all the *lo fons* work. I barely notice it any more. It only seems strong when the weather gets hot."

My mother helped me into the back seat of the car while my father got in the front and spoke haltingly to the driver. The driver was quiet for a moment, then said something I did not understand. My father cleared his throat and spoke again. This time the driver nodded his head and started the car.

In Hong Kong, in the kitchen we had shared with two other families, my mother had bragged that her husband was a restaurant owner. She made it sound as if we only rented our small room in Hong Kong so we wouldn't waste money on such a short stay, especially when we would soon be leaving for something much bigger and better. I wondered if my father's business would be as large and fancy as the dim sum restaurant in Toronto.

The taxi stopped in front of a row of stores. My father got out and held the door open for us. My mother had barely stepped out of the car when she slipped on a patch of ice and fell. I called out *Mah* and scrambled after her. It happened so quickly that my father had no time to break the fall and could only help her back up. He apologized over and over, until my mother gestured for him to stop. She brushed herself off and took my hand. My father picked up our suitcases and we followed him in the dark toward a brightly lit building.

There was a man, half hidden by some large leafed plants, peering through the window. The moment he saw us, he rushed around a counter and unlocked the glass front door. He was the strangest-looking man I had ever seen. The bottom half of his face had completely collapsed, his cheeks and chin looked as if they had been sucked into a hole below his nose, yet the top half was normal with a head of white hair, thick as a rug, and a pair of wire-rimmed glasses perched on his nose. He grinned as we walked past, and I saw that he had no teeth. My mother smiled for the first time. My father introduced us to his friend, Doon-Yat *Bak*, Uncle Yat.

Uncle Yat looked down and said to me, "If you forget my name, just call me Toothless Uncle." I leaned into my mother and smiled back. I liked Uncle Yat right away.

My father told us that Uncle Yat operated the kitchen and that together they shared the business. He also told us that once the business was large enough, my brother, Lee-Kung, would leave his job in Owen Sound and join us at the Dragon Café. But right now there was only enough work for him and Uncle Yat.

As young men from neighbouring counties in China, my father and Uncle Yat had each paid a five-hundred-dollar head tax to the

Canadian government just before the start of the First World War, and together they had boarded the same boat. Although they both wore wire-rimmed glasses, dressed alike in white shirts with rolled-up sleeves and black pants shiny with wear, it was impossible to mistake one for the other. Uncle Yat had a broad face with sharp, sunken cheeks and a grin that made the outer corners of his eyes turn down and disappear into creases. He was the one person at the café who could make my mother smile. My father, on the other hand, had a long, narrow face with round, serious eyes, and wispy grey hair. It was a severe face, but whenever he spoke to me, his voice was gentle and his eyes were kind.

Along one side of the restaurant ran a long Formica lunch counter. I went to sit on one of the red vinyl stools, to see if it might spin around, but my mother gave me a warning glance. I knew I had to behave. Past the counter stood two tables, while along the opposite wall ran ten wooden booths that stretched all the way to the back.

My father smiled nervously as he led us through a swinging door to the kitchen. In the middle of the room was a square work station with a giant wooden chopping block at one corner. Built above the work area were open shelves with neat rows of stacked dishes. Along the wall, closest to the dining room, was a line of deep stainless-steel sinks attached to a long draining board with a garbage bucket tucked underneath. I noticed the leftover food that had been scraped into the pail and made a face until my mother pinched my arm. On the other side of the work station was a large stove with burners, a flat grill, a vat filled with hot oil, and rectangular metal baskets hooked over a bar. Beside it were more burners with two of the biggest woks I had ever seen sitting on top. Uncle Yat told us that he spent a lot of time making French fries and hamburgers. He laughed and said that the *lo fons* couldn't get enough fried food. My father warned me in a serious voice to stay away from the cooking area, especially the hot oil. I looked up and saw pots hanging from ceiling hooks near the stove. My father told us that they had closed the restaurant early because of our arrival and that Uncle Yat had just finished tidying up the kitchen and washing the floors. The smell of soap and grease mingled in the air.

Uncle Yat returned to the dining room while my father took us upstairs to get settled. A door opened off the kitchen into a cramped hall. At one end was the exit to a tiny backyard. My father tugged sharply at another door closer to us. It seemed heavy and stiff, as if too large for its frame. Later I would find that I had to use both hands to yank it open and then pull from the other side to close it. A steep wooden staircase started abruptly inside the door. It was dark and narrow. Each step served as a shelf for buckets and jars. My mother and I had to stand to the side with our backs pressed against the wall while my father squeezed our suitcases past us. He struggled up the stairs, stopping every few moments, turning his head to watch us wind our way carefully past the restaurant supplies. My hand never left the banister as we climbed up and up.

The landing at the top widened into a windowless foyer. It seemed that everywhere I looked there were boxes. One wall was stacked high with them and I could see the front room held even more. My father told us that the room at the end of the hall was ours, and beside it was Uncle Yat's. He opened the door to our room and pulled on a string that dangled from the ceiling. A single bare light bulb revealed a small space dominated by a massive wooden dresser with drawers that curved out like a belly. The mirror above it was splotchy with cracked silver lines, reflecting a watery image of the three of us, our heads too small and our bodies too wide. Against the wall behind us was a metal-framed double bed with a faded brown woollen blanket spread over the mattress. For the next three years I would sleep in the middle of that bed, a parent on either side.

Heaving the suitcases onto the mattress, my father then turned to the bureau and pulled out two large drawers and one small one. He tapped at the small drawer that remained closed. "That's enough space for me," he said. "You and Su-Jen can have the rest for your things." My parents stood awkwardly for a minute. "When you've finished putting your things away, come down," my father finally said. "Uncle Yat has made some hot sweet soup." He hesitated for a moment and added, "I know it's plain, but we have everything we need." My father touched my cheek, his fingers lingering a moment, then stepped slowly down the stairs.

My mother sat on the bed and looked around the room, her face pale. She let out a deep sigh and muttered under her breath, "This town is so quiet you can hear the dead." Covering her mouth with her hands, she started to weep, her shoulders shaking. I stared at her; the lump that had been sitting at the back of my throat since we left Hong Kong swelled until I began to cry too.

My mother folded her arms around me, pressing my face against her chest. She buried her face in my hair and we sobbed together.

We went downstairs sometime later to find my father and Uncle Yat waiting with a pot of red bean soup. They served us steaming bowls at the table, Uncle Yat nodding and smiling. "I added a little more sugar than usual," he said. "Your father said little girls like sweet things." Though my eyes felt swollen from crying, I smiled at Uncle Yat and devoured the delicious soup. But my mother couldn't eat, and swallowed only a few spoonfuls. We didn't stay long at the table. When my mother rose from her half-empty bowl and motioned to me to follow her, my father looked disappointed and said that we must be tired from all our travels. I saw his eyes search my mother's face as he told her not to worry, that we were home and finally together.

Upstairs we quickly changed into our nightclothes. My mother placed her skirt and jacket inside the suitcase, sliding it under the bed. She hung my dress on a hook behind the door.

She folded the covers back from the bed and lay on the side next to the wall. She told me to lie down beside her, and pulled the blankets over us. I was still awake when my father came upstairs. I watched him in the light from the hall as he prepared for bed. Unaware that I was peeking out from beneath the covers, he took off his shirt and trousers, then reached into his mouth and pulled out his false teeth. I gasped silently as the lower half of his face collapsed, making him look as if he were Uncle Yat's brother. He put his teeth in a glass of water on a stool beside the bed, removed his wire-rimmed glasses, and put on a round woollen cap. He lay down beside me in silence.

On that first night at the Dragon Café, I was like a wall in the middle of the double bed. On one side my mother turned away from me, muffled sobs and shudders running through her. On the other side my father lay rigid on his back.

My father showed my mother how to do her tasks around the restaurant: how to wash the glasses in the stainless-steel sinks behind the Formica lunch counter, making sure she added a capful of bleach to the rinse water; how to clear dirty dishes and to wipe the tables clean after customers left; how to fill the china coffee creamers each morning, to fill sugar and napkin dispensers, to make coffee and wash out the pots. He told her that in time she would be able to wait on tables and use the cash register. In the kitchen I watched her peel potatoes, dry dishes, and scrape leftover food off thick white china plates with the side of a metal fork. Within a week she seemed to know all her chores, silently performing them day after day.

❧

SOON AFTER MY MOTHER and I came to Irvine, my father registered me for school. He had told me that Canada was a good country, that the government cared about the people, that school was free and children had to go until they were sixteen, unlike China when he was a boy where only the rich could afford to stay in school. Something else seemed to prey on his mind. "You need a new name for school, Su-Jen, a Canadian name," he finally said. When he saw that I didn't understand, he crouched down, putting his arm around my shoulders. "The principal of the school said so. We must listen to him. Don't worry, you will always be Su-Jen inside. Later we'll go and see Hardware Store Uncle. He will help us." My father was talking about the man with the apron who sipped coffee at our lunch counter late in the morning.

Mr. Swackhammer was the tallest man I'd ever seen, with watery blue eyes and a thick thatch of pale yellow hair, and hands so massive that when he picked up a cup and saucer, they looked like something from a child's toy china set. My father made a point of introducing my mother and me, later telling us what a nice man he was, always willing to help.

Swackhammers' was only next door, but my mother made me put on my coat against the cold. When my father and I entered the store, Mr. Swackhammer was at the back, unpacking a box. He looked up and started to walk toward us while we waited at the front between the cash counter and a shelf stacked with pots and pans. He grinned at me, reached into his pocket, and gave me a candy. My father hesitated before he spoke, struggling with the foreign sounds, trying to make Mr. Swackhammer understand that I needed a Canadian name for school.

Mr. Swackhammer nodded and listened with an expression of deep concentration. When my father finished, he said, "Call your daughter *An-nee*, Annie, after Annie Oakley." His voice boomed in the quiet shop.

"Annee Oaklee?" asked my father. "Who is she?" Mr. Swackhammer bent over slightly to catch his words.

"She was a very famous person," said Mr. Swackhammer. "In a Wild West show. Knew how to shoot a gun. Bang! Bang!"

"Oh?" said my father politely.

"There's a movie of her. *Annie Get Your Gun.* Best movie I ever saw, starring Betty Hutton. Here, I'll write the name on a piece of paper." He took a stub of pencil from behind his ear and searched the nearby counter for paper. "A good name," he said, handing the scrap to my father. "A good name for your daughter."

At the restaurant, my father explained to me and my mother what Mr. Swackhammer had said. He made me practise saying my new name. "An-nee, An-nee . . . ," I repeated.

"Sounds like a Chinese name," my mother said.

My father wrote my new name and my Chinese one in alphabet letters on a clean sheet of paper. "Remember, *lo fons* put their family name last," he said. "Not like us. For us, the family name is so important, we put it first." I printed *Su-Jen Annie Chou* over and over, saying the name of each letter out loud. When I looked up and returned my mother's smile, she kissed the top of my head.

Several years later I saw a picture of Betty Hutton in her cowgirl regalia. It seemed strange, a small, dark Chinese girl named after someone so tall, so very blonde and blue-eyed like Mr. Swackhammer himself.

Alexander Chiddie Public School was the only elementary school in Irvine. It sat at the top of a hill like a hat perched on a head. Constructed only a few years before our arrival, it was a flat-roofed, red brick building with clear shiny windows, surrounded by parklike grounds. Flowing at the bottom of the hill was Willow Creek, a meandering stream with clumps of sumac growing up the bank and willow trees along the edge, their graceful branches bending over and grazing the water. Large elms, maples, and a few red pines dotted the hillside.

The school was named after Alexander Chiddie, the first principal in Irvine. Hanging in the foyer, under pictures of the Queen and Prince Philip, was his portrait, a dark oil painting with a heavy gilded frame. Although his lips pressed down and his head thrust out from a tight-fitting white collar, there was something unthreatening, almost welcoming about him. He seemed to offer everyone who entered his warning and blessing.

Both my parents walked me to school on my first day. My mother made me wear extra sweaters under my coat and put on the thick boots that my father had bought at Reids' Five and Dime, a pair of ugly, brown rubber overshoes that buckled up past the ankles. Unlike the wide streets of Chinatown where the sidewalks were cleared of snow, the sidewalks in Irvine had large drifts along the side spilling on to the road. I wanted to run up and down along the ridge of snow, but my father held my hand and I knew he would not let me play. We walked up Main Street and continued through town to the bridge that crossed Willow Creek below the school. My mother seemed to hesitate, and glanced nervously at me before stepping on the bridge. As we started on the asphalt path that wound up the hill on the other side, she stopped again and turned around to stare at the icy creek with its cracks of melting water.

"You must be careful by the river, Su-Jen. Always hold the rail when you are on the bridge," she admonished, pointing to the iron railing, the muscles in her face tense. "And don't go near the water. Su-Jen, are you listening?" I nodded my head solemnly, and knew she was thinking about my water fate.

My father said nothing, but carefully led me around some patches of ice on the path while my mother followed close behind. The trees on the hillside were bare against the grey sky.

We entered the building and my father took us down an empty hall. It seemed endless, with ceilings high above us. In the school office a woman was sitting behind a large desk. She smiled at my father and spoke loudly to him. A man in a suit came out of a smaller office and shook my father's hand; he nodded at my mother. Both my parents seemed to shrink as they looked at this man who was so friendly. In appearance he wasn't unlike the other *lo fons* who came into the Dragon Café, the ones my father and Uncle Yat joked about, their large noses, pale complexions, and watery eyes. It was strange to see my father so meek, almost fearful.

I had never gone to school before and I was excited to learn how to read and write and to speak English. If we had stayed in Hong Kong I would have started school earlier, but my mother said there was no point in paying for just a few months. The man explained to my father that it was Friday and school was almost over for the week, that it would be better if I came back on Monday and he would take me to my Grade One class. All the way home, my mother told me how lucky I was. She said it was the most beautiful school she had ever seen. My father told me that I would have to study hard and to respect all my teachers and obey the man who was the principal of the school.

That evening Reverend MacDougall, who drank coffee every morning at the counter with Mr. Swackhammer, suggested that his daughter, Jean, walk me to school so that my mother would not have to take time away from the restaurant. According to my father, because Jean and her family believed in Jesus Christ, I would be well looked after. He said we were lucky to live in a town with such good-hearted people. My mother answered in a flat voice and told us about the missionaries she had met in China. They had taught her about Jesus and the importance of being kind to others. She added with a slight smile, "As if they were they only ones who knew about kindness."

On Monday morning I dressed in my winter clothes and waited in the front booth with my mother while my father sat on a stool in front of the lunch counter. The restaurant would not open for another hour and I began to fidget in the quiet. I was eager for Jean to arrive. I had wanted to see my classroom on Friday and had been disappointed that I had to wait. When Jean knocked on the door, my father rushed over and unlocked it, stepping back to invite her in.

My mother and I were ready to greet Jean with a smile, but instead we stared at her face. It was sprinkled so thickly with orange freckles it would have been almost impossible to find a place with enough clear skin to prick a pin. Neither my mother nor I had ever seen someone with skin like that. With her mouth shaped in a small *o* of astonishment, my mother said bluntly, "*Mot su gwon?* Her skin, what's wrong with it? Does she have a disease?"

"No, no," my father said, hushing her, "nothing's wrong. Some *lo fons* are born like that."

At age ten, Jean was almost as tall as my mother. She stood ramrod straight, her fine red hair held back from her face with a headband. She seemed more like an adult than a child; I could not imagine her playing or being naughty. My mother looked at my father and nodded her approval. Jean took my hand and said goodbye loudly to my parents as we left.

Partway to school, Jean and I stopped at a white house and picked up another girl who seemed about the same age as me. She had her coat on and was waiting inside the door with her mother. I liked Jonette Dooley the moment Jean introduced us, the way she made a little wave with her hand and smiled shyly at me. Mrs. Dooley kissed Jonette goodbye, did up her own coat, and marched in the opposite direction toward the centre of town.

Jean was very serious about her duty. She always made us hold hands and stay just in front of her as we walked; she made us stop at each corner to look for cars, making exaggerated gestures when I didn't understand her instructions. Whenever we broke into a run, Jean would catch up and make us slow down. This game of chase always made Jonette and me burst into giggles, feeling like conspirators against our watchful guard. For all the months that Jean walked us to and from school, I never saw her run, chase other kids, or laugh with other girls.

Miss Hinckley, a young woman with a glossy brown ponytail and wavy bangs, was in charge of my Grade One class. Each day she clipped in her hair a velvet bow that matched her outfit. She had large hazel eyes with long lashes. But in spite of her pretty face, there was something about Miss Hinckley that made me cautious. It was the way she smiled, how her mouth stretched into a fearsome grin even when she was angry.

On that first morning I watched as the girls formed one line and the boys another outside the school doors. I followed them in and found myself in a long hall that echoed with teachers' voices. The principal had shown us which classroom was mine. I watched the other students and understood that I was to remove my boots in the hallway. Miss Hinckley found me and showed me how to place them with the backs against the wall next to the last pair, to hang my coat in a large closet at the back of the classroom on a special hook with my name printed underneath. She clasped my hand and led me to a desk in the front row next to the window. Immediately I knew that it was for me, that it would not have to be shared, unlike my mother's school in China where students had to sit together at a long table. I was relieved to see Jonette sitting in the desk across from me. I looked around at the other students, some watching me, some whispering to each other. I turned to Jonette and she smiled.

Miss Hinckley tapped her desk with a pointer and made a sharp sound; the class became quiet. She motioned for me to come and stand next to her at the front of the room. Then she spoke to everyone, but the only word I understood was *Ann-ee*, which she repeated several times.

The morning was a blur of new sounds and faces. Once the rest of the class seemed busy at their desks, Miss Hinckley again took me by the hand and led me around the room, pointing to the different cards that were taped to places like the floor, wall, door, window, and cupboard. She read out loud to me each word that was printed on the card. I looked at her nodding head and taut smile, and understood that she wanted me to repeat what she had said. I opened my mouth and tried to copy her, stumbling over the foreign sounds. Miss Hinckley would say the word again, and once more I would try. As I improved, Miss Hinckley's terrifying smile grew larger. I sighed with relief. She showed me a book with pictures of pink-skinned people, and taught me the words *Mother, Father, Dick, Jane, Sally,* and *Spot.*

At my desk I watched Jonette and did everything she did: stood when she stood, sat when she sat. I thought how beautiful the classroom was with its tidy rows of desks and pictures posted on the walls. I could hardly wait to tell my mother about my desk, the sink at the back of the room, the books, the pictures, the carpet that we sat on. She had told me about the school that she had gone to as a child in China and I knew from her descriptions that it paled in comparison to mine, a superior school built by *lo fons.* On Friday she had been impressed with the little that she saw. Today I would tell her everything in detail.

I had been in Miss Hinckley's class for slightly more than a week when she put a red star on a page of my printing and tacked it on the bulletin board along with other approved work. I was so glad I had practised with my mother at home. As soon as Jean dropped me off at the front door that day, I rushed into the kitchen and told everyone my news. Uncle Yat winked at me and my mother clapped her hands. My father told me that if we were still in China I would one day sit for the imperial examinations.

Each school day started with "God Save the Queen." Miss Hinckley would blow into a pitch pipe and we would all sing together. Then we would solemnly bow our heads, close our eyes, and recite the Lord's Prayer. Next, Miss Hinckley would announce in a clear voice, "Clean hands only, boys and girls. Clean hands only." We would sit down and place our hands with our fingers spread apart on top of our desks. Miss Hinckley always started at the bottom of my row. I would listen to the slow, rhythmic click of her high heels against the floor, growing more and more anxious as the clicking drew closer. I sat studying my fingers and palms for any traces of dirt I might have missed. When she stood beside me, I stiffened and held my breath, ready to turn my hands over for inspection on both sides. As soon as she nodded approval and moved on, I would start to breathe again. Once, she had found dirt under Harry Platt's fingernails and sent him to the washroom to scrub. When he returned, she examined his hands again. While my English was still poor, I understood that his washing hadn't been good enough. She dragged Harry to the sink at the back of the room and scoured his hands with a brush. He returned to his desk, trying to act as if he didn't care about what had happened; when Miss Hinckley turned her back, he stuck out his tongue at her. But when he thought no one was looking, I saw him wipe his eyes. I then vowed to obey all the rules of the class. As long as I did exactly what Miss Hinckley expected, as long as I kept my hands clean, I thought I would stay out of trouble.

It was cold with a fierce wind on the day that Miss Hinckley leaned some pictures along the ledge of the blackboard. One was of girl sitting in a large chair with a man looking inside her mouth, another of a boy brushing his teeth, another of children eating apples, and finally one of children eating candy. I could tell from the pictures that Miss Hinckley was teaching a lesson about caring for our teeth. The tone of her voice told me that apples were good and that candy was bad. Miss Hinckley then surprised me by asking me to stand in front of the class. I was even more confused when she asked Paul Conway to stand beside me. She asked Paul to open his mouth wide and gestured for me to peer inside. I saw a pink tongue surrounded by an arc of tiny pearly teeth. I was suddenly self-conscious of the brown, decaying baby teeth inside my mouth and I pressed my lips together. She gave Paul the picture with the apples and me the one with the candy. Miss Hinckley looked at me as she pointed at Paul's picture and nodded her head, then pointed at mine and wagged her finger. I wanted to return to my desk, but she hadn't yet told me I could, so I waited while she picked up a paper bag from her desk. While the whole class watched, she brought out a tube of toothpaste and a toothbrush. Her exaggerated gestures told me to put paste on the brush, and to clean my teeth. "Every morning, every night before bed, and after ever meal," she repeated several times. My cheeks felt hot and my eyes began to brim with tears. Everyone was giggling and whispering. I wanted to run away. No one else had teeth like mine. All the *lo fon* children had been to the teeth doctor and I felt ashamed that I had never seen one.

That evening I stared in a smooth corner of the mirror in the bedroom that I shared with my parents. I opened my mouth wide and examined my ugly, brown front teeth. I thought of those perfect white ones in Paul's mouth and hated him for having them. I felt angry with my mother for not having taken me to a dentist. I wanted to get rid of all those teeth. I stretched my lips over them and wondered what it would be like to be toothless, like Uncle Yat. I had approached my father and asked him why Uncle Yat never wore dentures. My father told me how at first his own dentures had made his gums bleed and caused him much pain, but he kept wearing them and eventually got used to them. But Uncle Yat wasn't able to stand it, so his teeth ended up in his suitcase. It was a terrible waste of money, my father said.

I wiggled each tooth and found two in the top and two in the bottom that were loose. Over the next few days, I secretly moved them back and forth, twisting and pulling, until three broke free. The remaining one was loose, but felt unwilling to come out. I began to lose heart. I complained to my parents, but they both told me not to worry, that it would eventually come out on its own. My mother said her baby teeth had been decayed and her grown-up teeth grew in just fine. She couldn't seem to understand my urgency. I tried to explain that the teacher had made me stand in front of the whole class and look inside Paul Conway's mouth, but she said that I was too sensitive, the teacher was just trying to be kind.

Uncle Yat was the only one who understood, if not my humiliation, at least my need to get rid of my brown tooth. He said to me, "In China if a tooth was loose you took a thread and tied one end around it, and the other end to the handle of an open door. Then somebody would shut the door fast. Before you knew it, your tooth was out." Somehow I knew he wasn't telling me everything. I thought about how much it would hurt and all the blood that would gush from the gaping hole. But mostly I thought about Uncle Yat and the way he looked with his toothless mouth. I wondered how many of his teeth had been yanked out by using a thread and the slam of a door. But in the end I convinced myself that there was no other way.

Uncle Yat found a spool of black thread. He doubled a long strand, tied one end around my tooth and the other around the knob of the door leading to the hallway. He chuckled and told me I wouldn't feel a thing. I held on to a stool and shut my eyes tight; my mother stood behind me and put her arms around my shoulders. Uncle Yat slammed the door, and suddenly it was over. He showed me my funny brown tooth dangling from the end of the thread. I pushed my tongue against the soft impression left by my tooth and tasted blood. We grinned our toothless grins at each other, and he rubbed the top of my head. My mother held me for a moment longer, and then gave me some warm salted water for rinsing. I showed my tooth to my father and he said that with Uncle Yat's help there was no need for a dentist. Uncle Yat laughed and said that he hadn't had a toothache for almost twenty years.

I was happy to be rid of my ugly baby teeth. I could hardly wait for my second teeth to grow in. I knew they would be straight and white. Never again would Miss Hinckley be able to make me stand in front of a class and stare inside an open mouth of perfect teeth.

Everyone in my class loved Miss Hinckley; we were too frightened to do otherwise. But after the incident with the teeth, I admitted to myself what I had always secretly known: I hated her. I imagined kicking her shins and scratching her face. But when those feelings of resentment rose inside me, I became overwhelmed not just with hatred but with shame. My father had told me many times about the teachings of Confucius, about the importance of obedience and respect, of always listening to those who were older and wiser. "Su-Jen," he had said to me, "at home, you must obey *Ba Ba, Mah Mah,* and Uncle Yat. And at school you must obey and respect your teacher." I knew that if I ever acted on my hatred for Miss Hinckley, I would be in deep trouble at school. And worse I would bring dishonour to my family. I remained quiet and polite.

MAIN STREET IN IRVINE was a treeless commercial street, with rows of two-storey buildings on either side, stores or offices on the first floor and apartments on the second. All the important stores were on Main. Swackhammers' Hardware, with a television in the window, was next door to the Dragon Café, and Reids' Five and Dime was across the road. There was a shoe store and a drugstore on the same block as the Five and Dime. Richards' Clothing Store was kitty-corner to us, and Bensons' Dairy Bar down the road served hamburgers, fried chicken, fish and chips, and other *lo fon* fare like western sandwiches. The other two corner buildings at our intersection were banks. Farther down, on the same side as our restaurant, was a ladies' clothing store and Mr. Gildner's Jewellery and Watch Repair. Tucked in between the large storefronts were offices for the town lawyer and real-estate agent, and smaller stores like Sniders', which sold candy, comics, and bus tickets to the nearby small city of Urquhart and to Toronto. At the far end of our street was the Roxy Theatre, which showed a children's feature every weekend. The street was never very busy, not even on Saturdays. It was a plain street, and even though most of the buildings were made of red brick, the feeling was grey.

The architecture in Irvine may have been indistinct, but there was one way in which the town was unique. Pock Mark Lee, the Chinese vendor who drove the travelling grocery truck for the China Trading Company in Toronto, joked to my parents that he knew he was getting close to Irvine by the smell. The stench from the tanning factory was always in the air. During the winter, it faded to a distant odour, but in the hot, humid afternoons of summer, the smell became so thick it seemed almost to coat the inside of my mouth.

There was an alley between the rear of the stores on Main

and the backyards of the houses on Frederick. When the days grew warm, I played in the alley, careful to avoid the *lo fons* who used it as a shortcut. Sometimes there were glass bottles left on the pavement. If they were broken, my mother swept up the shards. Whenever I tried to help she would snap at me, "Leave it. *Eii-yah!* You'll cut yourself," and she would hurry over with the broom. Her reaction confused me, acting as if I were in grave danger.

I always liked our location on the corner of Main and Elm Streets. There was a fire escape outside the bedroom I shared with my parents. On either end of the platform were windows, one looking into our room and the other into Uncle Yat's. But our room also had a door opening onto it. In my mind this meant the fire escape belonged to us more than Uncle Yat. For the first few summers in Irvine, my mother and I would sit on the metal landing and fan each other during the hot summer nights. Uncle Yat sometimes poked his head out his window to check the weather. Later when my brother, Lee-Kung, arrived, he would climb out through his window onto the fire escape after the restaurant had closed and sit with his back against the wall smoking his Players cigarettes.

When I stood on the fire escape, I could look straight down beneath me to my mother's tangled garden. Before going to bed I sometimes curled into a ball and spied between the black wrought-iron bars on the people who cut through the alley below, sometimes I would even see couples stopping to kiss and then disappear into the lanes between the buildings. During the day I stood on my tiptoes so I could see across the alley over the thick green hedge into the leafy backyards of the mysterious *lo fons*: tidy flower beds, grassy lawns, swings and teeter-totters; for me, such things were like places in a faraway land, so unlike anything I had known. But whenever I was in the alley and tried to separate the tangle of branches to catch a closer glimpse of what lay on the other side, I ended up with scratches, fine white lines on my arms.

It was a Saturday, not long after I had started school, that Jonette Dooley and her mother came into the Dragon Café. Only Jonette's eyes were visible above a thick scarf wrapped over her nose. She was wearing her favourite hat, made of white wool and knitted in a pattern of puckers, which she said looked like a bowl of porridge. We giggled every morning on the way to school when its massive pompom would bob up and down as she walked, even faster if she ran.

Mrs. Dooley was a short woman, barely five feet tall, but she was as wide as she was high. She reminded me of a human spinning top, broad at the middle, small at the top and bottom, her tiny, fur-trimmed boots a precarious base. As she stood just inside the doorway of the restaurant, her eyes darted about the room. Not many women came into the restaurant on their own. Our customers were mostly teenagers and tired, dusty-looking men who ate alone.

My father was standing behind the glass cabinet as a man paid his bill. On top of the cabinet was a cash register with a handle that he sometimes let me pull down, making a loud ring as the drawer banged open. My father gave the man some change, then turned to Mrs. Dooley, an enquiring look on his face. He reached over the counter and patted the pompom on Jonette's hat. I left the back booth where I had been drawing pictures to come and stand beside my father. Jonette pulled her scarf away from her face and grinned at me.

Mrs. Dooley said, "Bake shop, bake shop" over and over, tapping her chest.

Then she pointed in the direction of their store and my father nodded and answered, "Ah-h-h."

Gesturing to me and Jonette, Mrs. Dooley pointed again in the same direction, saying several times over, "Annie, Jonette. Play together, play together."

I figured out before my father why she and Jonette were in the restaurant. "That girl is in my class." I said to him. "She walks to school every day with me and Jean. She's asking me to come and play with her."

My mother, who had been watching us over her shoulder as she rinsed glasses, dried her hands on a tea towel and turned around. She asked, "*Hoo mut-ah?* What does she want?" After my father translated Mrs. Dooley's invitation into Chinese, she nodded and said, "*Hola, hola,* good, good." Then she muttered under her breath, "How fat, shaped like a winter melon." When I giggled, Jonette giggled in return, not knowing the reason for my laughter.

Mrs. Dooley's eyes went back and forth between my parents as they spoke to each other in Chinese. My father nodded and spoke in English, "Ah-h-h, okay, okay, good, good," he said.

Then he held up his wrist and touched his watch, "Come home, four o'clock." He held up four fingers, emphasizing his words.

I put on my leggings, coat, hat, mittens, and rubber boots as fast as I could and skipped out the door with Jonette after her mother. We walked past the restaurant window, and I saw my mother watching through the branches of the jade plants. Jonette held my mittened hand and grinned. She made a little wave with her other hand and I saw that her mitten was knitted into three sections to make a puppet. The thumb and baby finger formed the arms, and the middle part had a face with blue eyes, red lips, and two yellow braids, made from other pieces of wool. When Jonette made her puppet clap, I laughed. She took off one of her mittens, and we exchanged, following Jonette's mother along Main Street for a block, then turning down Water Street to the bakery.

I loved everything about Dooleys' Bakery. The kitchen at the Dragon Café smelled of the oil that splattered from the stir-frying of chop sueys and chow meins and from the deep-frying of fish and chips. Even with the exhaust fan on most of the day, the air at the restaurant seemed heavy with grease, soaking into our clothes, hair, and skin. But the aroma that wafted from the ovens at the bakery was mouth-watering, sugary, comforting, dry.

The work space behind the store was a large, brightly lit room with high ceilings and long tables and huge mixing bowls big enough for me to hide in. On the floor at the end of one table was a giant-sized mixer with a round tub that came up to my chest. I would stare, mesmerized by the movement of two humming electric beaters, each thicker than a man's fist, churning batter for countless cookies and cakes. Along the entire back wall ran a row of ovens above a coal furnace that blazed red hot. Jonette's father placed trays of cookie dough, pans of cake batter, and loaves of bread on long wooden paddles and fed them into each of the ovens.

Mr. Dooley dressed in white cotton trousers, an undershirt, and a baker's hat, and whistled to songs on the radio as he worked. Every so often he would break out singing, making Jonette and me laugh. He was tall and skinny, with quick-moving hands. After the cakes were baked, cooled, and taken out of their tins, he would place each one on a round platform attached to a rotating stand; wielding a thin steel spatula, he would smooth the mound of icing that had been spooned on top. Next he would fill a white V-shaped bag with more icing and poise the tip over the cake, squeezing out frilly edges and flowers. There were cupcakes sprinkled with shredded coconut and others filled with lemon curd and dusted with icing sugar. At the restaurant, Uncle Yat made only three kinds of pies: apple, raisin, and cherry. I sometimes helped him scrape the fillings out of cans. Compared to Mr. Dooley's creations, they seemed so dull with their beige crusts. There were no surprises inside, no sweet icings, no dustings of sugar powder.

Jonette's mother operated the bread slicer. She made us stand with our hands behind our back when we came near. The machine had many vertical blades that shook like a row of sawing teeth. With one motion the loaves were forced through the blades, then caught in a paper bag.

Above the bread slicer, Mrs. Dooley had put up a picture of a beautiful girl dressed in a sparkly costume with a skirt that flared out in mid-twirl. I thought she was the winner of a beauty contest, but Mrs. Dooley explained to me that she was Barbara Ann Scott and had won the gold medal in figure skating in the Olympics before Jonette and I were born. She found pictures of other athletes and wrote the word *Olympics* on the back of an envelope. When I showed it to my father, he said, "The *lo fons* have a big contest. They run and jump, things like that, and give prizes to the winners."

Jonette took me out behind the bakery, where she twirled and jumped and struck different poses, pretending to figure skate. We competed to see who could leap the highest. On the asphalt of her father's parking lot, we skated and spun and pretended to be Barbara Ann Scott.

For the rest of our year in Grade One, Jonette and I played together almost every day. Whenever she visited us at the café, my mother would say, "She's a good, obedient girl. Just look at her with her small smile and not talking too much." Sometimes we sat in the back booth of the restaurant and drew pictures, or played in the alley behind our building once the weather turned warm. If my father gave us Cokes and bags of chips as a treat, Jonette smiled her "small smile" and always said thank you. But most days after school and on Saturdays, we played in her father's work room at the bakery. On Sundays, Mrs. Dooley took Jonette and me to church, both of us wearing our best dresses and matching white gloves. Mrs. Dooley once asked if my mother would like to join us. When I told my mother, she said Mrs.

Dooley was kind. She told me that Aunt Hai-Lan went to church every Sunday morning and that if we lived in Toronto she would go with her and believe. It was all right for me to worship and believe, she said, but for her there was no point. In Irvine, she would be in a room full of *lo fons,* unable to understand a single word.

For the first few weeks of the summer after Grade One, Jonette and I were together every day. Then in the middle of July, Mr. Dooley closed the shop for two weeks and took his family on a holiday. Jonette had been telling me about the Bay of Fundy in New Brunswick, where the tides were higher than their store and where going down a special magnetic hill made you feel as if you were going up. Mrs. Dooley explained to me several times what tides were, but I never really understood, beyond the fact that they had something to do with water and the moon.

My mother only added to my confusion. On summer nights we often stood on the fire escape outside the bedroom and gazed at the moon in the sky. "When I was born, there was too much moon in my fortune," she once said. "With you, though, there's too much water." She turned to me and said seriously, "Remember, Su-Jen, that water is your danger sign. You must always be careful when you are near." She mused about lunar phases that were good and ones that were bad, usually in relation to how she felt. To her the moon was a magical source of good and evil. But unlike Mrs. Dooley, my mother never said that it could move water from one place to another. It didn't seem to matter whether

I was spoken to in English or Chinese. The more I was told, it seemed the less I understood.

The Dooleys had been gone for several days and without Jonette the mornings and afternoons felt endless. Earlier I had watched my father fill sugar dispensers and helped my mother dry cutlery. I now sat in the back booth colouring pictures. The day before I had discovered *The Howdy Doody Show* on the television displayed in the window of Mr. Swackhammer's store. It was the only thing I had to look forward to.

Abandoning my drawings, I went and stood outside Swackhammers' window. At four o'clock, the Indian head disappeared from the television screen and *Howdy Doody* came on. I loved the antics of the marionette and Clarabelle the Clown. I was so busy laughing at the tricks they played on the grown-ups in the show I didn't notice a bunch of big kids surround me. They jostled for a view of the tv, scaring me with their shouting and elbowing. Two of them were eating ice-cream cones and one had a ring of chocolate around his mouth. A dark-haired girl with eyes blue-green like marbles towered above me. "Out of my way, chink," she sneered and pushed me down onto the sidewalk. I tried to get up, but she shoved me again. She stood over me, her hands in fists at her sides. She jeered over her shoulder at her friends, making them laugh. My English was now much better, but I was so shocked by what had happened that her words became meaningless sounds. My face burned with shame and my hands with scrapes from falling. I ran home in confusion and tears.

My mother was looking out the restaurant window as I returned. "What happened?" she demanded. "Those *sei gew doys*, dead ghost kids, what were they doing to you?"

I quickly walked past several booths filled with customers, keeping my head down and hiding my tears. Frown lines furrowed in her forehead. I didn't want to tell her about what had happened, about my shame and humiliation. There was nothing she could have done.

That evening while my father relaxed with the Chinese newspaper in a quiet moment after supper, my mother took my hand and together we approached him. Looking at the floor rather than at my father, she quietly said, "Su-Jen should have a tricycle. She can ride in the alley behind the restaurant." I looked up at my mother in surprise.

Without glancing up, my father shook his head and said, "They cost too much. For only a toy."

My mother was about to say something but seemed to change her mind. She gestured at the back booth and told me to go play with my crayons. Pretending to draw, I watched her point in the direction of Swackhammers' with one hand and fidget with the collar of her dress with the other. My father stopped his reading and stared at her. An instant later, he was sitting across from me. He put his hand on my shoulder and said, "Su-Jen, tomorrow we will go and buy a tricycle. You will not play on the street any more." I saw my mother still standing at the counter, smiling at me. Sliding out from the bench, I threw my arms around my father, then ran to my mother. She wrapped her arms around me and let out a long sigh.

It seemed lunch that day would never end, but once my father finished clearing and wiping the last table, we went to Swackhammers'. At the back of the store was a row of shiny new tricycles to choose from, some with baskets, others with streamers on the handlebars. My father smiled and gave me permission to choose my favourite. I sat on each one and compared the colour and the ribbons endlessly. It was the first new toy that I could remember being purchased for me. Finally I picked a red tricycle with the gold letters ccm on the steering column. My father carried it around the side of the Dragon Café to the alley, while I rushed into the restaurant, almost colliding with my mother, who was carrying a cup of coffee to a customer in a booth. "*Fi loy*, hurry, come and see," I called and ran through the kitchen into the backyard, where my father was waiting. My mother and Uncle Yat followed behind. I climbed on the seat and placed my feet on the pedals, my hands on the handlebars, expecting the wheels to move on their own. My father held me by the shoulders and pushed me down the alley. I watched my knees pump up and down, the cracked asphalt blurred under the speeding wheels. "Now you do it," he said.

My feet rested on the pedals, but nothing happened. "I can't," I cried.

"*Mo yung!* Useless!" Shaking his head but smiling, he showed me how to push down on one foot, then the other, propelling myself farther along the alley, riding over the cracks and the tufts of grass that grew in between. The grown-ups clapped and cheered at my efforts, then went back into the restaurant, leaving me on my own. I was concentrating so hard on pushing the pedals that I didn't see the girl with the mean marble eyes standing in the alley. She stepped in front of me and blocked my way.

"Hey, chink, where'd you get the bike?" she said. "Did you steal it?"

I tried to ride past her, but she grabbed the handlebars and thrust her face in front of mine, narrowing her eyes as she taunted, "Get off that bike before I push you off." I felt her hot, bubblegum breath on my face. I refused to let go and tightened my grip, but I was no match. She knocked me off my seat, then climbed on the tricycle and pedalled away. I got up and ran into the restaurant, calling my mother. When we came out, the girl was gone. My tricycle was lying on its side in the alley.

The next afternoon, my mother worked behind the restaurant in her small garden while I played. She stood up from a deep squat in the garden beds and watched me ride my tricycle several times up and down the alley. "*Ho lek,* very smart," she called out. I expected my mother to continue watching me, instead she returned to her garden. As I rode my bike back up the alley, the girl again appeared, blocking the road. She grabbed the handlebars and shouted at me to get off. This time I was prepared. I clenched my fists around my handlebars, took a deep breath, and kicked her with all my might. She yelped and let go and I tried to get away. But she grabbed my arm and dragged me off my tricycle. I fell on the asphalt, grazing my leg on some loose pebbles. She rode off, her knees jutting out, her body overwhelming the little bike. I got up and ran after her, crying out. My mother must have heard the commotion. She dashed up the alley, shouting at the girl, "*Nay sey gwei nah,* you dead ghost hag." Her bun had loosened and her hair was wild around her face. My mother caught up with the girl at the end of the alley, where she could ride no farther. With one hand, she grasped the handlebars and glared at the girl, hissing at her in Chinese. I had never seen my mother so fierce. The girl stumbled off the bike and backed away, her mouth gaping. She turned and ran, disappearing between the buildings. My mother gently looked at my scrapes and bruises. She put her arm around me, and together we wheeled my tricycle into our little patch of yard.

The girl did not come back to the alley again. When I returned to school in September and saw her in a crowd of big kids, my heart started to pound, but she never bothered with me. The way she looked past me, it was as if I were invisible. There wasn't even a flicker of recognition.

It's been a long time since I've thought about that girl; even now I can conjure up her face, those eyes, how the word *chink* shot from her lips, piercing me like an arrow. But with it there is my mother's fierce defence of me and the soft weight of her arm across my shoulders: one of the last moments in my childhood when my mother made everything right.

❧

AS A YOUNG CHILD I never really thought about my parents' lives in Irvine, how small their world must have seemed, never extending beyond the Dragon Café. Every day my parents did the same jobs in the restaurant. I watched the same customers come for meals, for morning coffee, for afternoon Coke and French fries. Fifteen minutes after the whistle blew at the tanning factory the bachelor diners would start coming into the Dragon Café for supper. Every other weekend my father and Uncle Yat counted on extra business because of payday at the factory. They looked forward to visits from Pock Mark Lee with his grocery truck, buying ingredients from him for the Chinese meals that we ate each day. My parents continued to read the Chinese newspaper that came in the mail and to talk about the Communists in China. The only excitement during those years was an overnight visit from my brother. Father had seemed happy to see him, but all through the visit he had worried out loud that Lee-Kung was losing money by taking an extra day off work. He had nagged about it so much that my brother had become angry and left early.

In that time, it also seemed to me my parents' appearances didn't change. My mother wore the flower-print dresses that she made herself and my father wore his black pants and white shirts with rolled-up sleeves. I must have been blind to any new lines on their faces. In the evenings my father told me stories from China about emperors, scholars, daring women, and great beauties. My mother complained about him forever talking about ancient things like Confucius, and the building of the Great Wall in China. She once said to me, "It's all right the first time you hear it, but then again and again the same stories. I don't want to hear them any more. You'll get sick of it. You'll see." I never shared her opinion, though. I never tired of listening to my father. I liked the way his wire-rimmed glasses would slide down his nose, his voice becoming like a singsong. I didn't care that she thought he was old-fashioned. For my parents one day was like the next. They settled into an uneasy and distant relationship with each other. Their love, their tenderness, they gave to me.

My life, on the other hand, was changing. I became taller and bigger, my second teeth grew in white and straight. At school I began to learn about my adopted country. I spoke English like a native, without a trace of an accent. I played, thought, and dreamed in the language of the *lo fons*. A few years later and I would no longer remember a time when I didn't speak their words and read their books. But my father and Uncle Yat still spoke the same halting English. My mother spoke only a few words. I began to translate conversations they had with the *lo fon* customers, switching between English and Chinese. Whenever I stepped outside the restaurant it seemed I was entering a world unknown to my family: school, church, friends' houses, the town beyond Main Street. I found it hard to imagine a year without winter any more, a home other than Irvine.

For my mother, though, home would always be China. In Irvine she lived among strangers, unable to speak their language.

Whenever she talked about happy times, they were during her childhood in that distant land. A wistful smile would soften her face as she told me about sleeping and playing with her sister in the attic above her parents' bedroom. She once showed me a piece of jade-green silk cloth that was frayed and worn around the edge. In the centre was a white lotus floating in varying shades of blue water, the embroidery so fine that when I held it at arm's length the petals looked real. I had been helping her store away my summer clothes in the brown leather suitcase from Hong Kong when I noticed a piece of shiny material in the corner and asked her what it was. She took it out and spread it on her lap. "My mother embroidered this herself. I was going to have it made into a cushion, but then my life changed and over here there seems to be no place for lovely things. It's all I have that reminds me of her," she said. "Maybe, Su-Jen, one day you will do something with it." I admired the cloth some more, then she carefully folded it and stored it back in her suitcase.

There was so little left from her old life. She said it was so long ago that sometimes it felt as if it had never happened. But she described her life with such clarity and vividness that I knew all those memories lived on inside her. There was so little in this new country that gave her pleasure. The good things she found were related in some way to China: an aria from a Chinese opera, a letter from a relative back home or from Aunt Hai-Lan in Toronto, written in Chinese, a familiar-looking script that I couldn't read and had nothing to do with my life in Canada.

There were times when I felt guilty about my own happiness in Irvine. We had come to Canada because of me, but I was the only one who had found a home. I reminded myself many times that I must honour my family and what they had done for me, that I must be *em jee seng,* not talk too much, be obedient, and not cause trouble, work hard at school.

Every Sunday my mother looked forward to the early closing. At eight o'clock, Father would lock the front door, bring out our Seabreeze record player, and put on a Chinese opera. Uncle Yat would prop open the door to the kitchen. The music would fill the air and comfort them as they swept the floor, filled sugar dispensers, washed ashtrays, or dried dishes. When my mother heard the long, drawn-out notes sung in a minor key accompanied by Chinese string instruments and the clash of cymbals, the muscles in her jaw loosened and she slowly came alive in a way that she never was during the rest of the week. The furrows in Father's brow softened.

While I found the music grating to my ears, and preferred the songs I learned at school, I looked forward to this moment when my parents seemed to relax and my mother's sadness lifted.

Hung Sing Nu was my mother's favourite singer. Her voice had a melancholy quality that appealed to her. She told me that Hung Sing Nu had recently left Hong Kong to visit mainland China, but the Communist government would not allow her to return to Hong Kong to pursue her career. She was like a captured bird, forced to make propaganda movies. In some way my mother must have identified with Hung Sing Nu, with the invisible cage that was now her life. My mother once showed me a picture of the singer in one of her magazines. I examined it for a moment and told my mother that she was even more beautiful. But she only shook her head sadly. "It does not matter, Su-Jen," she said. "Being stuck in this town my life would be no worse if I were ugly."

My parents listened to many operas, but their favourite was the *White Snake Goddess.* They found common ground in this piece of music, both complaining about the story in the opera, how it was unlike the folk tale they had known as children. My mother told me the one she knew best. It was about a young scholar who was wandering through a market and noticed inside a cage an exquisite white snake, unusual because she was weeping. The young scholar felt such pity for the snake that he bought her and released her. Whenever my mother told me this story, it was the image of the beautiful caged creature with tears in her eyes that remained in my mind. With powers of magic, the snake transformed herself into a young woman, whom the scholar fell in love with and married. For a while they lived happily, having a son together, until an evil monk exposed her true serpentine form. Both using their magical powers, the monk and the White Snake Goddess fought a duel. But the sorcery of the monk was stronger than that of the White Snake, so he defeated her and separated her from her husband and son, imprisoning her beneath the Thunder Peak Pagoda. Although the story ended happily when the son grew into a man and finally freed his mother from the spell of the monk, it was the aria the White Snake sang during her imprisonment that my mother liked the most. The high operatic notes, accompanied by the sad strains of the erhu, seemed to envelope her into a world that was her own. Entranced by the beauty of the music, my mother often sat next to the record player, her eyes closed and quietly weeping, as if she herself were the White Snake Goddess, trapped beneath the Thunder Peak Pagoda, lamenting her lost love.

AT SCHOOL JONETTE AND I played only with each other, rarely allowing a third person into our games. On Sundays the Dooleys always invited me to join their midday meal after we went to church. Mrs. Dooley made food unlike anything I had at home: roast beef, mashed potatoes, and boiled peas, eaten with a knife and a fork. My father carried dishes like that to the *lo fon* customers, but we never ate them ourselves.

Jonette and I bought comic books together at Sniders' with our weekly allowances and looked at the toys in Reids' Five and Dime. In the summer, without my mother knowing, we played barefoot in the shallow part of Willow Creek, leaping from rock to rock and catching crayfish and minnows. It seemed whatever our disagreements we would remain true to each other. But in the spring of Grade Four, Debbie MacLean entered my life and, in one brief moment, shifted my understanding of the world. My friendship with Jonette ended and I caught a glimpse of how others saw me.

Debbie's family had moved to a house in the new suburb at the edge of Irvine. She enrolled at Alexander Chiddie and joined my class. Mrs. MacLean drove Debbie to school in a shiny red convertible, dropping her off each morning at the bridge that crossed Willow Creek. Her father was a mechanic and had bought the local gas station and garage. It was obvious they had a lot of money. All the kids were convinced that they were the richest family in Irvine, even richer than the Beestons.

Once, as I was leaving Sunday school, I had heard some of the women in the neighbourhood call Mr. Beeston "Old Money Bags," saying that he had more money than anybody else in town. Beestons' tanning factory may have been responsible for the sour smell in the air that came from processing animal hides, but it was also responsible for almost every job in town. Every Christmas the Beestons held a party in the school auditorium. The children whose parents worked at the factory were invited, missing an afternoon of school and returning to class with orange moustaches and clutching a doll or a truck. Still, it was hard to believe that the Beestons were richer than the MacLeans. Hilary Beeston, the granddaughter, who was in my class, came to school in a navy blue wool tunic and a white shirt, or a green-and-blue plaid kilt with a navy sweater. Her plain leather oxfords looked dull and uninteresting next to Debbie's shiny black patent shoes with gold buckles. And Hilary never brought new toys to show off around the schoolyard.

Debbie told us that she had a pink princess telephone in her bedroom. I had never been to her house, much less her bedroom, but in my mind's eye I saw Debbie chatting on the pink princess telephone, propped up by fluffy pink satin pillows on a bed covered with a pink satin bedspread with matching pink satin curtains on the window. I saw Debbie smiling into her pink telephone, her finger twirling a lock of golden hair. I suppose the only thing I knew for sure was that her bedroom wasn't like mine. I knew that she didn't have to sleep in the same bed with her parents in a room upstairs from a restaurant, that she lived in a real house with a living room and a dining room. Debbie's home, I was sure, would be even fancier than Jonette's. The first time I had visited Jonette's house, I had known that I would never allow anyone from town to see the second floor of the Dragon Café.

I often wondered what it would be like to be Debbie, to have soft blonde curls that floated like a cloud around a lightly freckled face with a delicate upturned nose, to come to school so often in new clothes. But more than anything, I wondered what it would be like to be the centre of attention. The boys in my class were all secretly in love with Debbie. You could tell by the way they teased her, pulling her hair and chasing her without ever catching her. In the schoolyard I watched the boys from the corner of my eye, but they never seemed to notice me.

Debbie was the first girl to bring a Barbie to school. Everyone had seen pictures in magazines of this doll with the body of a woman. All the girls at school talked about her, and even the Grades Seven and Eight girls wanted one. The day Debbie brought her to school, we clustered around and watched as she undressed what looked like a miniature pink plastic manikin to reveal a pinched waist and two breasts jutting out from her chest.

Someone used the word *tits* and we all giggled. Every recess Debbie chose someone new to help change Barbie into yet another outfit, barking orders while the chosen person fumbled with the tiny hooks and snaps. *Watch what you're doing. You almost yanked her arm off. Not that skirt, stupid, the other one. Give her back to me.* I winced when I heard Debbie boss those girls in such a mean voice, but at the same time I knew, deep down, I wanted to be a part of that inner circle. I would not refuse, if given the chance.

Mrs. Dooley said the snowfall that year had been unusually heavy. By April, with the rain and the melting snow, the creek at the bottom of the school hill had changed from a wide, flat ribbon of ice to a raging torrent. Every day the principal's voice boomed over the P.A. system warning us to stay away from Willow Creek.

But the students didn't obey him – the excitement of the creek was impossible to resist. Jonette and I stopped on the bridge to join some kids who leaned over the iron railing to watch the water rush underneath. The last of the ice had melted and all week the water seemed to have gathered force. Like a living creature, Willow Creek swelled before my eyes, daily growing deeper and stronger, rushing to empty itself into the mouth of Irvine Lake. Frozen and asleep in the winter, it became full of menacing rage in the spring. Last year one of the McFadyen boys had drowned while playing on the soggy bank. They found him face down with his head wedged between two rocks. I told myself that he had been pulled in and swept away by accident, that there was no such thing as an underwater ghost. Still, I never told my mother about the drowning.

I peered cautiously over the side of the bridge. Jonette shouted and pointed at leaves and sticks being carried off by the force of the current. The power of the river frightened me. I thought of the warning inside the red book that held my fortune. My fate was lurking just out of sight, ready to pounce when I least expected it. I watched the surge of water rushing beneath the bridge, feeling myself become mesmerized, trapped by the powerful flow. As I looked in the river's current I saw the shapes of strong, muscular arms reaching out to drag me in and pull me down.

I shuddered and tugged at Jonette's sleeve to go. "Not yet," she said. "I want to look some more."

"Jonette, I'm going." My legs started to feel weak.

"In a minute," Jonette said, brushing me away.

I pulled myself from the railing and crossed the bridge alone. My heart was loud inside my chest and my palms felt damp.

Debbie MacLean ran up beside me. "Hi, Annie," she said, startling me. She looked at me as if she were surprised by something she had never noticed before. "Gee, I like your coat. Where'd you get it?"

"My mother bought it in Hong Kong," I said, pleased with her attention. I could tell she was impressed. My mother had kept my new jacket stored like a hidden treasure in her suitcase until I was old enough to wear it. Whenever she opened the case, she let me look at it – the red wool appliquéd with cloth flowers and lined with a shiny satin. For the past few years I had worn an ugly, hip-length navy coat with an imitation fur collar and a belt with a buckle. There was a matching hat with earflaps. They had been a gift from Uncle Yat. I remembered my excitement at seeing the large box from Eaton's on the counter. When I was told that Uncle Yat had ordered it especially for me, I could hardly wait to open it. But the moment I lifted the lid and spread the tissue paper, I hated the coat. I could tell by looking that it was too big, something that I would wear and grow into. It looked like a boy's coat. And worse, it was navy, a boy colour. I could tell that my parents were pleased and my mother immediately recognized that Uncle Yat had spent a lot of money. "Try it on," she said, pushing my arms into the coat. "Now thank Uncle Yat," she insisted. I turned to Uncle Yat and muttered thanks under my breath; he smiled his toothless grin. But I didn't care what the adults thought, I didn't care that the coat was warm and that the hat would cover my ears. I had wanted something pink and fitted at the waist, something pretty, something like what Debbie was wearing now – a new pink velvet jacket with pink pearl buttons.

"Annie, wait up," called Jonette, running up the path behind us.

Debbie and I turned around. "Where'd you get *your* coat, Jonette?" asked Debbie, her mouth curving into a thin smile.

I looked at Jonette and thought for the first time how shabby she looked in her faded beige corduroy jacket with giant white buttons and patch pockets. Almost all her clothes were from an older cousin in Toronto. I was relieved that I wasn't in my blue boy-coat. Breathless, Jonette looked down at her coat. "My cousin gave it to me," she said.

Debbie's eyes widened "You wear hand-me-downs?" she sneered.

"So?" said Jonette, her face flushed and confused.

Then Debbie turned to me and said, "You play with someone who wears hand-me-downs?" Without waiting for an answer, Debbie flounced on ahead to join another group of children. Gathering together, they listened as Debbie whispered, then they all turned and stared at Jonette, whose eyes welled with tears.

"Can't you ask your mum to buy you a new coat?" I said, embarrassed for her. Jonette looked miserable and said nothing, so we walked in silence to the top of the hill, passing our favourite spot in the yard, a clump of rocks worn into the shape of small chairs and arranged as if by magic to provide a conversation corner. She asked if I wanted to sit and play there until the bell.

"Maybe later," I answered.

The next morning I sat at my desk anxious for the recess bell to ring but dreading it at the same time. Yesterday before school ended, Debbie had passed me a note, all folded up into a tight, square-shaped wad. Opening the note, I had read *TOP SECRET*, underlined at the top of the page. Underneath she had written: *I'm bringing a surprise tomorrow just for you. Meet me at recess. Don't tell.* Debbie turned in my direction and smiled ever so slightly.

When we were told to get ready for recess, Debbie was the first one at the door. She stood holding a large cloth bag, and beckoned me to stand behind her. How could I tell Jonette that Debbie wanted to play with me and not her? I saw Jonette walk toward me, ready to play together as we always did. Then I heard Debbie announce, "Annie's playing with me today. I brought something special for her."

I looked up and saw Jonette staring at me, her mouth slightly open. I turned away. Today was my day to be chosen.

Outside, Debbie and I walked together to the base of the giant elm tree. Some of the girls she had chosen for friends earlier that week followed us. "What's in the bag?" they asked.

Debbie tossed her blonde hair and said, "You'll see." She reached inside and brought out two long bundles of striped flannelette: one pink and one blue. The girls clustered around, peeking over her shoulders. Debbie leaned slightly in my direction, the bundles pressed close to her chest. She gently edged her admirers away and said, "Here, Annie, this doll is for you."

Suddenly I felt uneasy. Debbie lifted the flannelette to show me her baby with its pink complexion and blue eyes. Then she reached over and carefully pulled down the blanket that protected the face of mine. It was almost identical to hers: the open-and-shut eyes, the paintbrush eyelashes, the perfectly rounded cheeks, the cute, tiny upturned nose, and the rosebud mouth with a small hole for inserting a miniature baby bottle. The difference was that my doll had brown eyes and deep-brown skin that resembled my own. I held on to it for a moment, then turned and shoved the dark object back in Debbie's arms with such force that she almost lost her balance. "I don't want it. Take it back," I said.

"What are you doing?" she shouted, her face twisted with offence. But I had already turned and was walking away.

I ran past the group of rocks shaped like chairs and headed toward the swing set. I hopped on a seat and started to pump with my legs as hard and as fast as I could. The air rushed against my face as I went higher and higher.

Yesterday the teacher had played a record of a woman telling the story of Rapunzel. As I listened, I had imagined myself locked up in the tower; my eyes were blue, and the hair that tumbled out the window was fair and golden, just like everyone else's. I didn't want the brown doll to be only for me.

I felt the wind blowing through my hair, drying my cheeks, and breathed in the smell of spring. Down the hillside, I saw trees covered with tiny yellow-green buds, the bridge with the creek flowing underneath. And beyond that was my home, a town filled with pink-skinned *lo fons*.

I was flying high, parallel to the ground, almost ready to go over the beam, when I saw the other kids racing toward the school. I knew that I had missed the bell. I dragged my feet on the ground and leapt off the swing. As I started to run for the doors, I saw Jonette running ahead of me. I wanted to call out to her, but couldn't.

When I returned home from school that day my father was unwrapping cartons of cigarettes. Inside the glass case, the stacks of pale blue Players, green Export A's, and red Du Mauriers were getting low. Carefully lifting the old packages, he placed the new ones underneath. My mother sat hemming a dress that she was making for me. I wanted to tell her not just about Debbie and the dolls, but about how wrong everything had turned out. No matter how hard I tried, I couldn't explain how I felt. In the middle of my story, Uncle Yat plunked a tray of wet cutlery on the table for my mother to dry. As she picked up her tea towel, she smiled at me. I knew she didn't understand my feelings. All she understood was that someone had brought a doll to school for me to play with. I had no reason to be upset.

When I met up with Jonette the next morning to walk to school, Darlene Atkinson, who sat behind me in class, was already waiting for her. Partway to school, Darlene asked if I would be playing with Debbie again at recess.

Things were never the same between me and Jonette. I went less and less to the bakery after school and only occasionally on Saturdays. I spent more time on my own, reading books and drawing pictures in scrapbooks that I bought from Reids'. Jonette started to play more often with Darlene Atkinson, and after the Easter holidays I walked to school with both of them.

BY NOW MY ABILITY to express myself in English had far surpassed my ability in Chinese. Through school and books my English vocabulary had grown. I came home wanting to tell my parents what had happened to me during the day, but I often found myself frustrated not knowing the Chinese words to explain what I had learned.

There were so many things I wanted to share with my family. But most of all I wanted to share, especially with my father, the stories I heard in church. I remember how people fussed over me when I began to go to church on my own. They told me what a brave girl I was. I would take my seat and gaze up at the high white ceiling and at the light that poured in through the stained-glass windows no matter what the weather. The air would always be still and my breathing would become slow and even.

Draped in his dark robes, with a Bible clutched in his hands, Reverend MacDougall would step up to the pulpit and the quiet whispers of the congregation would become silent. He would begin to speak, holding everyone spellbound with his voice. I didn't always understand what he meant, but that didn't matter. His sermons made all other thoughts leave my mind. One Sunday, the Reverend told us the story of Samson and Delilah: how Delilah had cut Samson's hair in his sleep, after she had tricked him into telling her that its length was the source of his strength. Shaking his fist, he told us about Samson's revenge once his hair had grown back. His face reddened and his voice thundered, "O Lord God, remember me and give me back my strength." But at the end of the story when Samson pulled down the pillars that held up the temple and killed himself and all the Philistines inside, the Reverend's voice dropped to a hush. He bowed his head and prayed with his arms held in the air, saying, "Amen" before crumpling like a rag doll on the carved wooden throne behind the pulpit. Immediately the choir stood and sang, their music soothing and restoring him so that he could rise and preach again, ready to tell the congregation even more about God's power and love.

I raced home that day and tried to repeat the story to my

father, but like all my attempts before – about the world being flooded, about Moses leading his people out of Egypt, about Elijah going to heaven in a chariot of fire, about Ruth and her fidelity to Naomi – it came out sounding choppy and flat, not at all the way it had been told in church. I found myself wishing, as I had many times before, that my father understood English better, the language that was now mine. Nevertheless he listened and smiled at my efforts.

When my father told me the story of Shao Kun, he transformed into the storyteller that I had wanted to be. His words embraced me and carried me off to ancient China, to the world of Shao Kun, a beautiful young woman who disguised herself as a man in order to lead an army of soldiers and defeat the barbarians. When the emperor of China discovered her true identity, he fell hopelessly in love with her. And I knew if I imagined myself as Shao Kun that she would have black hair and almond-shaped eyes just like mine.

&

POCK MARK LEE DROVE his truck filled with Chinese groceries from Toronto around a circuit of small towns and cities that took him as far west as London. He arrived in Irvine every other Thursday night, sometimes just in time to eat with us. If he was late, my parents always saved some of our Chinese meal for him. In all the years that I knew him, I never heard his real name. He was a stout man with big hands, his face and neck covered with tiny scars. My mother laughed and said that his skin was dimpled like deep-fried tofu. Once, when I was little, I didn't finish my rice and my mother had said to me, "Eat all your rice or you will end up with a husband who looks like Uncle Pock Mark. Every grain of rice left in your bowl will mean a scar the same size on your husband's face." After hearing that, I wondered if Pock Mark's wife ever finished hers.

My mother, more than anyone else in our family, looked forward to Pock Mark's visits. She bought dried shrimp, dried oysters, and dried mushrooms for soup. She cooked small pots of rice and steamed on top bits of Chinese bacon and dried pressed duck or salted fish chopped up with ginger and pork, which always filled the air with a pungent smell. Every two weeks we bought a gallon-sized metal can filled with large white cubes of tofu covered in water. For several days afterwards she would cook fresh tofu in soup or fried with vegetables. Since moving to Canada, my mother's concern about what we ate had grown almost into an obsession. Cooking was the only thing here that gave her real pleasure. Much of what she knew about food, she had learned from her herbalist father. She believed in the yin and yang qualities of food, in their medicinal as well as their nutritional value. Too much yin food and there wasn't enough vigour, fire. Too much yang food and you would become *yeet hai,* have too much heat in your body, and suffer indigestion, heartburn, and possibly rashes. She said that *lo fons* ate too much yang food with their French fries, hamburgers, deep-fried fatty foods, and chocolate. She believed in the importance of balance not just in the ingredients but in the cooking methods. A stir-fried dish needed to be balanced by a steamed one. She scolded me for eating ice cream because it was cold and tried to convince me to add hot water to milk so that it would be lukewarm and therefore not create imbalance. Every night my mother made soup. Soup was considered yin and it neutralized the effects of any stir-frying or overly rich food. She would not let me leave the table until I had consumed at least one bowl. One August when the peaches were in season, she warned me not to eat too many, to be careful of the yang nature of the high acid content. I ignored her, stuffing myself with one after another. When I broke into a rash she became angry. My academic accomplishments, normally a source of pride, became a source of frustration; she accused me of never listening to her and believing only what I read in the *lo fon* books. At school I had learned the importance of a balanced diet through Canada's Food Rules, a wall chart showing the number of servings of vegetable, fruit, meat, or its equivalent, the number of glasses of milk, and so on. My mother's knowledge, on the other hand, seemed to me more like sorcery, absorbed through the spirits of her ancestors.

During one of Pock Mark's visits, my father told him that my brother was coming to replace Uncle Yat at the Dragon Café. The restaurant where he worked in Owen Sound had been sold, and Uncle Yat had decided he was too old to work in a kitchen. He would sell his share in the restaurant to my father and my brother, and then join his son in Ottawa. I was sad that Uncle Yat would be leaving, but at the same time I was excited by the prospect of my brother coming to live with us. My father had said to my mother and me, his voice filled with enthusiasm, "It will be good when Lee-Kung comes. He is young and maybe with his energy this business will finally start to grow. He will look for a bride and then get married. In a while I'll be too old for this, and he will carry on. With his family."

My mother had told me that when my father first came to Canada, he had hoped to make a lot of money and to one day return to China a rich man. Because of the Communists, his plans had been ruined. He was no longer able to return home with the hope of building a business there. So he was pleased that Lee-Kung was moving to Irvine and saw his arrival as a new opportunity. "Things will be much easier with Lee-Kung," he said. "Our whole family will finally be together."

"It's good that's he's coming," said my mother. "It would be impossible for just the two of us to manage this place. We work hard enough as it is."

My father looked at me. "Did you know, Su-Jen," he said, "that when your brother was still a baby in Hoi Ping County, I had to return to Canada? I was still here when the Second World War started and I couldn't get back to China until it was over. By the time I got back, my son, he was almost seventeen. I am glad that he is coming to Irvine. I can tell from his letters that he is a hard-working man, that he will honour his family."

We had all expected many things of my brother then, each of us pinning our hopes of a happier future on his arrival. As I look back I understand how much our lives changed the day Lee-Kung walked into the Dragon Café.

OUR TEACHER TOLD US that this was the perfect spring. The temperatures were increasing gradually and flowers were blooming in the right order: the crocuses were almost finished, the daffodils in full bloom, and the tulips still in bud, not all at once as they did when the weather seemed to leap from winter to summer all in a week. The grass on the school hillside had changed from being soggy and muddy to firm and green.

I was doing my homework in my usual place, at the back booth underneath the Chinese movie-star calendar, eating an orange. I had become one of the best students in my class. I hadn't found a new best friend since Jonette, so I spent more time with school work and reading books.

I glanced up as a Chinese man wearing sunglasses pushed the door open with his foot. He was carrying a large suitcase in each hand. Right away I recognized my brother.

He stood inside the door, flanked by the two window ledges filled with dusty sansevieria and gnarled jade plants. He set down his bags, took off his glasses, and looked around. Dressed in blue cotton slacks and an unzipped tan jacket, he was even more handsome than I remembered, as handsome as one of the square-jawed Chinese movie stars in the Hong Kong magazines Pock Mark Lee sold from his truck. My mother had shown me a picture of Elvis, the *lo fon* singing sensation. With his crooked smile and his oiled hair combed back, my brother looked like a Chinese Elvis.

My father was pouring coffee for a customer as Lee-Kung walked into the dining room. As soon as he saw his son, a grin spread across his face. He returned the coffee pot to the burner and hurried around the Formica counter, clapping my brother on the shoulder, shaking his hand. My mother came rushing out of the kitchen through the swinging wooden door. I slid out from my booth and followed her. She stopped just for a moment to catch her breath, putting her hand up to brush back the few strands of hair that had loosened from her bun. She went to Lee-Kung and took his hand in hers. "It's good to have you here," she said with a smile, then turned to me, "Su-Jen, remember *Goh Goh*, Elder Brother." I nodded, unable to say anything more than yes. I didn't understand why, but I felt shy in front of this good-looking man who was my brother. I noticed that several of the customers were watching us.

My father couldn't stop smiling. He picked up one of Lee-Kung's suitcases. "Come now. *Choh-la*, sit down. Have something to eat." We followed him to the wooden booth at the back. My father seemed so pleased to have his family together at last. He got up and went into the kitchen to fetch Uncle Yat.

Uncle Yat pulled up a chair to the end of the booth. My mother exclaimed that in her excitement she had forgotten to make tea. A few moments later she called from the kitchen asking me to carry out a plate of biscuits, to set it in front of Elder Brother.

My brother drummed his fingers on the table and cast his eyes about the dining room. At the lunch counter, several men were drinking coffee and smoking. In the booth next to the window, some teenaged boys ate French fries, tapping their feet on the green-and-grey lino tile floor in time with the jukebox. It would be at least another hour before customers started coming in for supper. Elder Brother turned to Father, speaking in our dialect,

"I don't remember the town being so small. Does the restaurant have much business?"

"So-so," said Father. "But don't forget this business belongs to us. You are not working for someone else, you are working for your family."

"Don't worry," Uncle Yat said. "The most important thing is hard work, then you will have money. In ten, fifteen years open something bigger."

My father wagged his finger. "It's important not to waste your money on useless things," he said. "To be thrifty." One of the teenagers got up and popped a coin in the jukebox; loud, noisy music filled the room.

Motioning with his head in the two boys' direction, Uncle Yat chuckled and said, "Get other people to waste their money." My father and Uncle Yat got a special pleasure from joking about the customers in a language that only we understood.

Elder Brother's lips curled. "Yes, a real opportunity," he said dryly.

My mother, who was within earshot, returned with tea and started to fill the cups. She glanced up from her pouring and said to him, "Around here, there's no real place to spend your money. No difference even if you had any." He cocked one eyebrow higher than the other. Shrugging her shoulders, my mother met his gaze and smiled an upside-down smile.

"You can buy a lot of stuff in the store across the road," I protested.

My mother laughed. "Su-Jen, for you, yes, all those trinkets and toys. But there are no real stores, not here. Not like Hong

Kong, where the stores are open day and night." I slouched back into the bench. She was always talking about Hong Kong. Nothing here was as good as it was there. In the years that my mother and I had been in Canada, Hong Kong and China had for me become forgotten places. But my mother still talked about her old homes and when she gazed out the window at the near-empty street I knew she was thinking about them. She looked at Lee-Kung again, "Here, everything closes so early. Did you know that stores are closed all day Sunday? And on Wednesday afternoon?"

"Just like in Owen Sound," Elder Brother said. "But it didn't make any difference to the restaurants. We were open seven days a week. The hired help had one day off a week."

"And what did you do on your days off?" asked my mother.

My brother sipped his tea and smiled. "Go fishing, swimming, sometimes I took the bus to Toronto, but there wasn't really enough time and I ended up losing pay if I stayed over and didn't come back until the next day." He then turned to me, "But Irvine is much closer to Toronto, so when I have lots of money, Su-Jen, I promise to take you shopping there."

"And *Mah* too," I brightened and watched him light a cigarette.

"Enough talk about spending money," said Father. "We need to work and save. Then get in touch with a matchmaker and find a mail-order bride for you. It is time for you to get married and to start a family."

"Work and save. Work and save. That's all there is over here," said my mother with a small sigh and shake of the head.

Uncle Yat turned to me and smiled his toothless grin. "Now you, Su-Jen, you are a lucky girl," he said. "Only ten years old. You get to go to school. When you're grown-up, you can get a high-class job, like all the educated *lo fons*. You will make a lot of money and have days off. No *fuh gung*, bitter work, for you."

The adults in my family were always comparing Chinese people to *lo fons*. While we made fun of them, we all knew how powerful they were; they were the ones who lived in houses with backyards and drove cars. They were the important people in town, the teachers, the policemen, and the doctors.

"But she must work very hard at school," said Father, "at least twice as hard, maybe even ten times."

"Su-Jen, she is almost a *hoo sung*, a Canadian-born," said my mother, puffed up with pride. "She speaks like she was born here and she reads many thick books."

"Then Su-Jen is fortunate," said Lee-Kung. "The only choice I have is to work with my hands, spend my days in front of a stove and wok."

"It's true you must use your hands and not your mind, Lee-Kung. But if you are *ken hing*, hard-working," said Father, his voice becoming stern, "you will have a good life here too. You've been in Canada less than ten years and already you've saved enough to buy into this restaurant. You are a young man with many years left to grow this business. Things were much worse when Uncle Yat and I came to this country."

"Let's not talk about those things now," said Uncle Yat, trying to keep the peace.

"Remember, you could be back in China, living under the Communists," said Father.

"Yes, I guess we should all be thankful," said Lee-Kung with a shrug, "not to be in China."

He sucked on his cigarette and blew out a stream of smoke.

Elder Brother was different from my father and Uncle Yat – they both seemed content to spend their days in the restaurant. Only a few weeks after he arrived, Elder Brother went to Swackhammers' and bought himself a bicycle. When I noticed that there were wires around the handlebars, he told me that he had chosen a modern bike with handbrakes, not an old-fashioned one that stopped with pedals. One spring evening, he let me ride on the crossbar for a short after-supper spin around the block. The air was heavy with the scent of lilacs, almost masking the smell from the tannery. The breeze blew through my hair and I felt my brother's hot, smoky breath on the back of my neck. My whole body tingled. When we stopped in the alley behind the restaurant, my mother was waiting. As he held his bicycle steady, she put her arms out and helped me off.

"Okay, your turn now," Lee-Kung said to my mother as he patted the crossbar.

My mother playfully slapped him on the arm. "*Tsk,*" she said, before turning to me. "Now you must thank Elder Brother"

"*Ooh deah, Goh Goh,* thank you, Elder Brother," I said, lowering my eyes. But my brother wasn't listening to me, he was joking with my mother.

"When I lived in Owen Sound, I used to cycle around the town, and go fishing early on Sunday mornings with the cook from the other Chinese restaurant," he said.

"A bicycle's okay for you," said my mother, "but I think it'd be nicer to have a car."

"Just wait and see, a bike is only the beginning," said Lee-Kung. "One day, I'm going to buy a car, and I'll drive around like a big shot."

"Is that so," said my mother, smiling. "And where do you think you'll go in your fancy car?"

"I'll get out of this town. Explore. Go to Toronto. Maybe I'll even take you and Annie to some of those *lo fon* places."

"Really, *Goh Goh*?" I said.

"Want to go to Niagara Falls, Annie?" he said,

"Or we could drive away and never come back," joked my mother. My brother didn't answer; instead he looked at the ground, his face a little pink. I felt uncomfortable, but I couldn't explain why.

In between the moments of special attention that arrived like unexpected gifts, my brother ignored me. I found myself stealing glances at him, secretly watching what he did. When he wasn't working in the kitchen, he either sat in the back booth reading the Chinese newspaper or smoked cigarettes sitting on a stool in the yard, his face clouded by puffs of smoke. I wondered about his thoughts, afraid to interrupt his silence.

When Elder Brother came out of the kitchen and took a break in the dining room, he would sometimes lean over the lunch counter and talk casually with customers. His English wasn't perfect, but it was better than Father's or Uncle Yat's; he could laugh with the *lo fons* in a way that would have been impossible for them. Once I saw him and Mr. Swackhammer chuckling together at the lunch counter as they looked at a magazine. When they saw me staring at them, Mr. Swackhammer quickly closed it and put it inside his jacket.

Whenever I recall the time that Lee-Kung first came into our lives, the faith I once had in him now feels like a stone in my chest. My tall, handsome, brooding brother. Our future seemed to have so much possibility. In my foolish innocence I had hoped that even my mother might be happy.

A month after Elder Brother's arrival, Uncle Yat left for Ottawa. I didn't want him to go. I liked his lispy speech and the way he talked easily about his early days in Canada. I liked how he made my mother smile when he called her *Dai Ban Nang*, Lady Boss. Next to him, my father seemed stern and tight-lipped. The morning of Uncle Yat's departure, we walked him to Sniders', where he would catch the bus to Toronto and then to Ottawa to join his son. Lee-Kung carried his bags, then hurried back to the restaurant. I stayed with my parents until Uncle Yat boarded the bus. As if to himself my father said, "He is the most honest man I know. There are no snakes in his belly." Without Uncle Yat, who would make my mother laugh? I wondered.

That afternoon I sat at the lunch counter and helped my father fill the miniature china coffee creamers. "Su-Jen, we are *ho toy*, lucky, that our family's all here in Canada," he said. "Not like Uncle Yat."

"But isn't his son in Ottawa?" I said, worried about Uncle Yat living by himself.

"That's true. But his oldest son and daughter are still in China, along with his wife. Remember the picture he showed you? His oldest son is too old, so the government here won't let him into the country. And they won't let Uncle Yat bring over his daughter because she is married."

"But that's not fair," I said, not knowing anything about government rules.

"That's the law, Su-Jen. It's not up to us. It's too bad that his wife won't come."

"Why won't she? They must miss each other, being so far apart."

"When she was younger, maybe she wanted to come with Uncle Yat, but the government wouldn't let her. Now the government will let her, and she says she's too old. And Uncle Yat, he doesn't want to go back to China. Even though he's lonely, it's not really his home any more."

"I don't think Uncle Yat should go to Ottawa," I said. "He's lived with us for so long, we're more like his family than his real one." My father laughed, reached over and touched my cheek.

My mother, who had been tidying the front booth, walked by on the way into the kitchen. Without stopping she said, "Uncle Yat's wife, she's smart. Lucky to be in China. Not like me. Stranded here." The tone of her voice surprised me. Her words came out short and sharp, like darts, every one of them aimed at my father. He took a deep breath and his face grew hard. I wanted to reassure him that I was happy, that I wanted to stay here and didn't want to go back to China, but the words were stuck inside my mouth.

My father stared for a long moment at the coffee creamers. His face softened and he said to me quietly, "It's hard for your mother in this small town, not speaking the language, away from her own people, without anyone to talk to or to visit. You must remember to keep her company, Su-Jen, to help make your mother happy. The Communists forced us to leave our home and we have no hope of going back."

"But this is our home now," I said, frustrated with my mother.

My father stopped his work again. "You see, Su-Jen," he said. "Your mother's family was rich. And it's always hard to be rich first, then poor." He cleared his throat and added, "Without you she might have chosen to stay in Hong Kong and I could have sent her money. But she came to Canada because of you. She wanted what was best for you."

I was unable to meet my father's eyes. I knew he intended to make me feel better with his words, letting me know that my mother had put my happiness ahead of her own. But there was so much I didn't understand. My parents tried to explain how a government worked and at school my teacher had told us how the Canadian government was elected and how it made up laws. According to my father the government in Canada was good, while the one in China was bad, but I didn't know why except that it had something to do with the Communists.

Soon after Uncle Yat left, my father won a poetry-writing contest in one of the Chinese magazines. He read his winning poem to me in the singsong voice he used for reading verse, but the words were meaningless, written Chinese being so different from the spoken. I was pleased for him, but sad that Uncle Yat was no longer here to share his triumph. My father would miss those spare moments, sharing and discussing each other's writing, something I could not do.

Lee-Kung carried on in the kitchen, cooking the same fish and chips, clubhouse sandwiches, hot chicken and hot beef, and the Chinese dishes like sweet and sour chicken balls and egg foo youngs and chow meins. When we first arrived and my mother saw the "Chinese" food that was served to the customers, she was shocked. "The *lo fons,*" she said, "I guess they don't know anything about food." She didn't think much of the Canadian food either. It took her a long time to get used to seeing a big slab of meat served on a plate for one person. For her, there were two things that were essential to a meal. One was rice and the other was soup. I think she understood that *lo fons* substituted potatoes and bread for rice, but the thought of a meal without soup was unthinkable.

With my brother working in the kitchen, my mother joked even more about what the *lo fons* ate. My brother complained about the lack of business, but my father told him that for a business to grow it took many years.

Lee-Kung wanted to make changes to the menu, to introduce something called the combination plate. Customers would choose from dishes numbered one through five. Each choice would start with an egg roll and then a main course consisting of several items: perhaps sweet and sour spare ribs, chicken chop suey and guy ding, or soya sauce chicken wings, beef chow mein, and sweet and sour shrimp. "It's a new idea," he explained one evening after supper to Father. "The *lo fons* at the restaurant in Owen Sound licked their plates clean. Each dish, though, needs to have a sweet and sour on it. That's what they really love."

Father pressed his lips together into a frown and shook his head. "Business is fine. Why should I take a risk when I don't have to?"

A few days later, Lee-Kung again raised the topic during supper. This time when Father refused, Elder Brother grew impatient. "We'll never make any real money," Lee-Kung argued. "Don't you see? We need to look at what other places are doing. Try and keep up."

"So you know everything?" My father stared at him across the table. In a hurried voice, my mother told me to finish my rice.

"I didn't say that," said Elder Brother. "I just don't want to spend the rest of my life being a slave, working for nothing."

"How do you think I got the money to buy this place? To pay for the plane fares to bring everyone here? By taking big risks? No, I worked and saved. I never spent a penny on myself. I thought only of my family. I could have acted like a big shot, bought nice clothes, spent money on gambling, but you'd still be in China."

"What about me?" said Lee-Kung in disbelief. "Do you think I've been living like a big shot in Owen Sound? How do you think I got enough money to pay your toothless friend?"

"You don't know how easy you've had it," my father said angrily. "A job right away in Owen Sound, one day off a week, go fishing. You don't know half of what I've gone through, what Yat put up with. It's easy for you to talk about taking a chance. You're not the one who's had to live like a dog just to save a few cents."

"Things are different now. You don't have to live like a dog just to make some money," said Lee-Kung, banging the table.

It seemed that the fighting between Father and Lee-Kung went on for days; every evening one of them left the supper table in a huff. My father finally agreed to introduce three Chinese-food combination plates to the menu, but my brother had to continue with the Canadian daily specials. The new dishes, though, proved to be popular, especially with the bachelors who worked at the tanning factory. Many of them preferred the new additions to the old specials like hamburg steak and fish and chips.

Without consulting Father, Lee-Kung added a new dessert to the milkshakes, ice-cream sodas, and pies. In Owen Sound he had learned to make something called a Boston cream pie. When my brother first brought the new dessert into the dining room, Mr. Swackhammer and Reverend MacDougall were sitting at the lunch counter with their coffees. They each asked for a slice. By the end of the morning my brother had sold the entire pie. My father said to him in a gruff voice, "Okay, big shot." I didn't understand my brother's smile along with the *harrumph* sound in his throat.

The Boston cream pie sat behind the glass sliding doors on the top shelf of the stainless-steel cooler behind the Formica counter, like the queen of desserts for everyone to see. My mother said that it made the restaurant a little classier, now that we were serving something so exotic – a cake filled with vanilla pudding, iced with soft peaks of whipped cream, and decorated with maraschino cherries. The first time my brother gave me a slice, I ate the whole thing in three mouthfuls. I almost swooned, the flavours and textures blending so sweetly together, melting in my mouth, more delicious than anything from Dooleys' Bakery.

With the success of the combination plates and the Boston cream pie, my father didn't argue much about adding almond cookies to our menu. He emphasized to Lee-Kung that he had to continue making the apple, raisin, and cherry pies that the *lo fons* liked. But he later admitted that the cookies made our small-town restaurant seem more *goh seng*, high class, like the Shanghai and the Sai Woo in Toronto. Now whenever a customer finished a Chinese meal, we presented him with an almond cookie on a plate, a proper end to a meal.

Lee-Kung complained to my mother while they were washing up one evening. "I knew those new dishes would be popular. If we're going to make any money, we need to try new things. The way things are, we have money only because we don't spend it."

"That's the way these old men are," said my mother, shaking her head. "No imagination, just doing the same thing over and over, for years and years. Every penny goes in the bank. At least the old man's not washing clothes – some of these old men do nothing but wash and iron for fifty, sixty years."

"They basically work for nothing," said Lee-Kung. "You wouldn't get a *lo fon* to work for nothing."

I had been sitting on a short stool in a corner of the kitchen with a ball of yarn and a crochet hook. As I struggled with the wool, I listened to their conversation. I didn't like the tone my mother had started using when she talked about my father. I knew somehow that it wasn't right, but who was I to tell those who were older and wiser how to behave?

Before Elder Brother came, my mother had worked in the restaurant without saying much to anyone. During quiet moments she used to sit in the back booth, looking at a Chinese magazine and sipping tea. But now I often heard her complain to Elder Brother, speaking in a low voice as if she didn't want to be heard.

MY FAMILY IN CHINA was a mysterious, shadowy presence. There were only a few black-and-white photographs that revealed nothing of the people behind the solemn faces. I had no memory of ever meeting them, although my mother said they always asked about me in their letters, letters written in a script I couldn't read. Even Aunt Hai-Lan and Uncle Jong in Toronto seemed far away. Whenever my friends talked about visits from their grandparents, their aunts, uncles, and cousins, I listened with envy. These were real people who came to visit, whose voices and faces were familiar.

According to my mother, were it not for her, we would have all been trapped in China. When my father returned to China in

1947 after the war, he had expected to stay. He married my mother and they opened a store selling fabric, yarn, and other goods for making clothes. But as my mother often told me, she had a dream in the summer of 1949. *I saw the earth split wide open. People fell in and were devoured. I stood safely on one side and your father on the other. I then realized that your father had to go back to Canada.* My mother told me that when she had had this dream, the Communists had taken over almost all of China, but my father was still hoping for a Nationalist victory. She told him about her dream and that if he didn't leave soon it would be too late.

The Nationalists were defeated just a few months after my father's return to Canada. My mother told me that even though she had known that she was pregnant with me before my father left, she hadn't told him as she hadn't wanted to delay his departure. It wasn't until after his arrival in Canada that she wrote and told him about her condition. Six months later, shortly after my birth, my twenty-year-old brother, Lee-Kung, left China without us. More than four years passed before my mother and I left for Hong Kong and another two before we finally left for Canada.

I craved details about my family's past, the people back in China. I learned what little I knew from overhearing bits of grown-up conversation. I eavesdropped when my parents and my brother talked, gathering each piece of information and storing it inside me like a precious jewel.

I stood in front of the kitchen counter, spreading out egg-roll wrappers, while Elder Brother stirred in a large bowl a mixture of bean sprouts, shredded carrots and celery, and chopped cooked pork. Most of my chores at the restaurant involved helping my mother with things like drying dishes and scraping dirty plates. My brother had surprised me when he asked me to help him. We did not spend much time together despite living under the same roof. He was my Elder Brother, busy, distant, and unapproachable.

While he was mixing, he said with a small smile on his face, "You know what your mother calls the Chinese food on the menu? Fool-the-*lo-fon* food."

I didn't think what he said was very funny, but I laughed anyway to please him. Lee-Kung placed small amounts of filling in the centre of each square. I started to fold the bottom half of the wrapper up and the top down so that the edges overlapped. Elder Brother then showed me how to press the ends together, making sure the filling stayed in the centre. Watching him, I said, "I don't like egg rolls. I've never seen you or anybody in the family eat them. I've only seen *lo fons* eat them."

"You would eat them if you were hungry enough, little sister. During the war, there was never enough to eat. Sometimes I went for days without food. I'd have eaten anything," Lee-Kung said. He paused and with a sly grin added, "Even an egg roll."

My cheeks felt a little warm. I knew my brother was teasing me. "I've never gone for a whole day without food," I said.

"Once you've had that feeling of hunger, Annie, you never forget it. You're lucky to be here and not to be back in China." I didn't say anything for a while. But as I listened to my brother, I knew that I should once again be grateful to my parents and never complain. Compared to everyone else in my family, my life seemed so simple, without war or starvation.

Earlier in the day, I had joined my father on his daily walk to the post office. I found our mailbox on a wall covered with small silver metal doors engraved with numbers. My father gave me the key and I stood on my tiptoes to unlock it. My parents collected the mail every day regardless of the weather. They looked forward to news from China and my mother waited eagerly for Aunt Hai-Lan's letters. My father sometimes read the poems he and Uncle Yat wrote and sent to each other for comment. Today the weekly Chinese newspaper had also arrived. My parents would spend the next few days reading and rereading the paper. My mother would ignore her work, performing only the most pressing tasks.

In the dining room my parents sat at the back table absorbed in the paper. After I finished helping my brother I slid into the back booth with a comic book and a glass of gingerale. My father left to fetch an order from the kitchen, leaving my mother alone. A customer by the door quietly left without paying. She didn't notice until my father returned and accused her of not paying attention.

"How is this possible? Didn't you see him get up and leave?"

"Don't look at me. I thought you were watching. You didn't tell me you were getting up."

"What are you? Blind? Do I need to tell you everything – whether I shit or piss?" shouted my father.

"*Ei-yah!* It's only a few dollars," she shot back.

"Only a few dollars. I see, we make so much money we can

afford to feed the whole town." My father slammed the newspaper down on the table.

"So much money? We make no money," my mother hurled. "Look at you, worn like a shoe. How is it that you have nothing to show after all these years slaving in this country?"

My father spat back, "I spent all my money on my ungrateful family – to bring you over here."

"I'd be better off in China fighting for my life, here I just die a slow death."

I lost track of how many times they fought like this, I only know that the argument never changed, the intensity of their anger always climbed as they argued. This time the fighting ended when my mother rushed through the kitchen and ran upstairs.

Over the next few days my mother muttered over and over under her breath: this dead town, nobody around to talk to, nobody speaking Chinese and these ugly *lo fon* customers, work in life, work in death, and still no money. For days my parents didn't speak to each other, their silence weighing down so heavily that my breathing became shallow and my eyes watchful.

Yet we all continued in our roles. My father managed the dining room and supervised my brother in the kitchen. My mother ran back and forth between both places. During these periods she seemed to grow closer to my brother, sharing complaints about the "old man." My mother joked more with my brother, and lavished compliments on his cooking at supper. I helped with the odd chore, but mostly went to school, read my books, and kept out of the way.

My parents were always pecking at each other, tension bristling just beneath the surface. *Haven't you filled those sugar dispensers yet? Why's the fan still on? How come you turned the fan off?* During these times of deadlock, my parents would each complain to me. I began to feel like a fortress wall with a parent hiding on either side, each rising up without warning to take a snipe.

It was during this standoff that I learned the truth about Lee-Kung. I had returned from school and was sitting in the back booth with my book of cut-out dolls. On the weekend my father had given me thirty-five cents. He had opened the cash register and taken out the coins, patting me on the shoulder as he put the money in my hand. His eyes had looked sad as he told me to buy something for myself.

I had rushed across the street to Reids' Five and Dime. The store carried everything a person could possibly want: books, stationery, jewellery, bolts of cloth, toys of every kind. I had wanted to buy a book of wedding cut-outs. I had long admired the cover with its soft watercolour painting of the bride and groom, the bride with her soft blonde hair, resplendent in her white frothy gown, standing happily beside her handsome groom, both of them wearing wide Colgate smiles.

I had punched out the cardboard figures on Saturday: the bride, the groom, three bridesmaids, and three ushers. Each of them had two outfits, one casual and one for the wedding. But the bride had clothes for shopping, for tennis, for being at home, for swimming, for sleeping, and, of course, for the wedding.

Today I was going to cut out the men's clothes, then the bridesmaids' dresses, saving the bride's wardrobe and her wedding gown, the best, for last. I cut each item carefully along the dotted lines. I pretended I was arranging my own wedding, making plans for a fairy-tale future, the friction between my parents far away. I was cutting out the last tuxedo for the last usher when my mother sat down across from me. She plunked an empty metal tray and a damp tea towel on the table next to my paper cuttings. Shaking her head she said, "Look at you. Look at the mess."

"Don't worry. I'll clean it up," I answered without looking up.

"Nothing ever changes around here. It's the same day after day. Work, work, work and more work," said my mother. When I didn't respond she let out a deep sigh and said, "My life is never going to change. Stuck married to that old man and listening to his stories over and over."

"I like *Ba Ba*'s stories," I said quietly, concentrating on the paper tuxedo.

"You don't understand, Su-Jen, I had no choice but to marry your father. It was after the war and I had lost everything." She hesitated for a moment, then continued, "I've never told you this, but before you were born I was married to someone else and I had a son. My husband died during the war and we were left alone. I needed your father to help me raise him, and your father, he wanted a son for himself."

I grew anxious and confused, my cut-outs forgotten. What she was saying made no sense. "You never told me you were married before, that you and *Goh Goh* were left alone."

"No, Su-Jen, you don't understand. *Goh Goh* is not my son."

I felt as if the ground beneath me had shifted. Nothing was in its rightful place. My questions tumbled out one after the other. "Where is your son, then? *Ba Ba* was married, too, wasn't he? Where is *Goh Goh*'s mother?"

"I don't know where to start," said my mother. "You are right, your father had another wife before me. I never met her." Her voice started trembling. "Lee-Kung isn't your real brother. He's only half. He belongs to that other woman. He's not mine."

"But then where is your son and where is *Goh Goh*'s mother?" I asked again, my voice in a whisper.

"Your father's first wife died during the war. If she were alive, your father wouldn't be married to me. Su-Jen, there has been much sadness in our family. Your father had a son before Lee-Kung, but that child died when he was five, maybe six. I guess he hoped that my son would replace him." She bit her lip and added, "But then my son died too." Her eyes started to well with tears. My mother looked down at her lap. I was stricken by all this new information.

"How old was *Goh Goh* when his mother died?" I asked.

"He was thirteen or fourteen, I think. It was very hard. His grandmother was alive for a little while, and then I think he went to live with an uncle."

"But why didn't *Ba Ba* look after him?"

"He couldn't. He was stuck in Canada because of the war."

"What about you?" I asked.

"Me? I didn't even know your father then. I didn't marry him until he got back to China after the war."

My mother then turned away from me and refused to answer

any more questions, no matter how much I begged. There was so much more I wanted to know. My family had lived in other places and survived many hardships, but these new revelations had turned them into strangers, haunted by people I would never know. Their past felt unfathomable, it made me feel small and insignificant. Until then, I could not have imagined either parent being married to anyone except each other. I thought about what my mother had told me. Two more brothers, one even older than Lee-Kung. What were their names? I wondered what they had looked like. And how they died. If my father's first son were alive today, would he be married, with a family, working in the restaurant? And this other son, my mother's son, as I thought about him I was filled with regret. He could have been a brother, not much older, who would go to school with me, speak English, and share my world beyond the restaurant.

It seems that whenever I think about my childhood, sooner or later I end up at that summer. Until then I had assumed that I was the centre of my parents' lives. If you were to ask them, they would tell you that it was in fact so, that everything they did, they did for me, that all their sacrifices were for me, that they were here in this land of strangers only because of me. But that summer the belief that held us together would begin to change. My family had a past that did not include me, and the strain it placed on all of us would chafe at the threads that held us together.

IN PREVIOUS SUMMERS I had gone to Irvine Lake to wade in the shallows with Jonette and Mrs. Dooley. It was the centre of summer activity in our town. But this year, without Jonette, the hot days stretched out long and empty before me.

Almost everyone I knew swam at Irvine Lake. Families would gather for the day, bringing picnic lunches, spreading blankets on the steamy grass. Older kids I recognized from the Dragon Café would show up late in the day to swim and splash each other, the girls squealing.

The only person who didn't swim at the lake was Hilary Beeston. She told me that she vacationed every summer at her family cottage up north in some place called Muskoka. When I asked if she was sad to leave all her friends in Irvine and to swim by herself all summer, Hilary said that her mother wouldn't allow her to go in Irvine Lake. She told me that her mother called it a filthy hole and said she might get polio from it. I had to ask her what polio was, and she said that's what Mary Brodie had when she was three. Hilary said that before Mary was sick she could walk and run just like us. She was lucky she didn't die, but it was sad that she had to spend the rest of her life in a wheelchair, the whole town thought so. I felt bad for Mary too, but the truth was I never liked her. In the schoolyard I had been about to help push her wheelchair when she had growled in a low voice, "Don't touch my chair, chink." I had sucked in my breath and pulled back my hand. I was shocked, but the funny thing about Mary's anger toward me was that it made me feel closer to her. Not that I wanted to befriend her, but I now knew something about her that other people didn't.

My mother had never liked it when I went to the lake, but in the past when I had promised that Mrs. Dooley would be there to supervise and that I wouldn't go deeper than my knees, she had reluctantly agreed. There had been no real need for her worry since I was cautious of the water, unable to convince myself that my mother's warnings were only superstitions. Instead, Jonette and I had spent most of our time wading, splashing, and building sand castles. I had always loved the summer, but this year it had barely begun and already I couldn't wait for the endless days at the Dragon Café to finish, for September to arrive.

July started out warm and sunny, but day after day the temperature climbed and the humidity increased. By the middle of the month the stench from the tannery hovered in the air like foul breath.

My mother, who seemed never to perspire, had beads of sweat on her nose by noon of each day; by mid-afternoon the back of her clothing was damp. She wore loose flower-print dresses and her hair up in a knot on top of her head. However warm it was, no one in my family sweat like some of the *lo fon* customers who came into the restaurant. My parents commented on the men dripping with moisture and the women with the dark wet patches spreading under the arms of their blouses. My mother also complained that the *lo fon* aunts and uncles smelled different, stronger than we Chinese. My father said that it was because they drank too much milk and their bodies had more hair. I asked him how he knew. "Look at their arms. Look at Hardware Store Uncle," he answered.

In the kitchen, Lee-Kung kept a towel for mopping his brow. Only Father seemed unaffected; he simply washed his face more frequently and at night he stopped wearing pyjamas, dressing instead in a singlet and boxer shorts. In my three and a half years in Canada, I had seen his legs only once before. When I saw them now, sticking out from the bottom of his boxer shorts, their colour reminded me of the dusty grey plaster of Paris puppet that I had made in school. The skin made me think of crinkled wax paper with pale blue veins running underneath the surface like thin lines on a map. They were legs of an old man.

By the fourth day of the heat wave, people came into the restaurant complaining about record highs and weather forecasts. They were all convinced it had to break, that it couldn't last much longer.

When I told my mother how the *lo fons* complained, she shook her head disparagingly and said, "Tsk, this is nothing, compared to what it's like in the hot, rainy season in China. At least here it's a little cooler at night. At least here you don't have the floods. Every season I had to move everything from the first floor of the house to the second," she said. "People took turns watching the river, ready to call a warning when it looked like it was going to rise." I imagined looking out the window of the second floor of the restaurant and seeing the streets fill with water. "And after the water went down, we had to wait for everything to dry out. It was exhausting." she added.

"It's much better here then, isn't it?" I said, thinking for once she would agree with me.

"Su-Jen," she said with a sigh. "Yes, some things here are better, but even if this were the finest place in the world I would never belong. And I can't go back to China, not even if I wanted to. Everything there has changed. I'm stuck here, but I no longer have a real home." She shook her head and returned to wiping tables.

A few days into the heat wave, Jean MacDougall, who used to walk me to school, came into the restaurant for an ice cream. I was surprised to see her without her heavy coat. The winter before, Jean had been away from school for months with scarlet fever. When she returned in May, she was thin and pale, wrapped in a thick coat buttoned to the top, always wearing a hat. Even at the end of June, she had looked like a bundle of blankets. Most of the kids in her class ignored her, but some of them teased her and dared her to take off her coat. I walked with her for a while at recess one day, and asked why she had to wear her winter clothing for so long. She told me that after the scarlet fever she had developed something called rheumatic fever. The doctor was afraid that her heart might be weakened. He had told her parents that she couldn't afford to risk catching any kind of a chill so she had to be warmly dressed at all times. Jean then confided that she was praying to God every night. "God is testing me and I pray that he will give me the strength to endure all that he has in store for me," she said. "My dad told me I'm like the story of Job. Remember Job, from Sunday school?" I nodded at her, not sure how to answer. I knew the story, but hadn't thought things like that happened to real people. At that moment her illness had suddenly seemed like a badge of honour, that she alone had been chosen by

God. But in the middle of the July heat wave, as she took the ice-cream cone from my mother, her burden seemed like an awful lot to bear. "It's so hot, Annie," she said, raising her eyebrows at me, "the doctor told me I could wear just a sweater over my dress."

The second floor seemed to absorb all the heat from the kitchen below. It was unbearable lying in the bed between my parents, our bodies so close together, the air weighing down like a hot, invisible blanket. One night, my father took his pillow and spread a towel on the cot in the spare room. The next day my mother put fresh sheets on it. She pulled out the suitcase from under our bed and picked out a light blanket, leaving it folded at the foot of his cot in anticipation of the cooler weather that was bound to come.

The following night I slept close to the wall, my mother on the far side of the bed. There was now space between us, leaving me safe from the jabs and pokes of her elbows and knees during her night-time thrashing.

Lunch hour had finished; the restaurant would be quiet for several hours except for a few customers popping in for drinks, ice cream, and French fries. I stood and watched Lee-Kung lift a wire basket filled with French fries out of the tank of bubbling oil. The air was thick with the smell of grease. My brother had taken off his shirt and was wearing a white undershirt tucked into his pants. He reached for his towel to wipe the perspiration from his face and neck. "*Gotdamn,* it's like an oven. I'm going to the lake for a swim. Can't stand this damn place."

"Can I come?" I blurted, forgetting my shyness and my mother's fears. All I could think about was the heat and that I hadn't been to the lake all summer.

My brother seemed to consider it for a moment, then agreed.

"Can I go, *Mah*?" I said to my mother, who was sorting bean sprouts. I watched her face stiffen and knew she was thinking about my safety.

At that moment my father came into the kitchen to pick up the order of fries. "*Ba Ba,*" I said, "*Goh Goh*'s going to take me to the lake!"

He seemed pleased that Elder Brother and I would go together. "You must be careful," he said, then looked at my mother. "And stay close to the shore."

"No, I don't think so," said my mother, a frown on her face.

I pleaded, telling her I'd be careful. My body was sticky and my damp hair felt plastered to my head.

My mother hesitated and looked at my brother, then back at me, "You must not go past your ankles,"

"Don't worry so much. She'll be fine," said Lee-Kung.

"You must never take your eyes off her," said my mother to him. "And, Su-Jen, you must listen to what *Goh Goh* tells you."

Just before leaving the kitchen, my father bent to speak to me. "Su-Jen," he said, "you know how your mother worries about these things. You must promise to stay in the shallow part of the water."

I promised and rushed upstairs to put on my bathing suit and stuff a towel in a canvas tote. My brother was waiting for me at the lunch counter, an old nylon bag from Hong Kong slung over his shoulder.

Before we left, Lee-Kung again reassured my mother. He smiled and touched her on the shoulder, his hand lingering for a moment, his eyes holding hers. She stood outside the restaurant door and watched us leave.

My brother walked in long strides. He seemed unaware that I almost had to run to keep up. Waves of heat reflected off the pavement, hitting us in the face. The sun glared with such intensity that it was hard to imagine it would ever set. Earlier in the week Mr. Swackhammer had showed me a story in the newspaper about a sidewalk in New York that was so hot a man fried an egg on it. I told my mother and she laughed; when I asked if I could try it, she told me that I was *seen geng*, a mental case.

Irvine Lake was a short distance from the centre of town. Jonette and I had often followed Willow Creek from the bottom of the hill at school to where it turned into a marsh with grasses and bulrushes before widening into the lake. Just before the end of school my class had walked past it on the way to a picnic. Although the heat hadn't yet started to build, I had already been able to smell the decaying vegetation.

I looked up at my brother – he was such a contrast to Father, who didn't know how to ride a bicycle or how to swim. Lee-Kung was tall and held his broad shoulders back, his head high.

My father was slightly stooped, always looking as if he were carrying an invisible burden on his shoulders. Although I had never asked, I knew that neither of my parents swam, or even owned a bathing suit.

At the lake the grass was yellow and crunchy beneath our feet. On weekends the small beach was filled with swimmers and sunbathers, but today, a weekday, there was a choice of places to sit. The grassy field behind the strip of sand was scattered with trees for people who preferred to rest in the shade. Lee-Kung led me to the tree near the beach where he liked to spread his towel. I wanted to sit closer to the water, but I obeyed my brother. "Wait here while I go and change," he said. "Don't go near the lake, and no fooling around."

I watched him walk to the low concrete building and enter the men's changing room. When he came out in his swimming trunks, he passed two older girls lying on their stomachs on a blanket, hands under their chins, their eyes following him. I thought how rude they were to stare.

My brother dropped his clothes on his towel and ran toward the water. His whole body was tanned, his arms and legs so muscular. I got up and stood at the water's edge as he plunged in and effortlessly swam across the small lake.

I sat down at the shore and let the water lap over my legs. Lee-Kung came over and sat beside me, his body dripping. "This lake isn't much more than a pond," he said, shaking the water from his hair. "You should see a real lake, or even better the ocean. Now that's the best place to swim."

"I've never been in the ocean."

"One day I'll take you. After I convince the old man to sell the place, I'll buy something in a bigger town and make some money. We'll never make any here, this town's too small."

Suddenly the two girls, who had been staring at my brother, ran past us into the water, splashing us as they went. They stopped and turned, flashing their smiles at Lee-Kung. "Sor-ree," they sang out and dove into the lake, their ponytails swinging. I was annoyed, but my brother only watched them and said nothing.

My brother was silent for most of the afternoon. I watched him as he lay in the shade and drew on his cigarettes, carefully blowing smoke rings from his puckered lips. I knew he was thinking about those *lo fon* girls rather than talking to me. I was sure he wished he hadn't brought me. It was their fault that our afternoon was turning out like this, and I began to wish that we'd never come.

I woke up the next morning with my pyjamas damp and sticking to my body. My mother was already dressed. Her hair unclasped, she peered into the wavy mirror above our dresser. I got up to stand beside her and watch her reflection. She applied tiny dots of Ponds cold cream to her cheeks, chin, and forehead, spreading it over her face with her fingers.

She was a beautiful woman, with smooth skin, a full mouth, and dark, wide-set eyes. My mother turned to me and touched a spot below the inside corner of her right eye where the skin twisted into a small knot. It was the only blemish in an otherwise flawless complexion. "There used to be a mole here, instead of this scar," she said. "It's the worst place you can have a mole, a terrible omen. This is the reason for all my bad luck. It doesn't matter how much wealth or happiness I have, I end up losing it. My tears will wash everything away, just like a flood rushing through a house, carrying off all the furniture." She laughed sadly. "There was a fortune teller in China who said I have the nose of a rich woman – see how it's shaped like a change purse, the nostrils small and delicate. Not like some people with big flaring holes, all their money falling out."

"So that means we'll be rich one day," I said.

"No, Su-Jen. Whatever good fortune I have, it does not last. This mole means that I am doomed. My mother thought that she could get rid of the bad luck. When I was six, she held me down and a neighbour picked out the mole with the pointed tip of a knife." I made a face. My mother ignored me and continued. "But it was no use. There was no fooling the gods. Look at the joke they've played on me. Who would have guessed the day I was born that I'd be married to a poor man, living on the other side of the world?" She faced the mirror again and started to coil her hair in a bun and secure it with bobby pins.

"Well, I think we're lucky to be here. You're always talking about the Communists in China. We should be glad we're not stuck there like Uncle Yat's family," I said.

My mother turned away from the mirror, staring at me in disbelief. "You don't understand, Su-Jen. All of this is bad luck – the Communists, living here, everything." Then she softened, and extended her arm to stroke my cheek. "It doesn't matter, your life will be different," she said.

"What about me? Do I have any unlucky moles? Or lucky ones?" I asked, lifting up my pyjama top to inspect my stomach. My mother searched my back, then my front, under my arms, lifted my chin with her index finger to check my face and neck, brushing away my hair to look behind my ears, and finally examining the soles of my feet and in between my toes.

Muttering and shaking her head, my mother inspected every part of my body again. She frowned. "I've never seen anything like it," she whispered to herself. The tone of her voice filled me with worry and my mouth felt dry. My mother stared past me, a blank expression on her face. "There are no marks of any kind. Why did I not see this before?" she said. She looked at me, her expression a mixture of wonder and horror. "The gods have overlooked you."

My mother must have seen my distress because she lightened her voice as she held my face in her hands. "It's nothing. So you don't have any moles. It probably doesn't mean anything," she assured me. "*Mo sow*, don't worry."

Later that day I examined myself in front of the mirror, searching for a mole that my mother might have missed. But she was right, there was nothing. For the first time in more than a week, I slept wrapped in a blanket.

On summer nights when my father was still downstairs closing up the restaurant, my brother would climb through his window and sit on the fire escape. The faint smell of cigarette smoke would drift through our window. After the first week of the heat wave my mother began to join him outside after her bath. The creak of the fire-escape door and the murmur of their voices would wake me, but usually I went back to sleep. Sometimes, I got out of bed and sat with them on the fire escape, but I never stayed very long; they never seemed to notice me, interested only in each other, sharing jokes, a private language. I felt hurt and angry with my mother, who seemed to pay less and less attention to me. Sulking, I would return to bed, blocking out their voices with a pillow over my head.

One night the heat was unbearable and I woke up soaked in sweat. I noticed the other side of the bed was empty. I got up and opened the door onto the fire escape and saw Elder Brother and my mother leaning over the railing, looking down at the alley. I didn't move from the doorway. My mother turned to my brother and asked to try his cigarette.

Lee-Kung looked at her for a moment, then smiled and placed it between her fingers. Holding on to his gaze she brought the cigarette to her lips and inhaled. She coughed uncontrollably. My brother slapped her on the back several times and they both began to laugh. He glanced around and saw me standing by the door. "Hey, Annie, you want to try?" he asked with a grin, dangling his cigarette at me. My mother flicked him gently on the wrist and they laughed again. I turned to go back to bed and expected my mother to follow, but it was a long time before she came in.

The heat held steady for a third week. The air congealed, coating our bodies like syrup, while the smell from the tannery cloyed the air. With each passing day, people's movements became slower, their limbs appeared to wilt under damp clothes. The ceiling fan in the restaurant dining room whirred day and night, the cooler hummed as it worked overtime. Customers would press their cold glasses of Coke to their foreheads in an effort to cool down. My mother scooped ice cream out of the cardboard cylinders until she said her arm and shoulder ached. Strands of her hair loosened in the humidity; she reached up repeatedly and pushed them behind her ear with the heel of her hand.

I walked to the post office with my father in the sweltering heat. Although the sky was a brilliant blue, I no longer found it beautiful. The sun seemed cruel. I noticed for the first time in days that there were small white clouds around the horizon and I wondered if there might be an end to our misery on its way. At the post office was a letter from Hong Kong addressed to Lee-Kung. "Su-Jen," my father said in a rising voice, "a letter from the prospective mail-order bride."

"I didn't know *Goh Goh* was getting married," I said.

"I don't know if he is yet," said my father as we turned to leave the post office. "They're still writing back and forth, getting to know each other. If they like each other, then your brother will arrange for her to come to Canada and they will get married."

My father was in a rush to get back. "How can Elder Brother decide if he likes her if they've never met?" I asked, my footsteps quickening. "Doesn't he want to meet his wife before they promise to get married?"

"The girl is in Hong Kong, Su-Jen. They will get to know each other through their letters," my father said. "If they like each other, then your brother will apply to the government and bring her to Canada as his mail-order bride. Dates are for *lo fons*. They are not the Chinese way."

"Well, I'm going to meet my husband before I marry him. And I'll wear a white wedding gown and get married in a church," I said.

"Oh, they can have a *lo fon*–style wedding," said my father. "Aunt Hai-Lan can look after that since she goes to church. But the banquet will have to be at a Chinese restaurant."

"What about a honeymoon?"

"Oh, Su-Jen, we'll think about those things later, they have just started to correspond." My father quickened his pace. I hurried to keep up with him but caught my sandal on a crack in the sidewalk and sprawled on the ground. My father turned back and helped me up, brushing me off and scolding me for being so clumsy.

I followed him into the restaurant and saw my mother pouring coffee for Mr. Swackhammer, who sat at the lunch counter with Reverend MacDougall.

"Look," called Father excitedly. "A letter from the mail-order bride." My mother lifted her head, a blank look on her face, the coffee pot in mid-air.

My father rushed into the kitchen and waved the letter at Lee-Kung. "A letter from the mail-order bride. Hurry! Open it!"

Lee-Kung was standing over a small wooden barrel filled with dirty cutlery and hot soapy water, shaking it from side to side. "Just a minute," he said. He lifted the barrel, emptied its contents into a pile on the draining board, and poured several pots of boiling water over the knives, forks, and spoons. Father again waved the letter at him. After wiping his hands on his apron, Lee-Kung reached for his towel to mop his neck and face. He took the envelope and slit it open with a knife, removing the folded onion-skin paper.

"What does she say?" asked Father.

Lee-Kung didn't answer right away. He finished reading, stuffed the paper in the envelope, and tossed it on the counter. "You can read it yourself," he said.

Father picked it up, removed the letter, and started to read, nodding his head with approval. "*Hola, hola,* good, good," he said.

I peered over Father's arm. "What does the letter say?"

"The girl is telling your brother about herself," said Father. "She's been in Hong Kong for almost a year, has a job in a wig-making factory. And would like to come to Canada. She sounds like a good possibility."

I turned to ask my brother if he liked what the mail-order bride had said in her letter, but stopped when I saw my mother staring at him as she stood inside the kitchen door. I glanced back at my brother. Their faces were still, eyes locked. He reached into his shirt pocket for cigarettes and walked into the backyard. My father put the letter on the counter and returned to the dining room without mentioning my fall. My mother did not notice the scrapes on my knees and hands. When I showed her, she didn't fuss, she told me absently to go upstairs and wash off the dirt.

The ceiling fan droned without seeming to bring any relief. In the front half of the restaurant, teenagers sat with their legs sticking into the aisle. As soon as one set of rock 'n' roll songs was finished, someone would drift over and feed more coins into the jukebox. There was a tray of wet cutlery on the table between my mother and me, but I felt so depleted by the heat that even a simple task like drying knives and forks felt almost impossible.

My mother stared at the cutlery and shook her head. "The moment I stepped off the plane," she said, "I knew that it was *tu-thlai,* all wrong." Her remark filled me with dread, having heard it many times before. I knew the words building inside her head, soon to be spat from her lips. Her face was oily with perspiration, and her eyebrows had gathered together just above the bridge of her nose. The utensils clanged loudly against each other as she tossed them into their respective slots.

Without looking at me, she said, "What difference is it to him that we're here? Much better to have stayed in Hong Kong. And have that old man send us money." Since the heat wave, her complaints about my father and our life in Canada had grown sharper and more frequent, often triggered by what seemed like nothing.

The teenagers in the booth closest to us had left. I noticed my father taking longer than usual to wipe the table. Suddenly he stood over us with the wet cloth still in his hand. He threw it on the table, making a thwacking sound. "Who do you think you are? The Empress?" he said, glaring at my mother.

She stared back at him. Shaking her head, she picked up the newspaper on the bench and fanned herself, "I might not be the Empress, but I didn't expect to be in prison for the rest of my life."

"Stop complaining. It's not like I'm living a life of luxury." My father picked up the rag and stomped into the kitchen.

Afraid to say anything or to look up, I continued drying the cutlery, having heard the same exchange of shots many times before. I knew my mother hated living in this town, but there was nothing anyone could do about it. I sat silently while she continued to complain. I could not bring myself to defend my father against her because I knew she would think I was being disloyal. My father had explained to me many times all the different titles in a Chinese family: *poh poh,* grandmother on mother's side, *yeh yeh,* grandfather on father's side, *dai gwoy,* older aunt on father's side, *kew kew,* younger uncle on mother's side, and so on. "In Chinese," he said, "you know right away if the aunt or uncle is on your mother's or your father's side, younger or older. Not like in English, where a person's position in the family is not known." He explained to me that in a traditional Chinese family the father's side was always more *teng,* stronger. The tone of his voice told me that I should love him more, but I could only nod. Deep inside, I knew, even then, that my mother came first. Yet when my father told me stories from China, his words were like a soft breeze on my cheek. Just recently, he had told me again the story of the Butterfly Lovers, how their love was forbidden, and how finally they were united in death. I had listened and pretended that I was the ancient heroine, disguised as a boy so that I could go away and study at school, only to fall in love with one of my classmates and live in anguish, unable to declare my true feelings.

It was hard to imagine an all-consuming love, like the one in the Butterfly Lovers. I couldn't recall my parents exchanging a gentle word or making a kind gesture to each other. I didn't like it when my mother referred to my father as "that old man." On one of our visits to Toronto, I had overheard her telling Aunt Hai-Lan that back in China not long after she had married my father, they'd run into a schoolmate of hers at a teahouse. The friend assumed that my father was her father. My mother had been so embarrassed that she had not corrected her. A few months later, much to her relief, he left for Canada.

I was ashamed that I had felt the same way. Darlene Atkinson often came to the restaurant with her family for supper and had commented to me at school, "I always see your grandfather sitting behind the cash register."

Jonette, who had been standing next to her, spoke before I could answer. "That's not her grandfather. That's her father." The skin underneath my clothes had grown hot and prickly, my face warm.

"He's so old!" Darlene exclaimed, her mouth wide open in surprise. "I thought the guy in the kitchen was your dad."

"No," I answered. "He's my brother."

The Atkinsons reminded me of the Andersons in the television show *Father Knows Best* that I had sometimes watched at Jonette's. When they came into the restaurant, Mrs. Atkinson had her arm hooked around her husband's elbow, followed by their three children. If only I were like Darlene, with parents like hers, a teenaged sister like Lorraine and an older brother like Gary. I wished Mr. Atkinson didn't clap my father on the back and call him Charlie. And when my father grinned back, I wished it wasn't so wide and false. I wished he were younger, like Lee-Kung. My embarrassment about my father ran deep. But the shame that I had about my feelings was like a knife in the heart.

MY MOTHER AND I sat on the fire escape, our backs against the railing. The night had not offered any relief from the heat, and the smell from the tannery remained as strong as it was during the day. Lee-Kung rested against the brick wall as he sat across from us, his bare legs stretched out beside my mother's, almost touching. His head was tilted up, smoke rings rising from his mouth. The air was so heavy, the rings stayed suspended in their doughnut shape a long time before disappearing.

My mother glanced up at the circles hovering above us. "You think you're so smart," she said, smiling at my brother.

"Watch me. I'll show you how," said Lee-Kung. They leaned toward each other, and he puckered his lips, releasing a circle of smoke with each push of breath. My mother laughed, her trailing hair brushing his arm.

I fetched the bamboo fan from the dresser and waved it at the smoke rings, making them disappear. My mother made a soft huff of annoyance. Lee-Kung took the fan from me and gently waved it in front of my mother. She lifted her face to let the air glide over her. With her back arched, she let out a slow sigh of satisfaction. I didn't like the way my brother looked at her, at the thin silky pyjama fabric falling over her breasts. I snatched the fan from him and held it in both hands, flapping it up and down in my mother's direction. She sat upright, looking startled. They both laughed. They seemed to have forgotten I was there.

It used to be that when my mother came to bed, she smelled of Yardley's lavender soap. Now she stank of tobacco.

The air soon became so oppressive that it could no longer contain itself, finally erupting into a thunderstorm that night. My mother and Elder Brother had been sitting on the fire escape talking when lightning began to sear the sky and thunder rumbled in the distance. They came in the door as the thunder exploded and I jumped out of bed, startling them. My brother stood in our bedroom, wearing only boxer shorts and a T-shirt; he seemed uncomfortable and stared at the floor while trying to squeeze past the bed. At that moment Father appeared in the doorway. My brother quickly excused himself and brushed past Father toward the foyer. Father stepped inside our room.

"I guess the thunder surprised you, did it?" He said to my mother.

"Yes," she said. Then with a hardness in her voice, she added, "It did." They looked at each other for a long minute. I was afraid to breathe.

My father shook his head and walked across the foyer into the room where he slept, closing the door behind him.

My mother shut the door and seemed to sag against it. A flash of lightning lit up the window. My mother and I rushed over and watched the storm through the rain-streaked panes of glass.

Rolls of thunder piled one on top of the other, rising into a deafening crescendo. She encircled me in her arms and held my head against her chest, her heart throbbing in my ear, the smell of cigarettes in her clothes. When she let go, I looked up. Her thick black hair fell loose below her shoulders. Her cheeks were wet, but it wasn't from the rain. She closed the window and we went to bed. Usually I found the rhythmic patter of rain on the roof soothing, reassuring, but that night it took a long time for me to fall asleep.

I woke up suddenly in the middle of the night and found my mother's side of the bed empty. For a while I stayed in bed and stared into the dark. The rain had stopped. I finally got up and opened the door to the fire escape. No one was there. I stepped onto the platform and felt the wet wrought-iron slats pressing into my bare feet. I peered over the railing and gazed down at the empty alley below. I looked up and saw a hazy moon suspended over the houses on the other side. For the first time in days, the air felt cool against my skin. Everything was so still, broken only by the drip of water and the beating of my heart. I should have gone back inside, but instead I shivered in the dark as I leaned against the damp brick wall next to my brother's window.

Compelled forward by something I did not understand, I edged over and peeked between the half-drawn curtains. There they were. Lying together in the moonlight on his bed, my long, dark brother on top of my pale, slender mother, their naked bodies coiled around each other like snakes. I pressed my hand over my mouth and stared, then dashed into our bedroom, got into bed, and pulled the covers over my head, my heart racing.

When my mother finally came to bed, I pretended to be asleep. Her hair reeked of cigarettes, but there was something different lurking underneath. The smell made me think of the marsh where Willow Creek widened into Irvine Lake.

In the morning the air was thin and light. The sky felt higher and had a paleness that made me think of winter. People walked more briskly and were no longer mopping their brows. Customers came into the restaurant expressing their relief at the change in weather. Normally I would have shared their feelings; instead I found it hard to concentrate on what they said. All I could think about was what I had seen the night before. Whenever I looked at someone in my family, I was filled with shame. I carried a terrible secret that I could never tell anyone.

All day my mother seemed to be living in another world. She took longer than usual drying the cutlery, stopping to stare into space for no apparent reason. She was so distracted that when she filled the sugar dispensers, several of them overflowed.

But that night and for several more after, my mother came to bed freshly bathed, fragrant with Yardley's lavender soap, smelling familiar again. I began to doubt myself. Maybe I hadn't really seen my mother and my brother together. Maybe I had only dreamed it. Then it began again: she came to bed in the early hours of the morning, bringing with her the smell of smoke and a lingering hint of salt and marsh.

From the outside it seemed that nothing in our family had changed. My father worked in the dining room, Lee-Kung in the kitchen, and my mother in both places. It was business as usual in the restaurant, with more customers on the weekend and busiest of all on payday at the tannery. The same bachelor diners came in for supper. Mr. Swackhammer and Reverend MacDougall came in for coffee most mornings. But our lives upstairs from the Dragon Café had changed forever. My father did not return to our bedroom and my mother's nightly absences became regular. I avoided my brother; I felt such a mixture of confusion and anger toward him, this brother whom I had once secretly adored and had expected to lead us to better days. Without intending to, I began to withdraw slowly from my family, pushing away my mother's sporadic hugs and spending less time listening to my father tell his stories.

To the people in Irvine, we must have seemed the perfect immigrant family. We were polite, hard-working, unthreatening, and we kept to ourselves. As far as the townsfolk were concerned, there was nothing about us that would upset the moral and social order that presided over them. Even when things started to go wrong, we blended so seamlessly into their everyday life, we remained invisible.

WITH SEPTEMBER APPROACHING quickly, my mother offered to make me a new dress for school. We crossed the road and went into the back of Reids' where the yard goods were displayed. I looked at shelves filled with bolts of cloth, thinking how I had shopped for fabric with my mother earlier this summer and how it seemed like a very long time ago. I chose a pale pink material with a pattern of small green leaves for my dress, knowing that my mother would have preferred a darker colour, something sensible, that wouldn't so easily show the dirt. She agreed to my selection and also to the yellow yarn for a sweater. I had chosen the colours to spite her; I had wanted her to object and argue with me, but she said nothing and paid the saleswoman as I hung back sulky and quiet. My feelings about her had changed in ways that I didn't understand. I only knew that I didn't like the way I felt. I wanted my love for my mother to be like it was before.

School started soon enough and I was glad to join the Grade Five class. Each day I did my homework at the back table in the restaurant, books and papers spread around me, spending more time on my assignments, keeping my head lowered and concentrating on my work. My parents rushed past me without stopping as they carried dishes back and forth from the dining room, no doubt pleased that I was so involved with my studies. When I stood in front of the mirror in the bedroom and looked at my reflection through the cracked silver lines, the face that stared back at me was mine. I was unable to detect anything different, yet I no longer felt the same, haunted by the secret that I kept.

I had walked into the kitchen and found my mother and Lee-Kung standing across from each other at the chopping block, slicing vegetables. Their heads were almost touching and they were talking and laughing in a soft, tender way. I left the room without either one noticing me. From then on I began to make a loud noise or cough before entering the kitchen. I hated protecting them, but I didn't know what else to do, I didn't want my father to find out.

Yet as time wore on, those moments of secret affection seemed to change. Lee-Kung no longer talked with my mother about buying a car and taking us to places like Niagara Falls. If they were around other people, I noticed a stiffness in her body. Her eyes never met Lee-Kung's. There was a new irritability between them. Once, when my mother took longer than usual scraping the dishes, Lee-Kung said to her, "Let's finish this tonight, not tomorrow." In the past my mother would have made a joke of it, but she snapped at him, "If you don't like the way I work, you can do it all yourself, then what?" Lee-Kung looked at her and shook his head. My mother sucked in her breath and bit her lower lip, looking as if she were ready to burst into tears.

I spoke to my brother as little as possible, and only when necessary. My mother frequently seemed preoccupied and often I had to say and ask things more than once. She became quieter and fought less with my father, but when she did she was vicious with her words. During one of their worst fights, she screamed at him, "I would kill myself and kill Su-Jen too rather than leave her here with you." My mother upset me, but I felt no anger, only sadness and emptiness. Even then, I must have understood something of my mother's sense of powerlessness. It was only later I came to realize that in an odd, twisted way, she was expressing a fierce love for me, but back then I had failed to see the depth of her unhappiness. At the time I saw my father, a man I was growing to love a little more each day, standing alone, his eyes filled with pain. I wanted to go to him, yet could not.

&

MY FATHER ONCE TOLD me a folk tale about the expression *ngeng hay*, to go along with things, to be uncomplaining. At its worst, this meant repressing all your bad thoughts, holding in the bad air, and allowing nothing to slip out.

There was a young girl who was about to get married. Before the girl left to go to her new home, her mother told her that if she wanted to have a happy marriage she should *ngeng hay*. Of course the mother meant that her daughter should overlook minor irritants, be uncomplaining. But the daughter misunderstood and thought that she should never release any bad air from her body. When the mother saw her daughter several months after the wedding, the girl had changed from a plump, rosy-cheeked girl to a thin, drawn wraith with a greenish tinge to her skin. Naturally the mother was alarmed. She asked her daughter what the matter was. The daughter said nothing was wrong, everyone was kind to her, she was only doing what her mother had told her. By being *ngeng hay*, she had not released any bad air; she hadn't passed any wind since she left home. The mother couldn't believe her ears.

It so happened that at a nearby village fair there was a farting contest, and the family decided to enter the girl as a contestant. She broke the longest, noisiest, smelliest fart of anyone there.

And it just so happened that the prize was a purse filled with gold. As it turned out, her idea of *ngeng hay* paid off after all. The girl then became plump and rosy-cheeked again. And everyone lived happily ever after.

This was one of the few folk tales from my father that my mother liked. The humour was obvious, but my mother made me uncomfortable the way she laughed and laughed, showering the poor bride with contempt.

My mother considered herself so different from my father. She felt he was mired in the past and saw herself as far more modern. At the time I didn't realize that their attitudes to life were, in fact, similar. They both talked about *hek fuh,* to swallow bitterness, and *ngeng hay*. For my mother, it seemed that she had swallowed bitterness for most of her life, in China and in Canada. It was odd that she saw herself as *ngeng hay,* as she bristled and fought so much with Father, complaining to me afterwards, but perhaps I didn't count. I guess what she meant was that if she didn't *ngeng hay,* she would have fought even more with him. "So much I keep inside myself because of you," she said. "If it weren't for you, I would leave." It seemed that by saying these words she wanted to tell me how much I meant to her, but they only made me resentful; I knew that she now stayed not just for me, but also because of my brother.

At school I was learning about the solar system. I learned the names of the planets, about the moon and its orbit around the earth. I finally understood the reason for the movement of the ocean tides that Mrs. Dooley had once tried to explain to me. Science class taught me that most things in the world could be explained by facts and observations, that proof was needed to make something real. I liked using words like *apparatus, procedure,* and *conclusion.* My mother, though, clung to the beliefs that she had brought with her from China. She talked about our dead relatives, about her encounters with them back in the village in China where she and my father sent money. She remained concerned about the omen inside the pages of the fortune teller's red book, reminding me again of the shadow that water cast over my life. She became obsessed with the mole that had been dug out from the inside corner of her right eye, the source of all the bad luck in her life, and fretted over my absence of moles. Frequently I would find her consulting with the book of face readings. She once said to me, her voice filled with dread, "The *fung shu,* the wind water, in the restaurant is wrong. The air is at odds with the moon."

When she shared those thoughts with me, I tried to dismiss them. I told myself that they made no sense, that they conflicted with what I was learning in school. But each spring as I crossed the bridge on the way to school I saw in the current of the river the shapes of underwater ghosts.

FOR SEVERAL MONTHS we had been savouring the harvest from my mother's garden. She had made one of our favourites, her winter melon soup, for supper. But that night, Father didn't seem interested in what my mother had cooked, he was busy questioning Lee-Kung instead. "Have you written back to Fu-Ling yet?"

I knew Father was referring to the letter Elder Brother had received more than two weeks ago.

Without looking up, my brother shook his head and shoved more rice into his mouth.

"*Jeet doo nay,* I can't believe you," said Father. "You are taking too long to answer. She's going to think you're not interested. What if she decides not to come? Then what will you do? All that time wasted."

"I'm a cook, not a writer. It takes time to decide what to say."

My father put down his rice bowl and chopsticks. "But you must find the time," he said. "What's so difficult about writing a simple letter?"

"Well, then why don't you write it?" my brother said defiantly. My mother looked away. I winced at Lee-Kung's words. Father believed strongly in the importance of children obeying their parents; although my brother was an adult and worked hard in the restaurant, I knew that his behaviour toward our father was not what was expected from a good Chinese son.

Father took a deep breath and stared at him before speaking. "Lee-Kung, I am your father," he said, his voice shaking. "It is the duty of a son to obey his father. I know what is best. A man needs to think about more than just himself, he must think about his family. You are thirty years old, not eighteen. You don't have all the time in the world. You must do as I tell you."

"I know what to do. You don't need to lecture me," said my brother as he stood up and walked into the kitchen with his chopsticks and rice bowl. During their exchange I stared at the table and ate my dinner. But I, too, wanted to shout at my brother; I, too, wanted him to get married. Anything to stop my mother from going to him in the night.

Father banged his fist on the table and looked at my mother, her chopsticks poised over the snow peas. "I want you to talk to him."

My mother shrugged her shoulders. "What more can I say?"

"Do as I ask."

I watched her back stiffen as she lifted some peas.

My mother and I stood in the kitchen, bent over the garbage pail, scraping uneaten food off a pile of dirty dishes on the draining board. Over the scratching sound of forks against plates, she told me that she was sending a small sum of money back to China for a wedding ceremony for my dead brother.

My heart sank. "*Mah,* what are you talking about? Why are you sending money to dead people?"

"Su-Jen, even dead sons must be married in order to have companionship," she said impatiently. "If my son were alive, he would now be old enough. He needs to get married, just like your father's first son. Once he has a wife in the ghost world, he won't be jealous of the living. And maybe he will look after us, take away my bad luck."

"But who's going to want to marry a dead man?" I asked loudly, emphasizing my disbelief.

"*Eiii-yah!*" she said. "There's so much you don't understand. If we were living in China, you would know about these things. The bride won't be alive. She'll be dead too, but she'd be the right age if she were alive. Just like the bride was for your father's dead son."

I ignored the tone of her voice and said, "How can you believe these things? You talk about ghosts as if they're real. If any of the people in town knew these things about us, they'd think we're crazy."

My mother held her plate and fork apart for a moment and looked at me. "You are becoming too much like the *lo fons,* Su-Jen. We are Chinese and we believe in the spirits of our ancestors. It's important to respect them. There's more to life than what you learn in school. You especially should be thankful to the ancestors for all the luck in your life. Going to school every day, playing with friends." She picked up another plate and continued her scraping. "Back in China, before the war when I was young, people were always telling me how lucky I was. I was the most beautiful girl in the village, probably in the county. My father, he said to me many times, *If I declared my daughter the third most beautiful girl in the village, no one would dare claim second, much less first spot.* I was betrothed when I was three. My father was a herbalist and he arranged a marriage into a very wealthy family. Before I was married, the wedding cakes and biscuits that were sent to the village were the best we had ever seen, and beautifully wrapped in red paper with gold lettering. I gave them out to every family in the village, I had so many." She stopped for a moment, seeming to be lost in the memory of better times. "We killed a hundred pigs for roasting and there was a three-day celebration before I went to Nanking to be married. I was only sixteen. A few months later, just before the Japanese invaded the city, I visited my sister in Canton. Everyone said that I was lucky to have been away, but they were wrong. Those hateful Japanese, they burned down my house and killed my husband. They destroyed the city. Because of them I ended up a poor woman with no husband, and no home to return to. When I discovered that I was going to have a baby, I had no choice but to stay with my sister and her family, but after she died, her husband saw me and my baby son as little more than beggars. Even the jewellery I was wearing, I had to sell. Aunt Hai-Lan had more luck than me. And now she is in Toronto with other Chinese people. She has no idea what my life is like here. Sometimes, Su-Jen, I think that I was unlucky to have survived the war. I had to marry your father, an old man, just to survive." Her impatience had faded and she now sounded crushed by sorrow. "I married him for my son. I wanted him to go to school, to have a future. But now he's dead and I am here. *Mo tin, mo meung.* No money, no life."

I continued my work, unable to look up, to respond. My mother added the cleared plate to the stack on the draining board. She tossed her fork into the cutlery barrel filled with soapy water, wiped her hands on her apron, and left me to finish scraping the plates, the screech of metal against china echoing in the empty kitchen.

&

THERE WAS AN UNSPOKEN but understood social hierarchy at school. The Kennys, the children of the town doctor, and the Barkers, the children of the local lawyer, looked down from the peak. At the bottom were the Pikes, a ragged family of fourteen children. There was at least one in every class. I heard rumours of Mr. Pike getting drunk all the time and never leaving his wife with enough money for groceries. Marion Pike, who was in my class, was quiet and mousy, but the other Pikes got into fights and caused trouble. All of them were filthy. The rest of us at school floated around in an undistinguished middle ground with people like Debbie MacLean occasionally rising to the top.

There were two people at school who lived beyond this social order. One was Hilary Beeston. Except for going to school and church it seemed that her life had very little to do with the town. Every Saturday her mother drove her to Toronto for violin lessons and in the winter they continued on to their chalet for skiing. She had to go home every day after school to practise her music. She was the only person I knew who took violin lessons, and I was unaware of any other family in town who went skiing. In the summer she went to Muskoka. She never seemed comfortable with the girls in her class at school. At recess she seemed to prefer to watch rather than to join in the games, even when she was invited.

The other person was Charlotte Heighington. She had an aura of self-assurance that enticed and challenged you to be as daring as she. She didn't cause obvious trouble in class, yet she defied the teachers in her own way. Unlike the rest of us who answered hesitantly, Charlotte replied with confidence and an unwavering stare. But the teachers seemed to like her. She appeared to understand jokes the rest of us didn't. I found myself wondering what it would be like to be so unafraid, to be that self-possessed. Charlotte read more than any other student in the class, and when she picked up a pencil or a crayon, the pictures that emerged were unlike anything I had ever seen. Some horses she had sketched from a photograph in a book looked more alive in her drawings, as if they were able not only to run but to fly.

Even Charlotte's looks stood out from the other girls in our class. Her face, I now realize, was too beautiful, too mature for her age. Her bones had a strength and angularity that didn't belong on someone so young, her mouth too full, her eyes too knowing.

Most of the girls in my class were careful around Charlotte, keeping her at arm's length. Charlotte's separateness reflected her family's position too. They didn't seem to have a clearly defined place in town, not fitting into one category of family or the other. It may have been because the Heighingtons never went to church or because they were poor, though not as poor as the Pikes. Several of the kids from school took weekly piano lessons from Mrs. Heighington. They talked about how much they hated going, saying that the house was dirty and disgusting. Jonette, who had been her student for a year, said to me, "The smell in that house is enough to make you gag. But my mother makes me go. She keeps saying it's so sad about Charlotte's mum." When I asked Jonette why, she told me her mother had said Charlotte's grandfather was so mad at Charlotte's mum for marrying who she did that he hadn't left her a penny of his money when he died.

Until that fall I hadn't had much to do with Charlotte. We were in the same grade, but hadn't been in the same class before. We slowly began to become friends; slowly because I was cautious by nature and her fearlessness made me nervous.

The Heighingtons lived on the street behind ours, their backyard ending at the alley that ran behind the restaurant. That first summer in Irvine I used to gaze into their yard, along with others, from the fire escape outside our bedroom, dreaming that it was some kind of earthly paradise. Now, going over for the first time after school, I realized their house was a shambling, rundown place, covered with what looked like fake brick. It was not at all the place of perfection that I had imagined. The front yard was a patchy mixture of grass, weeds, and dusty dirt. But on either side of the front door were two thick climbing rose bushes that bloomed great clusters of red flowers in early summer and filled the air with their fragrance.

I followed Charlotte around the side of the house, stepping over her two younger brothers as they pushed Dinky Toys around in the dirt. They didn't look up as Charlotte led me through a screen door into a small vestibule cluttered with tools, beer bottles, children's toys, and a baby stroller. I was struck by the oversweet scent of apples on the verge of rot. I would soon learn that the air in the Heighington house was always like that, strong and heavy, no matter what the season.

When Charlotte opened the kitchen door, their collie dog, Juno, ran toward us, barking and wagging her tail. Charlotte laughed as she bent down and allowed the dog to lick her face. I stiffened as I watched them; I was fearful of dogs. For years my mother had filled me with tales of dogs roaming wild in China; she frequently showed me the scar on her knee where she had been bitten as a child.

Charlotte's mother was sitting at the kitchen table reading, her feet propped up on a chair. On the table was an ashtray brimming with old butts, a cigarette smouldering on its edge. Mrs. Heighington wore a faded cotton dress that fell over unshaven legs, her bare feet in a pair of rubber flip-flops, exposing toes with peeling polish. Simmering on the stove was a huge pot of something that smelled like stewing meat and vegetables. She seemed completely absorbed in her book. Charlotte called out to her and Mrs. Heighington looked up and smiled at us. She was a thin woman with a pale, freckled complexion and dull red hair. Her skin had a quality that I had seen in some older *lo fon* women: an onion-paper thinness with fine, delicate lines around the mouth and eyes. She told me that she knew all about me, that she was glad to meet me. Her eyes were dark and warm. She made me feel immediately at home.

The Heighington place, even though it had a typical living room, dining room, and kitchen, felt different from the other houses I'd visited in town. For one, the kitchen table was cluttered with dirty dishes, and there were books everywhere, some open and some closed. I soon learned that aside from my father, there wasn't anyone who loved stories as much as Charlotte's mother. She recounted fairy tales, Greek myths, and Bible stories to us. Even though she didn't go to church any more, she told me that her favourite stories were from the Old Testament. And she was always listening to music on the radio. She said it was classical and she loved it, even when Mr. Heighington yelled at her from the other room to "turn that crap down."

One Saturday after lunch Mrs. Heighington, with the baby on her hip, handed Charlotte a brown paper bag and told us we'd have to sing for our supper by collecting cigarette butts. We spent the next few hours with our heads down, searching the sidewalks and the gutters of Irvine. I knew that none of the other girls in our class would do something as grimy as this, nor would Charlotte ask them.

We found some butts on the way to the Community Centre, but the best hunting ground was the grassy lawn around it. Our eyes grew keen at detecting squashed white cylinders nestled in the grass or lying in the grooves between sections of pavement. On the way back to the Heighingtons' we came across a gold mine. Somebody had emptied a car ashtray in the gutter next to a Stop sign. "What a find!" crowed Charlotte. "Some of them are barely smoked."

Bringing our bag into the kitchen, we sat at the mottled grey Arborite table with Mrs. Heighington and spread our harvest on the table. We cut off the burnt ends and snipped open the butts with scissors, then scraped the dried tobacco into a bowl. Mrs. Heighington scooped up the tobacco and rolled it in fresh papers. The baby had fallen asleep in her playpen in a corner of the room. From where we sat I could hear the television in the living room where Charlotte's father, her two brothers, and her grandparents watched wrestling. Mrs. Heighington was listening to a broadcast of the opera. I found the singing just as strange as in the Chinese operas my parents played on Sunday evenings.

Mrs. Heighington caught me staring at her as she worked, placing just the right amount of tobacco on the paper and rolling it without loosing a shred. "You didn't know rolling cigarettes could be an art form, did you, Annie?" she said, a small, crooked smile on her face. I accidentally dropped some tobacco on the floor. Juno rushed over and licked it up. Charlotte and her mother laughed. Mrs. Heighington tickled the dog under her chin and said, "Are you trying to take up smoking, poochie?" I listened to them laugh again, and I knew I didn't want to go home, I wanted to help Charlotte's mother make cigarettes for the rest of the afternoon.

After we finished, I scrubbed my hands with soap. My fingers smelled of tobacco and I didn't need my mother asking me questions, though it was unlikely she would have noticed.

Before I left, Mrs. Heighington said to me, "Annie, you are indeed a boon companion." Although I didn't know the meaning of boon, the warmth of her words made me feel welcome and wanted. I adored her.

I LEANED AGAINST the red brick wall of the school, waiting for the morning bell. The air felt gentle and I could tell that it was going to be one of those last warm days in October before the cold settled in.

I didn't see Charlotte coming until she was almost in front of me. She looked sad and preoccupied, her face puffy and splotched. When I asked her what was wrong, she said quietly, "My grandpa died in the night. My grandmother woke up this morning, and he was there lying next to her, dead."

My mouth dropped open in alarm. "That's terrible. Was he sick?"

Charlotte took a shaky breath. "No. He just died in his sleep. The doctor thinks it was a heart attack."

I felt terrible for Charlotte, but I wondered what it would be like to lose someone I loved; all my grandparents were long dead before I was born.

"Oh, Charlotte." It was all I could say. I took her hand in mine and gave it a squeeze.

"My grandmother couldn't stop crying. The funeral is tomorrow. Tonight there's something at the funeral home where we all say goodbye to him. Will you come, Annie?" She looked me in the eye.

I hesitated, avoiding the question. "I've never seen a dead person before," I finally said.

"Well . . . he looks the same," Charlotte's voice dropped to a hush. "But when I touched him, he felt cold. His fingers were stiff." Her breath was warm against my cheek. I was horrified to think that Charlotte had touched a dead body. Charlotte leaned her head slightly toward mine, drawing me in. "Will you come to my house after supper? And come with us to the funeral home?"

I couldn't move. I prayed that the bell would ring before I had to answer. Charlotte's face looked pale and sad, yet she continued to hold my gaze.

My mother was convinced the dead were to be feared, that they had powers beyond our comprehension. I thought about the wedding in China my mother felt she had to have for her dead son in order to appease his spirit. Although I had argued with her about her beliefs and I said they made no sense, there remained within me a nagging doubt, making it impossible to completely deny the existence of spirits. Now, faced with the possibility of seeing a dead person, I was truly afraid and reluctant. I worried I would be tempting fate by going near someone who had just died. But Charlotte had asked me to be with her, to be her friend. I could not refuse. I agreed to go.

If my mother found out that Charlotte's grandfather had just died, she would not let me go to the Heighingtons'. There was trouble enough dealing with the spirits of the dead in our own family. What unknown rituals would have to be performed for my protection if she knew that I had gone into a house where the soul of the recently deceased might still be lingering?

In order to go to the funeral home with Charlotte, I would have to convince my mother to let me eat before the rest of my family. Supper hour was busy in the restaurant, meaning that we ate after the customers left, rarely before seven-thirty. Today would be no different. My mother would not be pleased that I was missing our family supper, a proper Chinese meal. I decided to tell her that Charlotte and I had been chosen to work on a special school project, and then ask her to make me a snack so that I could leave and work at Charlotte's house.

When I arrived home, there were only a few customers in the dining room of the restaurant. In another half-hour, at quarter to five, the tannery whistle would signal to grown-ups the end of work and to children the end of play. My father was drying and putting away glasses on the shelves above the stainless-steel sinks behind the lunch counter. He called after me as I rushed past. In the kitchen my mother was slicing vegetables in preparation for the supper hour.

My mother seemed annoyed at my request to eat early. Although she never said as much when I visited with Charlotte, I knew she would have preferred me to spend time with other girls. She still talked about Jonette with the small smile, and she liked the way Darlene looked in her freshly ironed clothes. But she called Charlotte the girl with the devil eyes. In the summer, Charlotte had come to the restaurant for ice cream. When my mother handed her her cone across the counter, Charlotte stared back at her, something that a good Chinese girl would never do.

Before she could say no, I blurted out that the teacher had chosen Charlotte and me over other kids for an assignment, and that it would mean extra marks. She finally agreed and settled for making me a hot chicken sandwich. I knew she relished the idea of her daughter, an immigrant, doing so well and working on special projects, ahead of other *lo fon,* Canadian-born children who were the same age. I was a good student and she was proud of my report card filled with A's. My father constantly reminded me how hard I had to work, that if I wanted to compete with the *lo fons* I would have to work twice as hard, be twice as good, maybe even ten times. My parents had long decided that I would become either a lawyer or a doctor, elevating myself and them above the restaurant business.

Several times she walked past the back booth where I was eating. Each time she hesitated for a moment, as if she wanted to say something to me, but I focused on my sandwich and pretended not to see her. I felt nervous and excited and had to force myself to finish the meal.

At the Heighingtons' I found Charlotte's father waiting at the kitchen table, gently rocking the baby buggy. He looked uncomfortable in his good jacket. The boys stood in front of their mother, having their hair combed. Their faces were shiny from being scrubbed and their clothes were clean and pressed, unlike how they often were at school, scruffy from spending the lunch hour playing in the sandbox. I almost didn't recognize Mrs. Heighington. Her hair, freshly washed and parted at one side, fell in loose waves around her face. She wore a plain black dress, nylon stockings, and black shoes. I wondered if this was the real Mrs. Heighington, a glimmer of the young woman I had seen in an old photograph in the living room. It was strange seeing them all dressed up. They seemed like a different family. Mrs. Heighington smiled sadly at me and told Charlotte to hurry and change into her dress.

I followed Charlotte out of the kitchen past a pile of dirty laundry, with the sleeves of shirts and legs of pants wriggling like snakes onto the floor, and through the large room where Mrs. Heighington gave her piano lessons. Past the dining table covered with knickknacks and piles of books was the piano. There seemed to be an invisible line drawn around the music area. There were no laundry baskets or piles of clutter. The top of the piano was clear except for a lamp, a vase, and an ashtray.

Charlotte took me into her grandparents' bedroom. From the doorway I could see the room was dominated by a double bed, still unmade, with blankets pushed toward the foot, exposing a rumpled bottom sheet. There was a depression in each of the pillows, cradling an invisible head. Which side had her grandfather slept on? I had seen the double bed where Mr. and Mrs. Dooley slept; unlike this one, it had always been made, their private lives hidden by a smooth white bedspread. My parents used to share the same bed, but I had always been there in the middle, protecting them from each other. Here, along with the rumpled sheets, the smell of acrid sweat hung in the air, stale cigar smoke mingled with layers of old perfume and pee. I could feel the grandfather's presence. What was I doing in a dead man's room? I could hear my mother's voice admonishing me, "*Seen geng,* crazy!"

Charlotte's grandmother was sitting in the corner of the room, staring at the empty bed. She filled the oversized and faded brown velvet chair so completely that it was hard to tell where it stopped and where she began. The old woman wept silently into a handkerchief as Charlotte went to her and put her arms around her.

"Oh, Charlotte! You're a treasure, a real treasure." She looked up and saw me hanging back in the doorway. She extended an arm. Without thinking, I rushed over and knelt down, burying my head in her bosom. I could feel the folds of flesh under her black lace dress. She wrapped her arm across my shoulders, and I smelled a mixture of camphor and the same Evening in Paris perfume I had given my teacher at Christmas. As she stroked my back, she said tearfully, "You're a good friend, being with our Charlotte today." At that moment, in spite of the death of her grandfather, I envied Charlotte. I envied the warmth and easy affection that flowed in her family. I liked the way they were talking about her grandfather: how much they loved him and would miss him, but also funny little things like his love of cheap cigars and the humbugs covered in lint that he kept in his pockets. Charlotte released herself from her grandmother's embrace and stood up, saying she had to get ready. I reluctantly followed Charlotte out and up to her bedroom.

Being in Charlotte's room was like being in another house. Her bed was made, with the sheets smoothly spread beneath a nubbly baby blue cotton cover. The floor was swept and the drawers in her bureau were closed. The walls were covered with line drawings of horses, ready to spring off the paper. There were pictures of fantastical animals, of made-up places and creatures. Looking at those pictures, I entered a place unlike any other. I had travelled across the world, and I knew that the ground was always beneath my feet and the sky above my head. But in Charlotte's imagination none of that would be true.

Charlotte brought out from her closet a dress made from shiny black taffeta that shimmered when it caught the light. Charlotte held it against her body, the full skirt billowing out. "What do you think?" she asked. I stretched out my hand, carefully touching the smooth, silky fabric. It was beautiful. "My mum made it for me."

Charlotte's mother had the hands of a magician, one minute rolling cigarettes, the next minute sewing princess gowns. My mother made dresses for me, but nothing like this, one that shone and sparkled. Charlotte undressed and put her clothes away, wearing only her panties and undershirt. Her breasts were starting to show. I could see two reddish-brown centres pushing against the thin material. Charlotte put on her dress, then fished a white lacy crinoline from her closet and slipped it under her skirt.

I looked at Charlotte in her new dress as she combed her hair off her face and clipped it back with two silver barrettes. I noticed for the first time the deep green of her eyes and how they were flecked with caramel, the same colour as her hair. I turned and caught a glimpse of myself in the mirror: my plain skirt and red cardigan, my navy knee socks and my black shoes with their single straps. I saw a round face, with narrow eyes and a broad nose. I would never look like Charlotte. I knew that my hair would always be straight, and I wondered if my chest would always be flat. Charlotte put on her jacket and we joined the family downstairs.

Wilkinsons' Funeral Home seemed set apart from all the stores on Main Street, with a remote and dignified feeling. Charlotte and I walked behind her family to the front door of the building. The grass was green and cut short. The shrubs surrounding the front of the whitewashed brick building were carefully clipped, giving the effect of a border of green ruffles.

Mr. Heighington opened the heavy wooden door and we walked into a foyer. Against the wall was a polished wooden table with a gleaming silver vase of yellow chrysanthemums and white roses. Through the arched doorway was the most beautiful room I had ever seen. Hanging from the ceiling was a glass light in the shape of a flower with many petals. At one end of the room, thick burgundy curtains were drawn across a curved window. At the other end, resting on top of a long table with a white satin skirt, was an open wooden coffin.

Charlotte's grandmother sat down in an armchair closest to the coffin, clutching a rumpled hankie. Mr. Heighington stood next to his mother with his hands behind his back and his head down. I didn't see him very often around their house. During the week he worked for a construction company and on the weekends he was either watching television in another room or drinking with his friends at the Irvine Legion. Sometimes Charlotte had to go to the Legion to tell her father that supper was ready. I found myself staring at him again. The jacket and freshly pressed pants seemed to make his movements stiff, and his face looked raw from a recent shave.

Mrs. Heighington lifted the baby out of the carriage and stood beside her husband. She told her sons to sit on the couch that was near their grandmother and to be on their best behaviour. Charlotte and I hovered just inside the room.

Neighbours began to arrive. Some of them stopped to speak to Charlotte before moving on to the other family members. I noticed that Mrs. Heighington did most of the talking, while her husband seemed awkward and silent. I saw Jean MacDougall and her mother hesitating under the archway. When Mrs. Heighington saw the minister's wife, she passed the baby to her husband. Mrs. MacDougall seemed to draw herself up before walking over with her daughter. She nodded stiffly at Mrs. Heighington. "Margaret," she said, then moved Jean along and spoke to Charlotte's grandmother. I was surprised to see Mrs. Heighington turn red and quickly wipe her eyes.

If I stood on my tiptoes I could see the outline of Charlotte's grandfather rising above the edge of the coffin. I could tell that he was dressed in a suit, probably not unlike the one worn by the town lawyer when he came into the restaurant for coffee and pie. I had only ever seen her grandfather dressed in pants that hung below his belly and an undershirt that exposed his loose, flabby arms. Charlotte took my hand and whispered that she wanted to see the body up close. I was terrified. I knew I was tempting this dead man's spirit just being there. I wondered if Charlotte could hear the hammering of my heart. I wanted to go with her as she approached the coffin, but couldn't, my feet seemed nailed to the floor. Charlotte dropped my hand and walked toward her grandfather.

She stood in front of the coffin and stared back at me. I told myself there was no reason for me to be afraid, but I was. I shook my head, imagining the still, waxen face framed by folds of white satin. My mother's voice echoed inside my ear, telling me that I was crazy, to leave at once. But I stayed and watched as Charlotte extended her arms along the edge of the coffin and bent over the side to kiss her grandfather's face.

When I went home that evening I marched straight past my parents and went directly to the second floor, rushing up the stairs. Dodging the boxes on the steps, I hurried into the bathroom and filled the bathtub with hot water, undressing as quickly as I could.

I lay in the tub of hot water, shut my eyes, and saw the inside of Charlotte's house, the piles of books, the stacks of unwashed dishes, and baskets of dirty laundry. I saw again and again the image of Charlotte bending over the coffin with her arms resting along the edge. I looked down at my naked body stretched out in the water and ran my hands over my chest, grazing the flat tips of my nipples. I felt for the first time a slight swelling beneath the skin. I remembered the day my mother pointed to the scar in the corner of her eye. Going with Charlotte to the funeral home seemed like such a foolish thing to have done. I was sure I had tempted fate by going. I felt guilty lying to my mother and putting myself in danger. And yet this lie, this secret that I cradled inside my chest, gave me a strange sense of power. My skin prickled in the hot water. My thoughts about my mother were like a knot of tangled yarn. I sank deeper into the tub.

THE DINING ROOM of the restaurant was empty, and without anyone putting dimes or quarters into the jukebox, it was eerily quiet. We were used to eating supper to the music of Ricky Nelson or the Everly Brothers, but tonight we listened to the hum of the refrigerator, the sound broken only by the howling winds outside. A November snowstorm had caught everyone by surprise. Lee-Kung had been shovelling snow from the sidewalk when I returned from school that afternoon, but drifts had gathered once more against the building. I could see peaks of snow along the bottom of the front windows. The bachelor tannery workers had rushed in after the whistle and eaten quickly, not bothering to linger over coffee and cigarettes. Likely because of the storm the later regular customers had stayed home. Even the teenagers who met each other almost every night in our restaurant were nowhere to be seen.

The quiet evening had given my mother and Lee-Kung the time to prepare a special meal. When they could, they made intricate dishes, experimenting with different combinations of ingredients. One of my brother's favourites involved soaking sheets of dried bean-curd skins in water until they were soft and pliable, then curling them into rolls filled with minced fresh shrimp and pork, and finally braising them gently in a sauce of chicken stock and scallions. Tonight there were dishes of steamed chicken chopped with dried mushrooms, of broccoli stir-fried with abalone, and a soup from pork stock with sliced carrots and dried bok choy. At the supper table, my mother placed the best dishes in front of my brother. It was obvious to me that they made these special efforts for each other. But how could my father not see? Of course he never let on that anything was wrong. Instead, he praised their efforts. In good Chinese families certain things were never said. To do so was to violate the face of the family, a sin of the gravest order. But looking back, I think my father must have known earlier than I gave him credit for. Why else would he have been so concerned about my brother's marriage?

I was wrenched from my thoughts by the tone of Father's voice.

"Spent all that money – for what? For nothing!" He spat the words like stones from his mouth.

They were talking about Fu-Ling, my brother's mail-order bride, the woman on whom my father was pinning his hopes. In the afternoon Father had trudged back from the post office with his head tucked into his chest against the blowing snow, carrying a letter from her.

My mother said, without looking up from the table, "Isn't it better that Lee-Kung find out now? He can start again, be married in another couple of years."

"If only we had found out ahead of time, before we spent all that money on her," said Father, shaking his head. I knew the matchmaker in Toronto had been paid for her services and that money had been sent to Fu-Ling as a goodwill gesture and probably for English lessons.

"We can't ask someone to send results from a chest X-ray with the very first letter. Lee-Kung is still young," said my mother, dismissing his concerns. Then she turned to me, noticing that I had almost finished my soup. "Su-Jen, do you want another bowl?"

I shook my head, seething. I saw through her words. I wanted to shout at her, I wanted my father to insist that my brother get married as soon as possible. But I said nothing, silenced by the iron yoke of our family code, weighing us down and locking us in our places.

"*Ba*, you don't usually find out these things until you've been corresponding for a while, not until you're close to applying to the government. You have to agree that it's better we find out now, not after I'm married. Then I'd be stuck paying medical bills for a wife who can't work," said Lee-Kung, jabbing with his chopsticks to break off a large piece of the minced steamed chicken.

"I know that," Father said to Lee-Kung. "But it's the time that you've wasted. You really should be getting married this year. You're not getting any younger. In another few years you will be considered less eligible. By then you'll be thirty-three, close to thirty-five. You have to start a family, and think about taking over the business. I am not a young man."

"It's not my fault," snapped Lee-Kung. "Stop blaming me."

"You are not taking this seriously, Lee-Kung. You have responsibilities," said Father, sounding exasperated.

Lee-Kung picked up his empty rice bowl and chopsticks and left the table. He kicked open the kitchen door. It swung back and forth behind him.

"Pock Mark's grocery truck will be here tomorrow," said Father to no one in particular. "I'll have a talk with him. Maybe in one of the small towns, there is a young girl we don't know about, looking for a husband." My mother stared at the table as if she hadn't heard.

After supper my mother and I were removing the pins that held the paper patterns to the pieces of cloth she had cut out and would later sew into a dress for herself. I asked why the mail-order bride wasn't coming.

My mother looked around her. This seemed an odd reaction since the only other people who could understand Chinese were the ones in our family and the restaurant was empty. Lee-Kung was in the kitchen washing dishes and Father was filling sugar dispensers behind the lunch counter. She dropped her voice to a whisper. "Your brother got a letter. The mail-order bride, her X-ray showed traces of *fuh loh*." She told me that it was a dreadful disease that people died from, so horrendous that the Canadian government wouldn't let you in if you showed even the slightest trace. In my mind, *fuh loh* took on terrible proportions. I came to the conclusion that it was leprosy, the unspeakable disease I'd read about in the Bible. I suddenly felt sorry for this phantom bride who would probably develop sores all over her body and whose nose, fingers, and toes would all drop off. Nevertheless, I was grateful to the Canadian government for saving not just my brother but our family from such an ill-fated marriage.

It wasn't until many years later, when someone translated *fuh loh* into English for me, that I realized the Canadian government had rejected my brother's mail-order bride because she had tested positive for tuberculosis.

Thinking about Lee-Kung's failed mail-order bride, I wondered if my parents would one day insist on choosing a husband for me. I couldn't imagine marrying someone I had never spoken to, or even kissed. Not that I knew what it was like to kiss a boy. I'd only seen real kissing in the movies at the Roxy, but it wasn't at all like the dry peck I'd seen between Jonette's parents. Walking home from school a few weeks earlier with Charlotte, we had stopped on the bridge and she had suddenly asked me if I knew what French kissing was. I leaned over the railing and said nothing. I hadn't wanted to admit that I didn't know.

Charlotte picked up some stones and tossed them over one at a time into the stream. She glanced around and said in a low voice, "That's when someone kisses you and he sticks his tongue in your mouth."

My jaw dropped as I turned and stared at her. "What! That's totally disgusting!" I said.

"Well . . . ," said Charlotte. "It all depends on who you do it with."

"How would you know?" I scoffed.

"None of your business," she said slyly.

I felt my face turn red. "I'm not letting anybody put his tongue in my mouth," I said with a huff.

"Oh brother, Annie," she said, rolling her eyes and shaking her head. A moment later she raised her eyebrows and added in a purring voice, "I'll bet your parents do it." She leaned over the railing and dropped another stone into the water.

I didn't say anything. Suddenly I understood that my mother kissed like that. But not with my father. I picked up a rock and hurled it into the water.

Not everything I knew about the bodies of men and women came from listening to Charlotte. I already knew that babies grew inside women's swollen bellies and I had seen boys pee behind the school. But Charlotte seemed to know all the adult secrets, speaking with such authority that I listened in awed silence about thick hair growing in private places, men with appendages the size of cucumbers dangling between their legs, babies slimy with blood being pushed through women's vaginas. More than anything, though, it was her voice: hushed and intimate, like the serpent in the Garden of Eden, inviting me to enter the secret society of grown-ups. I think back to how I devoured her talk, collecting all this mature information, trying to understand what I then could not.

At the time it was more interesting than anything I learned at school, and more thrilling than anything I talked about with Jonette or Darlene Atkinson. If my mother had her way I would be friends only with girls like Jonette or Darlene. But especially Darlene, a *nice* girl. She was the kind of girl who glowed from the top of her golden hair to the bottom of her polished shoes. With her soft pageboy framing her face, she looked like the girl on the Breck shampoo bottle. She had the best handwriting in the class. When Darlene's family came to the restaurant for supper, my mother commented, "What a nice family. Such polite children." There were times when I envied Darlene, when I wanted to be like her to please my mother. But in my heart of hearts, I knew I wanted to be as bold and fearless as Charlotte.

The next day the snowstorm was still blowing. In the night the last elm on the hill below the school had split and toppled over. Our teacher told us that the elm trees in Ontario were dying because of Dutch elm disease and that was why each year our trees had more bare branches and the leaves looked brown and dry. After school Charlotte and I walked past where the tree had fallen. Workmen from the town had already cleared away the branches and sawn off the spiky trunk, leaving behind a smooth, flat stump. I couldn't imagine a worse day for working outside.

The wind that had gathered and sculpted the snow along one side of the creek bank into long waves of rippling white drifts must have bitten into their hands and faces.

I walked with my scarf wrapped twice around my neck and my hat pulled low over my forehead. My cheeks were stinging from the cold as Charlotte and I went into her house through the side door. We found her mother looking out the kitchen window into the backyard. Mrs. Heighington had pounded a metal pole with a table feeder on top into her yard. On it she had scattered seeds for the birds. She gestured to us with her arm to approach the window. A gorgeous male cardinal was standing on the feeder, his deep-red coat, his black beak, his pointed crest in sharp contrast to the white snow. "Look at the cardinal," she said, laughing. "He's so beautiful, and so bossy, the way he chases the other birds away from the seeds. Look, Annie, there's his wife." Next to her husband, she seemed so plain with her muted reddish-brown coat.

It was as if Mrs. Heighington had read my thoughts. "In the bird world, Annie, the male is always the flamboyant one. We female humans tart ourselves up to attract the opposite gender, but female birds are plain so that when they nest their eggs, they're camouflaged."

Charlotte's mother told us that earlier in the afternoon she had taken the baby in a sled for a walk around the lake. She said, "The first snowfall is always magical, a winter wonderland."

It was still snowing so much that in the short walk home from Charlotte's house, I became covered with snow. I was just inside the door, still shaking the snow from my hat, when my father expressed concern about Pock Mark's journey through all those stops between London and Urquhart. Father was worried he would not make it to us that night. It had only happened a few times before, but if the weather was really bad Pock Mark would sleep in the truck and come to us the next afternoon.

Pock Mark Lee's truck was more like a caravan. Attached to the back of the cab was a huge rectangular box on wheels, fitted to allow customers to explore his wares inside. The moment he opened the back doors, a sharp, pungent mingling of smells like dried mushrooms, oysters, shrimp, salted fish, and fermented bean curds prickled your nostrils. If it was night, Pock Mark switched on a light recessed into the ceiling. The adults would hunch their bodies to enter. Built-in shelves were filled with Chinese groceries: packages of dried roots and herbal medicines, dried red dates and pouches of lotus seeds for soup, strings of Chinese sausages, the flat carcasses of dried duck and salted fish for steaming. Pock Mark carried medicinal teas and vials of tiny pink *Po Chai* pills expected to cure everything from headaches to diarrhea. There was a shelf filled with Chinese movie magazines, newspapers, and Chinese books. Pock Mark sold seeds in the spring and narcissus bulbs just before Christmas. In a back corner of the truck he kept a refrigerator that stored fresh vegetables and a large tin pail of water filled with fresh bricks of tofu. During each visit Father bought me a small package of *moys,* plums and apricots soaked in a syrup of sugar and anise, then dried and individually wrapped in thin, wrinkly paper. My mother always took time to go through the movie magazines before choosing one to buy. It was never an easy decision. I watched her shake her head and mutter to herself, "Maybe this one. It has more stories, but that one has more pictures of Hung Sing Nu." Whatever the selection, the purchase never made her happy. After reading about lives that were faraway and more exciting than hers, she would look around the cluttered kitchen or dingy dining room and complain. She often talked about how different her life would be if only she had been born at another time. She once told me about a family friend who had married into a wealthy family, but had died before the war when she was only thirty. My mother always felt that in spite of dying young, the woman had been lucky, that her short life had been filled with good fortune and that she had known no suffering.

That night, miraculously, Pock Mark pushed through and arrived at the Dragon Café only an hour later than usual. We were about to begin our meal as he came in, stomping the snow off his shoes. Father insisted that he join us for supper. "Hurry, hurry, come sit down, old friend. Come and eat." He motioned with his arm at a chair. My mother went into the kitchen and came out with a bowl of steaming white rice and a pair of chopsticks.

Pock Mark hung his coat on the rack and rubbed his hands together. "*Eem gwoi, eem gwoi,* no need to fuss," he said. "What a terrible night. I didn't know if I would make it. But look how fortunate I am, to have supper waiting for me, and a beautiful girl like Su-Jen to sit beside. Who would have thought an ugly old thing like me would be so lucky?"

My mother smiled and shook her head. "Talk later. Eat while the food is hot."

"We're just about to start," said Lee-Kung. "We'll give you the order after we finish." My mother and Lee-Kung always made a list of the items they wanted from the travelling grocer: special rock sugar, soya sauce, rice noodles, and so on.

Father seemed barely able to contain his impatience. "Do you know of any good girls?" my father said the moment Uncle Pock Mark paused from his rice to take a sip of soup. By "good" I knew he meant a girl who was unmarried, who was obedient, and stayed at home with her parents. Pock Mark often talked about his travels through the province. He sold groceries to all the Chinese families in the small towns of Southern Ontario, and he was among the first to know about the arrival of a son, daughter, or wife. Pock Mark wasn't an official matchmaker like those who had contacts in Hong Kong; his services depended on knowing of young, unmarried Chinese women already living in Canada.

Pock Mark seemed surprised. "Good girls? For who? I thought Lee-Kung was corresponding with that girl in Hong Kong."

Lee-Kung shook his head, but Father answered, "No, that one's not coming." Then he lowered his voice and added, "*Fuh loh.*"

Pock Mark frowned with concern and leaned closer. "Don't even think about it, better that you know now."

"That's what I say," interrupted Lee-Kung. "But my father can't get over the money we've spent."

Pock Mark turned to Father. "*Hi-lo,* yes. It is a loss, but you don't want to go near that kind of trouble. It's one thing if you're already married, but what if they hadn't found the *fuh loh* and she got sick over here, then what would you do? You'd all be stuck. And think of the money Lee-Kung would have to spend on doctors. You never know about these girls. Did I ever tell you about the fellow who owns the restaurant in Hespeler? I heard this from his brother. His mail-order wife from Hong Kong apparently has some kind of skin condition: when she gets up in the morning, the bed is cover with dead skin. *Eiee* . . . the thought makes my stomach churn. Sounds like being married to a fish, leaving scales all over the place. Much better to know these things ahead of time."

I grimaced at Pock Mark's story. Turning to me, he wagged his finger. "Su-Jen, I'm not *gon ei wah,* I don't talk fat talk. I always tell the truth."

"But we've invested a lot of time and money," Father answered, adding a sigh of exasperation.

"Let it go," said Pock Mark, gesturing with his chopsticks. "Better to know now than too late."

"So then, old friend, do you know of any good girls?" asked Father again. I noticed my mother exchange a glance with Lee-Kung, then pick up her spoon and dip it in the soup bowl.

Pock Mark had another mouthful of rice, and didn't speak for a few moments. "Let me think . . . yes, yes, over at the restaurant in Bambury," he said. "The daughter has just arrived from Hong Kong. Maybe eighteen or nineteen. Too old for school. I met her just last week. Shy, very quiet. *Em jee seng, em jee seng.* Doesn't talk too much. The kind of girl you're looking for."

Setting his chopsticks on the table, Father smiled at Pock Mark. "Could you approach them?" asked Father. "Tell them about Lee-Kung, how hard-working he is, what a fine son-in-law he would make." I watched the change in Father's face, he seemed like a man whose wish had finally been granted. Lee-Kung held his rice bowl to his mouth, hiding his face. Father waited for him to say something.

My brother took a long time to swallow. "Yes," he finally said, echoing Father. "Tell them what a fine son-in-law I would make."

"I'm going there tomorrow. Do you want me to talk to them?" asked Pock Mark. He picked up a toothpick and cleaned between his teeth. My mother stood up to clear the table.

"Yes, yes," answered Father. "This might be a real opportunity. We can't afford to lose any more time."

"Good girls like this are hard to come by," said Pock Mark, looking pointedly at Lee-Kung.

"I know," said Father. "A girl raised over here wants to choose her own husband. Won't let the parents pick for her." Then he turned to Lee-Kung and added, "You just might be lucky."

"When I'm old enough I'm going to pick my own husband," I blurted.

My father and Pock Mark looked at me and laughed. Pock Mark then said, "Of course, Su-Jen. A Canadian girl like you, so modern, not *guloh,* old-fashioned like us, tied to the old ways."

"That's right, Annie, you'll get to live your life like a *lo fon,*" said Lee-Kung, "Not like me, living in a new country, but chained by old rules."

Father ignored him and smiled at me. "Of course Lee-Kung himself will decide. He has to like the girl." My brother looked away.

Pock Mark became serious as he turned to me. "We Chinese believe in arranged marriages, Su-Jen, in the wisdom of our parents. Love is like tea. It starts out weak, but with time it grows stronger."

Father smiled at this explanation. My mother opened the kitchen door and told me to bring the rest of the dishes from the table.

As I got up, Pock Mark reached over and patted Lee-Kung's shoulder. "Things might turn out after all." Then he said to Father, "It's good if you can find a bride here. Much faster, no government work, and best of all, you don't have to pay the plane fare."

&

IT WAS THE SUNDAY evening after Pock Mark's visit and the restaurant was closed; music from the *White Snake Goddess* filled the air. All week Father had been fussing about the girl in Bambury, wondering about her family, how quickly she and Lee-Kung could wed, what a good addition she might make to the restaurant. He was wiping tables, expressing his thoughts to my mother and Lee-Kung. From where I worked at the back booth filling the sugar dispensers, I could see the kitchen through the open door. Lee-Kung had his head down, focusing on his task, not responding to Father's comments. I could smell the bleach he was using to disinfect the wooden chopping block.

"Next week when you go to Bambury, be sure to make a good impression," Father called to my mother behind the counter. He stood with his cloth in his hand and added, "Do you think Lee-Kung should wear a tie? If we had a car he could drive there instead of taking the bus. If everything works out well, the girl will take on some of the kitchen duties and learn to do the cash register. And they should start a family right away."

My mother was bent over the sink. "What makes you think a nineteen-year-old girl would want to spend the rest of her life in a place like this?" she snapped.

Father seemed surprised and stared at her back as she continued her washing. He recovered his wits. "Maybe for a queen like you this place isn't good enough, but this girl's parents are restaurant owners, not *goh seng*, high classy, like your family," he said with a sarcastic edge to his voice.

"My life isn't so *goh seng* any more, is it? All I do is work from the time I get up until the moment I drop into bed," my mother said bitterly, looking at her wrinkled hands.

"Here, everybody has to work. To survive you have to be able to *hek fuh*, to swallow bitterness." Father was now wiping the lunch counter behind my mother.

"Don't talk to me about *hek fuh*. I know all about bitterness." My mother turned around and glared at Father. "I lived through the war while you were safe over here." From where I stood at the back of the dining room, I could hear the ashtrays rattling against each other as she threw them in the sink.

"All right, all right!" said Father, pointing his finger at her. "Just remember when you go to visit next week, be careful about what you say. Just because you don't like living here, you don't have to say bad things about this place. Keep your thoughts to yourself. Remember, this is not for you. This is for Lee-Kung."

"Don't worry, I won't say a word." After a moment's silence, she spoke again, her voice thin, like the blade of a knife. "When the girl comes and sees this place and this dead town, I won't need to say a thing."

Father said nothing. He took out his accounting books and his abacus and sat down at the back table. No one sang along with the arias that hung in the air. When the music was over, Father did not bother to turn over the record. My mother was still at the sink washing glasses; she lifted her arm and rubbed the base of her neck. I finished filling the sugar dispensers and tiptoed around the dining room, delivering them to the tables and the lunch counter. I set one down where my father was working. I put my hand on top of his. He looked up and tried to smile. His cheeks were slack and the corners of his mouth sagged. All his anger was gone, only sadness left.

When I walked through the kitchen to go upstairs, Elder Brother was no longer there. I turned in the hallway and saw his dark silhouette leaning against the open doorway to the backyard, the tip of his cigarette glowed red against the night.

WE TOOK A NEAR-EMPTY Gray Coach bus to Bambury to meet the prospective bride and her family. Father stayed behind to manage the restaurant. He said there was no need to close the business since he could handle a quiet Sunday afternoon on his own.

Lee-Kung sat across the aisle from us, smoking cigarette after cigarette. My mother had brought a couple of Chinese magazines with her and flipped absently through the pages, stopping only to fuss that I hadn't worn a scarf and hat. This morning I had seen the dark circles under her eyes and had felt the same way. The previous night I had slept very little, kept awake by her tossing and turning. I sat next to her in a silent sulk. I had only agreed to go with them because of my father. Most of the way to Bambury, I sat with my nose pressed against the cold window, watching trees dusted with soft, silvery frost speed by.

Yesterday I had helped Father plant the narcissus bulbs he had bought from Pock Mark. He showed me how to place them in a glass bowl on a base of pebbles so that the green tip of each bulb curved inward. This, he told me, was so that they would provide support for each other as they grew. I held the bulbs in place and watched him carefully spread the rest of the pebbles around and in between each one, leaving only the tips exposed. He poured water into the bowl until the stones were covered. My father loved these flowers, called *su sin far,* clear water flower, as they reminded him of China. It was while we were working that he told me to go with my mother and my brother to Bambury. My first thought was that I would have to be alone with them, the second was that I had already planned to spend the afternoon with Charlotte. "Why do I have to go?" I protested.

My father looked at me and said, "We are a family. We do these things to help each other." I felt a pinprick of shame as I understood all that was unsaid, and nodded my head in agreement.

I had been through Bambury before with my mother on the way to Toronto to visit Aunt Hai-Lan and Uncle Jong. I could tell the town was larger than Irvine because it had a longer, busier main street and two Chinese restaurants. My mother seemed flustered as she stepped off the bus. She suddenly remembered that she had left her magazines on the seat and had to rush back.

The wind was especially strong that December day. The sidewalks were bare, the snow from the early storm now gone. My mother walked, clutching the top of her coat with one hand and the kerchief that was knotted under her chin with the other, her magazines under her arm. His shoulders hunched against the cold, my brother carried a bag filled with gifts for the Chongs. When we reached the Pearl Café, I looked up and saw the sign swinging back and forth above the restaurant window. Mr. and Mrs. Chong were watching for us. Mr. Chong opened the door and greeted Elder Brother with a hearty handshake, speaking in a Four Counties dialect. Stocky and well built, he was dressed in grey woollen trousers with a vest over a shirt and tie. Mrs. Chong was a round-faced woman with a small, tight smile. She was wearing a simple printed dress with a pale blue cardigan. I noticed that around her neck she wore several gold necklaces, one with a large jade pendant. There were gold studs in her ears and a diamond ring on her finger. Except for her wedding band, my mother did not wear jewellery.

My brother handed Mr. Chong a bag filled with oranges, a box of almond cookies, and a bottle of Johnny Walker Red Label Scotch.

"Thank you. Thank you," said Mr. and Mrs. Chong almost simultaneously. "*Em soy huk hay.* You needn't be so formal. We're almost neighbours."

"It's nothing. Very small," said Lee-Kung.

Mrs. Chong then looked at me, but spoke to my mother, "This is your daughter? Very pretty."

"Oh, so-so," said my mother. Whenever people complimented me in front of my mother, she always smiled but objected. I once told her my teacher said that a compliment should be received with a thank you. My mother answered with a *tsk* and said that was all right for *lo fons,* but for a proper Chinese girl to agree so directly would be boastful, showing a lack of refinement. A proper Chinese girl must always be modest.

The Pearl Café was similar to the Dragon Café in some ways. It had a lunch counter with seats and a row of booths along one wall. But the seats were modern, cushioned and covered with vinyl, rather than old-fashioned and wooden like ours. There was no central jukebox, instead what appeared to be miniature jukeboxes were mounted against the inside wall of each booth. The overall effect of the restaurant seemed brighter and more prosperous than ours. I wondered if the Pearl Café was as nice as Bill Woo's business in Urquhart. I'd never been there, but Pock Mark had said that Bill Woo's was the biggest and fanciest in the area. He also said Woo was about to make a lot of money because he had been granted a liquor licence from the government. My father had been impressed, saying that a liquor licence was something given only to *lo fon* restaurants or the fancy Chinese ones in Toronto.

Mrs. Chong took our coats and hung them on the coat tree at the back of the restaurant. I saw that my brother was wearing a sports jacket over a shirt without a tie. I had never before felt that he looked shabby, but next to Mr. Chong with his new-looking clothes, Elder Brother's seemed worn. Mr. Chong invited us to sit down at one of the back tables while his wife brought tea and a plate of sweet pastries and sliced fruit. Then she went into the kitchen and called their daughter.

Valerie Chong walked out from the kitchen just behind her mother. Her head was slightly bowed and she nodded at each of us without meeting our eyes. Mr. Chong made the introductions, then said to Lee-Kung, who was halfway between sitting and standing, "*Choi-la,* sit down, no need to stand on ceremony." Valerie slipped into the chair beside me. My brother's face was expressionless, but my mother wore a smile unlike any I had ever seen. It stretched across her face and made the cords in her neck stick out. Valerie clasped her hands in her lap, seeming almost afraid to look up. I was surprised to think that she might be a marriage prospect. Pock Mark had said that she was eighteen or nineteen, but she appeared not unlike some of the girls in my school. She had a slight build and was rather flat-chested. Her dress seemed a little large and the cuffs on her sweater were rolled. There was something about her that reminded me of the drawings of the round, peaceful Buddha-like faces in my mother's red book.

Mrs. Chong held up the teapot and nodded at my mother, "*Yem chah,* tea?"

"*Em-gwoi,* thank you, please," said my mother, her lips still in a tight smile. Mrs. Chong poured tea into thick white china cups with a green stripe around the top, just like the ones we used at the Dragon Café. She gestured to Valerie, who picked up the plate of pastries and offered them first to my mother, then brother.

"Your restaurant is very nice," said Lee-Kung, looking around at the few customers that were at the counter and in the booths. "You look like you have good business."

"*Mah-mah dei,* so-so," said Mr. Chong with a shrug of the shoulders. "I have only two cooks and one waiter. The waiter is off today, Sunday not so busy. I work in the dining room most days. My wife and Valerie have to help out, though. It's such a shame."

My mother turned deliberately to Valerie, "A young healthy girl like you, I'm sure you don't mind helping your parents, do you?"

"Oh, I don't mind," said Valerie, shaking her head. "But I'm not much use. I can't wait on tables or anything like that. I don't know if I'll be able to learn English."

Mr. Chong spoke before Valerie could say anything more. "What about your business? I'm sure it must make ours look very small."

"Not at all," said my mother. "Your restaurant is much larger and fancier."

"We have a family business," said Lee-Kung. "My father, my stepmother, and I manage it together."

"Our restaurant is sort of like yours," I said.

Mrs. Chong smiled and turned to me, "And what do you do to help in the restaurant?"

Before I could answer, my mother put her hand to her chest. "Oh, no, my daughter goes to school. She studies very hard," she said. "I would never make her work in the restaurant. Once in a while she might help out, but just for fun."

"I help out with some things," I piped up. "My father says that we should do as much as we can ourselves, rather than pay —"

I never finished; my mother tapped me firmly with her foot under the table.

"I can see you are from a hard-working family," said Mr. Chong. "I always say that if you want to have money, you need to make it *and* save it."

The smile on my mother's face stretched tighter. She turned and said to Valerie, "How do you like Canada?"

"It's very cold," said Valerie. "I haven't been outside much. It's hard not speaking any English." Her voice was barely above a whisper.

"You'll get used to the cold. And you'll learn English very fast." My mother spoke in an unfamiliar voice, sugar-coated and falsely reassuring. "Young people like you. Look at Su-Jen, she speaks like she's Canadian-born. No accent at all."

Mrs. Chong's smile was now almost as stiff as my mother's. "Your daughter was a little one when she came," she said. "But Valerie, being older, will not have the opportunity to go to school."

"That is true," said my mother, "but she is young, with the road of life stretching before her."

"And that is why we must be careful and make only the best decisions," said Mr. Chong, jumping into the conversation.

"Everyone wants to make good decisions," said Lee-Kung. "We need to think carefully and take our time."

"Valerie is our only daughter," said Mr. Chong. "Whatever we decide must be good for her and the family. When her older brother got married, both families were happy with the arrangement."

"How lucky to have a son, as well," said my mother. "Does he work here?"

"No," said Mr. Chong. "He just started his own business."

"Very small though," said Mrs. Chong quickly. "In Brampton, outside Toronto."

"You must be very proud," said my mother.

"Well," said Mr. Chong, putting up his hands. "You can't stand in the way of a man wanting to make money."

"Yes, money is important," said Lee-Kung. "But for us family has always come first."

"That goes without saying, but in order to provide for his family a man must make money," said Mr. Chong. "And the more the better," he added with a wide-mouthed laugh.

"There is no life without money," said my mother bitterly.

Mr. Chong looked uncomfortable. "Let me show you the kitchen," he said to Lee-Kung. He stood up quickly and my brother followed him.

Mrs. Chong offered my mother more tea and told us that in China her family were farmers.

"I was born in Toishan City," my mother said, "but my father moved us to a small village to start his practice as a herbalist when I was just a girl."

"A doctor's daughter," said Mrs. Chong. "Well, we were just poor farmers. My father didn't own much land, only about fifty *mow*."

"Fifty *mow*!"

"The land wasn't very good though. We barely made enough to look after the servants."

"You must find it hard working in the restaurant after having servants," said my mother in an overly sympathetic voice.

"Well, the Communists changed everything, didn't they?"

My mother agreed. I looked away at the mention of the Communists and rolled my eyes. Oh brother, I thought to myself. I might have known that sooner or later the Communists would be brought up and blamed for everything that went wrong in China.

Valerie gave me a look that told me she, too, had heard all this before. She smiled and said to me, "I wish I were going to school. I would be if we were still in Hong Kong." She was going to say something more, but her mother interrupted her and asked her to pass the pastries.

Mr. Chong was explaining their new automatic dishwasher to my brother as they returned from the kitchen. Lee-Kung nodded politely, then looked at his watch and announced that it was time to leave, that he had to get back for the dinner hour. Mr. Chong asked him where he had parked his car.

"We took the bus," answered Lee-Kung.

"Ah," said Mr. Chong, unable to keep the surprise from his face.

Lee-Kung added, "I'm getting my driver's licence and should be buying a car soon. Easier for business, don't you think?"

"I didn't know we were getting a car," I said, looking at my mother. She scowled at me, a signal to be quiet.

"Yes, yes," agreed Mr. Chong as if trying to gloss over a mistake. "A car is very useful, for going to Toronto, for shopping. Yes, yes."

"When did you decide to buy a car, Kung? Have you spoken to your father?" my mother said as we rushed through the cold to the bus station.

"I don't need to ask him," said Lee-Kung. "That damn Chong couldn't stop bragging about his son starting his own business. It's all fat talk. Pock Mark told me that he gave his son the money. Not like me, the other way around, giving all my savings to my father for a restaurant in a nowhere town." My brother spoke between puffs of smoke, pinching the cigarette between his thumb and index finger. His face was dark and angry. My mother reached out to pat him on the arm, but he shrugged her off. By the time we walked the block and a half to the bus station, he'd smoked the cigarette down to the filter.

On the bus my mother and my brother said very little to each other. At one point I heard her say, "Eighteen or nineteen? Looks to me no more than thirteen." Partway through our ride she clasped my hand in hers. "Her father owned fifty *mow*," she muttered in disbelief. "Funny, how everyone over here was so rich back home."

Lee-Kung got off the bus first and walked ahead of us toward the Dragon Café. As my mother stepped onto the sidewalk, she took a deep breath and steadied herself. She looked exhausted.

We came in the door just as Father was handing change to a customer. He began to question us even before we removed our coats. "Did everything go well? Was the girl suitable?"

My mother answered, "Okay, I guess . . ."

Father frowned and looked at Lee-Kung. "What do you think? Is she right for our family?"

"She seemed fine. Very young. She didn't talk much." My brother's voice sounded strained, as if the words were caught in the back of his throat.

"I thought she seemed nice," I added.

Father smiled at me. "Ah, Su-Jen, I'm glad you were there. Maybe this will work out for your brother. It is important that the families like each other."

My mother said in a dismissive voice, "She's small, flat-nosed, with a face a little like a steamed bun." She handed me her coat and motioned to me with her arm to take it upstairs. It was obvious she didn't want me around. I thought Valerie had a shy, peaceful look about her. I had watched her sneak glances at my brother. I could tell that she felt self-conscious and it made me feel sorry for her, to be put on display and judged like that. I couldn't help thinking that if she were a few years younger, she would be in school, with the possibility of an entirely different life. In a way she was like my mother, born at the wrong time.

The following Sunday afternoon the Chongs came to visit us at the Dragon Café. Father had rushed around all morning tidying the dining room, shouting at my mother to check the sugar dispensers and empty the ashtrays. He had stayed up last night hanging Christmas garlands made of tinsel between the lamps and above the sliding doors of the stainless-steel cooler.

I was behind the lunch counter pouring a cup of coffee for a customer when Father hurried past me to hold the door. The Chongs had arrived earlier than expected. Mr. Chong came in, followed by his wife and his daughter. He was carrying a shopping bag with some oranges inside and a bottle – I could tell from the shape of its neck – of Scotch. Mr. Chong smiled and told me in his hearty voice how pleased my parents must be with my help in the restaurant. My father invited our guests to sit at the back of the dining room and told me to fetch Lee-Kung and my mother.

My mother was at the chopping block cutting potatoes into French-fry strips for Lee-Kung to cook in the deep fryer. Even with the exhaust fan running, the air was thick with grease. I heard a sharp exchange of words that stopped when I entered the room.

"The Chongs are here," I said.

Lee-Kung looked at my mother and quickly lifted the basket out of the bubbling oil. Removing his apron he walked out to the dining room. My mother continued cutting the potato into strips. I stood inside the door and watched her. "Go. Tell them I'm coming," she hissed.

My father had pushed together the two back tables for us to sit around. He placed a pot of tea and a plate of almond cookies in front of Mr. and Mrs. Chong before tending to the last customer and locking the door. In the past whenever we had visitors, they waited through the supper hour and ate with us when it was finished. This was the first time that I had seen my father close the restaurant because of guests.

My mother entered the dining room and greeted the Chongs in a cheery, breathy sort of voice, and offered another cookie to Valerie, who shook her head in response, her eyes downcast. My mother sat down across from me, beside Lee-Kung.

"As you can see," said my mother with a wave of her hand, "our restaurant is very plain, not as fancy as yours."

"Oh no, no, no," protested Mrs. Chong, "not plain at all, very nice."

Mr. Chong added, "Big restaurants just mean more work and money to look after. A year ago I hired another cook and I may soon have to hire another waiter. I worry too much about my business, if I will make enough money to pay everybody and such. But with your place, you only have to make enough to look after yourselves." He paused and added in a joking voice, "Everybody thinks a big restaurant means more money, but sometimes it just means more headache."

"We bought this business only a few years ago. We are simple, honest people," said my father. "With time and hard work our business will grow."

"Yes, hard work is very important," agreed Mr. Chong. He nodded and said to his daughter, "Valerie, it will be just like at home here. I can see you will be expected to help out."

"But not work too hard," said my father quickly. "Your daughter will have time to relax and enjoy life. Su-Jen's mother shops in the stores in the town. And she often goes to Toronto to visit her aunt."

"Is this the only shopping street in town?" asked Mrs. Chong.

Before anyone could reply, Mr. Chong turned to his daughter

again. "Living in a small town wouldn't be so bad, Valerie. With so few places to shop, think of all the money you would have in the bank," he teased. Valerie sat quietly, her hands still in her lap, her cheeks slightly pink.

Mr. and Mrs. Chong obviously thought my brother was a good-enough marriage prospect to visit and evaluate our offerings. I looked around the dining room and remembered the Chong restaurant; ours really did seem shabby in comparison. The linoleum tiles that lined the floor between the lunch counter and the booths appeared even thinner and more worn than they had the day before. The Christmas decorations dangling between the lamps only made things worse. The bright festivity seemed so false in our restaurant. I wondered if the Chongs were disappointed.

During supper my father sat at the head of the table, with Mrs. Chong on one side and Mr. Chong on the other. I noticed that his wife was wearing all the gold jewellery she had worn on the day of our visit to Bambury.

Lee-Kung brought out the last dish, sat down beside me and across from my mother. I looked at the steamed fish, the sliced white chicken, the stir-fried shrimps with mixed vegetables, and the beef hot pot with dried bean curd – my mother's favourites. Father placed the best dishes in front of Mr. and Mrs. Chong. My mother picked up the largest shrimp with her chopsticks and placed it on Mrs. Chong's plate. Next she chose a plump piece of chicken for Mr. Chong.

Mr. Chong turned to Lee-Kung, "Everything is delicious. You have a real talent."

"Compared to the fancy restaurants in Toronto, though, this must seem very simple," said Lee-Kung.

"Mr. Chong is being kind," said Father.

"I'm only telling the truth," said Mr. Chong. "Your son should open his own restaurant in the big city."

"I understand your son has his own business," said my mother. "You must be very proud. Two businesses in one family. As my husband mentioned, ours is so small that we can manage it ourselves. Not like your place, three hired workers living upstairs." The muscles around my father's mouth grew taut. "The Chongs live in a house," she continued, lifting her eyebrows at Father.

"Do you have anyone upstairs?" asked Mrs. Chong.

"That's where we live," I answered.

"My son is a hard-working, thrifty man," Father interrupted as he looked at Mr. and Mrs. Chong and then my mother. "Given time he will have money to buy a house for his family. It takes a long time to make money. It's not easy over here."

"What your father says is right," said Mr. Chong, turning to Lee-Kung. "Wealth doesn't mean happiness. A man who works hard will never starve."

"Sometimes there's little choice but to work hard, unless you have a *lo fon* education," said Lee-Kung. "Things could be worse. I could be working for someone else instead of myself."

"Of course," said Mr. Chong. "You are right. It is always best to own a business."

"We Chinese have not had it easy over here," said my father. "When I arrived from Hoi Ping, I had no money and had to work at very low-paying jobs. In places like Timmins and Pembroke."

"Oh, I remember those early days," said Mr. Chong, nodding his head.

"Your family is from Hoi Ping?" said Mrs. Chong. "Then we're neighbours. My husband and I are both from Hoi Sun."

"Oh, the richest of the Four Counties," said my mother. "And your father owned fifty *mow*."

"But the land was very poor," said Mrs. Chong, blushing a little.

"It makes no difference whether you're from the rich county or the poor county once you're over here," said Mr. Chong, smiling at everyone around the table. He turned to his daughter. "Valerie, have you tried the fish? It's very good."

Valerie nodded and said, "Yes, your son is a very good cook."

"If you live here, you will always be well fed," joked my father.

Throughout the meal I watched Valerie, sitting quietly next to her mother, occasionally lifting her eyes from the table. Contrary to my mother's remarks, she was actually very pretty, a moon-shaped face framed with hair that appeared newly taken out of rollers. She was wearing a white cardigan over a pink dress with a round collar. It was hard to imagine her being married.

I noticed how my brother was toying with his food, not really eating. I wasn't sure why until I bent over to pick up my paper napkin that had fallen on the floor and saw my mother's leg stretched across the space under the table, the tips of her stockinged toes between my brother's thighs. I looked away and sat up.

When everyone finished eating, I helped my mother clear the dishes from the table. She brought a large pot of oolong tea from the kitchen and poured out cups for everyone. Reaching to pass tea to Mrs. Chong, my mother knocked a full cup over Valerie's lap. Valerie jumped up making little squealing noises, holding her wet skirt out from her lap. My mother seemed to hold her breath as she stood up from the bench. Lee-Kung pulled out the table, away from Valerie. I ran to the counter to get a dishcloth to mop up the spill and heard my father say several times, "I'm so sorry! How clumsy. Please excuse us."

Mr. Chong protested, "My daughter is fine. The tea wasn't that hot." Mrs. Chong made fluttering motions with her hands as she slid out from her side of the bench and let Valerie out.

My mother took the cloth from me and said in a firm voice, "Take Valerie upstairs. Find some other clothes for her to wear."

I led Valerie through the kitchen and up the flight of wooden stairs. She hung on to the banister, carefully avoiding the boxes and jars. Her eyes darted around as we passed through the dim foyer. The harsh glow from the light bulb in the bedroom revealed Valerie, her hands clenched together, staring at her squashed reflection in the warped mirror above our dresser.

I purposely chose to show her my mother's best dresses. I was sure my mother had spilled the tea on purpose, trying to ruin Lee-Kung's chances, whatever they might be.

When I brought Valerie downstairs she was wearing my mother's favourite dress, made from a print of white daisies on a dark green background. Although it was too large for Valerie she looked sweet rather than foolish.

Father smiled with relief at her. "This has been most unfortunate," he said. "Are you all right now? I hope Su-Jen was helpful."

"I'm fine, thank you. You must not worry," said Valerie softly. I saw a look pass between her and her mother.

"Yes, please, you must not think about it," said Mrs. Chong. "It was only a small thing."

"Keep the dress," said Father, looking at my mother. With a thin smile, he added, "Su-Jen's mother has too many dresses and nowhere to wear them. She tells me this all the time."

My mother straightened her shoulders and glared at me and at Father. She turned to Mr. and Mrs. Chong and spoke through tense, smiling lips, "I have many. Keep the dress."

"No. No. No," they said together, each waving a hand in protest.

Valerie sat down and took a small sip from her freshly poured cup of tea. For a moment no one said anything, then Mr. Chong looked at his watch and said, "We must go. We have imposed on your hospitality long enough."

"Yes, we must be going," agreed Mrs. Chong.

"It's not late at all," protested Father. "Stay as long as you want."

But Mr. Chong hurried his family along. They put on their coats, got into their car, and returned to Bambury, Valerie clutching a brown paper bag that held her sodden pink dress.

Father could barely contain his anger. As soon as the front door was shut, he shouted at my mother, "*Jeet doo nay!* Damn you! How could you be so clumsy? Have you no idea how important this was?"

"And it's my fault?" She was ready for him.

"Spilling the tea over that girl. It's a bad luck way to start." My father shook his head.

"You don't get it, do you?" My brother sounded exasperated. "There is no start. Your talk about thrift and hard work doesn't mean anything. They want a husband who has money now. How you both pretended that it doesn't matter that they're from Hoi Sun, and we're from Hoi Ping, that it's all the same over here. I didn't believe a word. He's looking for a rich man for his daughter." Lee-Kung then stomped into the kitchen without waiting for Father to respond.

We all went about our usual evening tasks with a heavy silence. The shiny red-and-green garlands that were draped between the lamps looked so ridiculous, I wanted to rip them down.

The silence was broken only by my father slamming chairs into place. Then the slow, melancholy notes of the erhu filled the air and the White Snake Goddess began to sing. The inside of my throat felt swollen; the music made my heart ache and long for a home I no longer knew. I turned and saw my mother sitting in the back booth, next to the record player. Her black eyes stared out from her pale ivory face.

That night my mother rested beside me on the bed at first, but soon she tiptoed out of our bedroom. I heard upset whispers coming through the wall, then my mother crying. After that, there was nothing.

Over the following few days, my mother seemed to gloat. There was a smugness about her and a briskness in the way she worked. I resented her undeclared triumph.

She came upstairs one evening and sat down across from me at my homework table in the foyer where I sometimes worked.

"Su-Jen," she said, "I must to talk to you."

"I'm doing my homework," I said, continuing to write in my notebook.

"Put your pencil down." Her tone was firm, but her voice wavered. I looked up at her. "Last night when I came to bed, I noticed the door to our room had been left open. You must remember to always close it," she said.

"Why does it have to stay closed?" I said, even though I already knew the reason.

"Don't ask why, just do as I tell you."

"Is there something you want to hide from someone?" All colour drained from my mother's face. My breath was short and shallow. I wanted to take my words out of the air, but my mother stood abruptly and left. I stared after her for a moment, then put my head down and cried.

A week or so after the Chongs' visit, my mother's dress arrived in the mail. By then my father had already written to ask the matchmaker about eligible young Hong Kong women.

In March, Pock Mark told Father that Valerie was engaged to Bill Woo's oldest son. When Father shared this information over supper, my mother gave a short *ha* of disgust. Lee-Kung set down his rice bowl and said, "Now do you understand?"

Before Father could say anything, my mother said, "I wouldn't want them in our family anyway. There was something about the shape of Mr. Chong's mouth that I didn't like, that told me he was false. Even when they were here, he was probably thinking about Bill Woo's boy." She laughed. "He's willing to marry his daughter to Woo's son just because he owns a restaurant that sells liquor. He doesn't care the boy isn't smart. Pock Mark told us the boy couldn't pass in school, even though he came to Canada when he was only twelve. What kind of a man does that to his daughter?"

Glaring at my mother, Father said, "You can say all you want, but who would want to marry into *this* family after what you did?" He got up from the table and walked over to the cash register, where a customer was waiting to pay his bill.

LEE-KUNG AND MY PARENTS were in the back booth of the dining room, huddled in what seemed to be a serious conversation. We had finished supper and the table had been cleared. A few customers were sitting at the lunch counter smoking and drinking coffee, a couple of teenagers were sprawled in the front booths. My brother called me over from the back table where I was reading a Nancy Drew mystery. There was something about the tone of his voice that made me suspicious. My brother stood out from the booth and gestured in a grand way for me to sit beside him. I slid warily into the empty space.

On the table were two black-and-white photographs, each of a young woman. The pictures were from the matchmaker my father had written to after the mess with Valerie Chong. Waving his hand over the photos, Elder Brother said, "So, Annie, who will it be? Who will be the one to marry your brother? You decide for me, little sister." I looked at Father, whose face was set in a frown. I leaned over to study the pictures.

On first inspection, the images were similar. Both girls had their hair permed into curls, both were seated with their hands in their lap. Both had clear complexions, no moles to darken or to enhance their futures. I turned toward my brother and he raised his eyebrows at me. My mother's face was stony. I felt everyone's eyes on me, waiting for me to speak.

I peered more closely at the photographs and noticed that one girl looked directly at the camera with a hint of a smile, as if she held a secret. The other had little expression on her face, what seemed an unwillingness to reveal herself, or perhaps a hidden stubbornness. I knew from listening to conversations over supper that both girls came highly recommended: both were healthy, obedient, quiet; both knew how to cook and sew, had completed several years of high school in China. But which stranger offered a better chance of happiness, I couldn't tell. I began to understand the weight of my brother's decision. If this was all he had to decide from, did it really matter who was chosen? The courtship would be the same, driven by money. As he did already for Fu-Ling, my brother would make the initial monetary gestures and, if things succeeded, this time he would send money for clothes, for the bride's family, for a pre-wedding banquet in Hong Kong, for the plane fare, and more.

I picked up the picture of the mysterious one and said to my brother, "What about her?"

Not waiting for Lee-Kung to answer, my mother shook her head and said, "Su-Jen, somehow I knew you would choose that girl, the one with the pretty looks. But your brother has decided to write to this girl." Pursing her lips together, my mother tapped the corner of the other photograph.

"Yes, someone solid and dependable to take care of you in your old age," Lee-Kung said snidely, glancing at my mother and drawing on his cigarette.

My mother snatched the photograph from the table and again examined her candidate. "She is the better choice," she said. "She looks reliable and hard-working. The other one is too skinny, probably wants too many expensive things."

Father, who had not yet spoken, agreed with her. "Yes, I think she is a good choice. We need someone willing to help out in the restaurant." He reached over and patted me on the shoulder. He then turned to Lee-Kung. "You must write to her now, get married as soon as possible. We have waited long enough."

Elder Brother's cloud of smoke hung over us as my father continued his planning. I was angry that my brother had included me in his decision. I'd had enough of his false gestures.

EVERY SPRING MY MOTHER looked forward to planting. Over the years she had worked hard to create a garden in our tiny yard. Some seeds my mother harvested herself, others she had bought from Pock Mark as early as the middle of March. She always talked about how much she hated the winter, and allowed weeks to go by without stepping outside. But in the spring she spent as much time as she could in her little garden, seeming to find solace and calm in the dark earth. I had seen Mrs. Heighington work in her backyard dressed in an old pair of trousers and a shirt; she knelt down and leaned across to her rows of plants. My mother, on the other hand, squatted when she worked, her dress falling in between her thighs.

In our small patch of ground my mother grew bok choy, mustard greens, Chinese broccoli, snow peas, amaranth, red and green peppers, fuzzy melons, and winter melons. She preferred the taste of the vegetables that she grew herself, saying the ones from Pock Mark were bigger and looked better, but the fertilizers the local Chinese farmers used diluted the taste. Even though I didn't really like vegetables, I enjoyed the musky flavour of her winter melon soup simmered with large chunks of carrots, sliced ginger root, and meaty pork bones. My mother put amaranth in a pot with an inch of boiling water and turned the leaves over with a pair of chopsticks until they were just cooked and wilted, then served them with a drizzle of soya sauce and sesame oil. Whenever I eat them, I still taste a hint of soil, reminding me of my mother's garden.

Many times I had listened to her describe the gardens around her home in Nanking: beds of bright peonies, purple lilacs, climbing roses that grew in clusters she called the seven sisters, ginkgoes and willows bent over blue ponds. It sounded like a heavenly place. When I was younger, those descriptions of her long-ago home had made me sad, and desperate to show her that pleasure could be found here too. In the fall I brought home colourful leaves, and in the spring, bouquets of dandelions, all to no avail. But as I grew older, I began to feel annoyed whenever she told me wistfully about her life in China.

By mid-May the soil was warm enough to dig. The trees had finished flowering and were covered with new pale green leaves. The air was redolent with the sweet scent of lilacs in bloom from the gardens beyond the hedge. I was returning home from church along the back alley and had stopped just before our backyard to remove a stone from my shoe when I heard voices.

Through the branches of a large bush, I saw my brother turning over the soil in our plot. My mother followed behind him with a rake, smoothing out the ground, chatting happily about the produce they would grow. She then squatted and ripped open a package, spilling tiny black seeds into her hand to sprinkle over the freshly raked earth.

Lee-Kung stopped and rested against the shovel. He took a cigarette from his package of Players and lit it, inhaling the smoke deep into his lungs and laughing at my mother's pride in the small garden. My mother stood up and stretched, looking tired but pleased with her work. My brother took a step toward her and brushed a smudge of soil from her cheek with his fingers. She smiled and placed her hand on top of his, lingering for a moment. I had caught them unaware, absorbed in their tasks and each other. Their mutual contentment was something I had never seen in my family. Instead of sharing their happiness, I felt nothing but dread. I wanted to get away from them, but as I turned to go, still unnoticed, Lee-Kung leaned close to my mother and said urgently, "After I get the car we can leave." My mother looked at the ground and said nothing. She took the rake and started to break up more clumps of soil. "Please, Jing. Why don't we leave, without telling anyone." He was pleading with her. I stood still and strained to listen.

My mother lifted her head. "Don't say that," she said, placing her hand over his mouth. "You know it's not possible. You make things worse with your talk. We have no choice but to stay here." My mother started to rake again.

"But we do have a choice. We don't have to live like this. I have money in the bank, enough to go somewhere faraway, maybe Vancouver. We could start all over again."

"You forget I have a daughter. What about Su-Jen?"

"We can take her with us," Elder Brother argued.

"It is not that easy. We're only fooling ourselves."

"You're always saying how much you hate it here. So why do you want to stay? Don't you see that soon we really will be trapped?" My mother stopped her work and looked at my brother.

"Kung, I've been through the war, I've lost my home more than once. I cannot do it again. And I have a daughter to think about." Her voice became strained.

My brother's temper flared. "What about me? You're not the only one who's been through the war. I've lost many things and made sacrifices. I should just leave, leave this damn place without you."

"Please, Kung, please, let's not fight." My mother placed her hand on my brother's shoulder. He looked away and turned over another clump of soil.

Unable to move, I stared for a moment longer. I remembered my excitement and shyness when my brother first arrived in Irvine. He had been so good-looking, it was as if a movie star had come to live with us. At the same time he had seemed so remote, I had been afraid to approach him. And when he betrayed our family, I had slammed the door shut, avoiding any situation where I might be alone with him. But now I was seeing a side of him I had never seen before, hurt, angry, and pleading with my mother.

I slipped from behind the bush and stole around to the front of the building. I licked my lips and tasted blood.

SNIDERS', THE SMALL VARIETY store a few doors away from the Dragon Café, was run by an unmarried brother and sister. Even though I had been going there to buy candy since I first arrived in Irvine, I still entered the store reluctantly. The air was stale with the smell of many meals made in their apartment behind the store. The brother, a squat, pear-shaped man with no neck and thick wet lips, sat like a massive toad behind the cash register. The sister, a crooked-back woman with a head of thin greying curls growing on a shiny scalp, walked with a limp as she served customers. She did not like children and always wanted us out of the store. Whenever I saw her bony hand reach for the candy inside the glass-fronted case, I shuddered and thought of the witch in *Hansel and Gretel.*

Sniders' also sold comic books. I had been happy following the adventures of Superman and Archie and the gang until one day Charlotte introduced me to love comics. I had seen them on the shelf, but I had felt shy about even opening the pages of stories that seemed so adult. From the first one I read, however, I became enthralled with the tales – almost always about a beautiful heroine succumbing to the attentions of a strong, manly hero who deserts her for adventure in a faraway land, only to return when he realizes there is a void in his life without his own true love. I imagined myself in her place, wrapped in the arms of a man with a straight nose, square jaw, and rippling muscles.

When I started to buy love comics of my own, Miss Snider would level me with a stare at the cash register. I could not meet her gaze when I handed her my money, but Charlotte looked her straight in the eye. Charlotte noticed my discomfort. "Why are you so embarrassed, Annie?" she said. "She's the one who's selling them." Charlotte was right. I wished I understood the world so clearly, with such assurance. It seemed that there was a time when I might have, but everything had shifted: up and down were no longer where they were before.

Last week my mother had found me on the fire escape with a stack of love comics at my side. She leafed through a few of them and said to me, "Why are you reading this garbage?"

"How do you know it's garbage?" I said, feeling guilty. "They're written in English."

"I don't need to read them to know that they're nothing but trash. Did you get these from Charlotte?"

Suddenly I became defiant. "I bought them with my own money," I said, "the money you gave me for helping in the restaurant."

"Then you are wasting it. Do not bring this filth home again."

I turned away from her and didn't say anything more. I didn't listen to her either. I bought more comics and hid them in the sleeve of a sweater or jacket, then locked myself in the bathroom above the restaurant and pored over them in secret.

I went to Charlotte's house almost every day after school and curled up with her in her room, reading about love that appeared doomed but somehow ended up being right. Charlotte read the passages out loud in exaggerated voices, making fun of the characters. "'And for months I roamed the same streets that we had walked together, waiting for *him* to return to me.'" I howled and hooted along with her, but underneath something drew me to these happy endings.

One afternoon Charlotte's mother came into the bedroom while we were reading. She was carrying the baby on her hip and held a small book in her other hand. "You girls really like reading that junk?" she asked good-naturedly.

"'He took me into his arms and kissed me passionately on the lips,'" Charlotte read breathlessly and fell back on the bed, clutching the comic to her chest.

Mrs. Heighington just laughed. "Look, you goose, I'm reading poetry to your sister. She loves it."

"But she doesn't understand it, does she?" I asked.

Mrs. Heighington sat down on the bed with the baby on her lap and held the book open in front of her.

Within my Garden, rides a Bird
Upon a single Wheel –
Whose spokes a dizzy Music make
As 'twere a traveling Mill –

He never stops, but slackens
Above the Ripest Rose –
Partakes without alighting,
And praises as he goes,

"You just love Emily Dickinson, don't you, darling?" she said to her baby. Then Mrs. Heighington looked at me. "She doesn't have to understand. She likes the sound of the words."

I picked up her book and read the poem, saying it softly to myself. It was beautiful, unlike anything I had ever heard. The words danced through my mind like music, even more enchanting to me than my favourite stories.

I was pulled from my thoughts when Charlotte asked, "Mum, can you read the poem 'Will There Really Be a Morning?'"

Mrs. Heighington took the book from me and flipped to the right page. I looked at Charlotte's face as her mother read, and at Mrs. Heighington with one daughter on her lap and the other nestled to her side, and I felt the void between my world and theirs. When I was younger my father had read his poetry to me, but written Chinese was a coded formal language I had never learned and couldn't understand.

Before I left I asked Mrs. Heighington if I could borrow her book of poems. That night I tried again and again to write a verse about my mother's garden. But in the end I ripped up the paper into tiny pieces.

I dried the last tray of wet cutlery from the Saturday lunch hour and left quickly to spend the afternoon at Charlotte's house. The lilacs were past their peak and the blossoms were turning brown. I found Charlotte and her mother at the kitchen table snipping old cigarette butts. Sounds of the wrestling match on television floated down the hall and mingled with the Saturday-afternoon opera. Just as I was about to sit down and help, one of her brothers came rushing into the kitchen. "Come quick! Dick the Bulldog Brower is killing Whipper Billy Watson!" Charlotte dropped what she was doing and we hurried into the living room. Her mother shook her head and laughed but stayed behind.

When Charlotte and I returned to the kitchen, Mrs. Heighington said to me, "I've been thinking, Annie, now that the good weather is here, we should teach you how to ride a bicycle. Charlotte knows how and you should too."

"Do you think so?" I said, looking at Charlotte, who crossed her eyes at me, making me giggle.

"Absolutely, every Canadian girl should know how to ride a bike." Mrs. Heighington stopped her cigarette rolling and looked at me. "And you *are* a Canadian girl, Annie." I beamed at her words.

My father and my brother had talked about buying a car for some time. They agreed that Pock Mark would be soon retiring and most likely would not be replaced. My father emphasized that owning a car would increase Lee-Kung's eligibility to a prospective mail-order bride, so the purchase would be money well spent. I pictured my brother behind the wheel, a cigarette dangling from his lips, acting like the big shot he craved to be. I thought about warning Father of Elder Brother's wish to leave town, but I could not bring myself to say it. Part of me didn't believe he would ever do it, especially if my mother refused to go with him.

So that spring, while Mr. Swackhammer taught my brother how to drive, I learned how to ride a bicycle. I practised on the sidewalk outside the Heighington house with Charlotte and her mother, a cigarette in her hand, running after me. By the time my cycling was steady, Lee-Kung had bought a car.

He had chosen a beige Chevrolet Bel Air with shiny chrome and whitewall tires, and I a second-hand bicycle at Swackhammers', purchased with the money I had earned and saved from working in the restaurant.

One Sunday in May I rode around the block to the Heighingtons. Charlotte's brothers were playing outside. They stopped what they were doing to talk to me, to admire my bike. They had never paid such attention to me before. One of them ran into the house, calling the family. Charlotte came out with her grandmother, father, and mother, holding the baby in her arms.

Charlotte wheeled her bicycle out from the shed behind the house, and I followed her on a ride that took us from one side of town to the other. I watched her pedal without hands, her arms dangling at her side. She turned around and laughed, daring me to copy her tricks. On my bike the world seemed like a new place. The air felt soft against my face as I explored unknown streets and watched houses speed by. I took a deep breath and tightened my grip on the handlebars, ready to change direction at a moment's notice.

WHENEVER I DRIVE a particular stretch of highway that passes Irvine on the way to Toronto, I am reminded of the first trip my family took to the city in Lee-Kung's brand-new car. The car was two weeks old when my father had decided to close the restaurant so we could spend the day in Toronto. Except for Christmas, this was the first time the restaurant had been closed for an entire day. Our first Christmas in Irvine we had stayed open and had had only ourselves for company. Not one customer had come into the dining room.

We left before noon. My brother was seated confidently behind the wheel, my father beside him. In the back seat my mother took my hand for a moment as we gathered speed. I remember she was wearing a white pleated skirt with a flowered top that she had sewn herself. Her hair was wound up in the usual knot at the top of her head, but it was secured with the beautiful tortoiseshell clasp from Hong Kong that she only wore on special occasions.

Lee-Kung drove out of town toward the main road. Highway 401 stretched out in front of us, its two grey bands running east and west on either side of a grassy ditch. My father marvelled at the speed of the cars whizzing by. When the highway was being built, Mr. Swackhammer and Officer Grisham, the new policeman, had talked about it almost every day as they sat at the restaurant counter drinking coffee. They told me with great excitement they would be able to drive to Toronto in under an hour because they wouldn't have to pass through all the small towns. They said that the road would be like the big highways in the United States where you could drive at seventy, eighty miles an hour.

In Chinatown we parked outside Aunt Hai-Lan and Uncle Jong's house on D'Arcy Street. All the houses had front lawns with large trees, but stood as close together as the stores in Irvine. Everything in the city felt crowded compared to our town: the buildings, the cars, the throngs of people on the main streets. But it was also the noise from the clanging of streetcars, from people's voices, and the heavy traffic, relentless and inescapable, that always jarred my senses.

We walked with Aunt Hai-Lan and Uncle Jong along Dundas to the Shanghai on Chestnut Street for lunch. My mother seemed pleased to be in Chinatown. She strolled along, chatting easily to Aunt Hai-Lan. "It's so nice to be here. I miss having someone to talk to. You are lucky, Auntie, to hear Chinese spoken all around you. When I go shopping in that small town, if what I want is on the shelf, I can manage," my mother said with a small laugh, "but if I need to ask for anything, I must take Su-Jen."

I had been to Toronto before, on the bus with my mother for her visits twice a year with Aunt Hai-Lan, and Lee-Kung caught the bus occasionally on a Sunday to visit with his friend from Owen Sound who had moved to Toronto, but I had no memory of Father ever leaving Irvine. He looked uncomfortable walking on Dundas Street with its rushing cars and mobs of thick pedestrian traffic. Uncle Jong, however, was at home, calmly leading the way to the restaurant. Jong was the envy of his peers. He first came to Canada as a young teenager and spoke an accented but fluent English. He had a government job working steady shifts at the post office, where he sorted mail. But it was the regular days off, paid holidays, and full government pension when he turned sixty-five that made everyone jealous. Aunt Hai-Lan looked after children during the week and they rented out rooms in their house. Their two sons were married and lived in homes of their own.

At the Shanghai, a man in a grey suit shook hands with Uncle Jong and welcomed us to the big city. He led us to a round table covered with a white tablecloth. The restaurant was packed with Sunday diners. Children were running in between tables, people talked in Chinese and laughed in loud voices. My mouth watered as I watched waiters in burgundy-coloured vests and black bow ties shuffle past carrying plates of steamed dumplings and fried noodles.

My father asked Jong to order and soon the waiter brought us *har gow, shui mi, char shu bow, cheung foon*, and *nor my guy*. I looked at the steamed pork and shrimp delicacies wrapped in thin rice-flour pastry, steamed white buns filled with barbecue pork, all cooked and served in small, round bamboo baskets, Chinese food that could be found only in the city, so unlike the Chinese food that we served in the Dragon Café. Outside, my father had seemed overwhelmed, but now that we were seated he looked relaxed, pleased to be surrounded by familiar sounds and Chinese faces. He joked with the waiter, telling him that we were visiting from a small town.

Her mouth full of pastry, Aunt Hai-Lan turned to my brother, "Kung, when are you inviting me to your wedding? Uncle Jong and I are getting old. And your father, he wants grandchildren and a daughter-in-law to look after him in his old age."

I was surprised to see Elder Brother blush. "I have not been very lucky so far. If everything goes smoothly, maybe in a few years," he said.

"I hope earlier than that," said Father. "We expected him to get married this summer, but you know what happened. Kung is now writing to a girl in Hong Kong. If all goes well, this time next year you'll be toasting at a wedding banquet." I darted a quick glance at my mother.

"I'll drink to that," said Uncle Jong, lifting his teacup.

"The sooner the better, nobody's getting any younger," teased Aunt Hai-Lan, nudging my mother with her elbow.

"Maybe third time lucky," said Lee-Kung with a half-smile. "Besides, how could I go wrong? Su-Jen's mother picked the bride this time." My mother and I sat stone-faced while everyone laughed at his joke.

We spent the afternoon wandering the busy streets until we ended up at the China Trading Store, the company Pock Mark worked for. The inside of the store was like another world, ancient and mysterious, dimly lit, filled with wooden shelves and huge wooden barrels containing dried oysters, shrimp, salted fish, mushrooms, and thousand-year-old eggs, the air thick with their earthy, salty odours, more pungent than Pock Mark's truck. It would have been hard to imagine a grocery store less like the iga in Irvine with its produce displayed on stainless-steel shelves under bright lights, tightly packaged, and without smell.

The China Trading Store seemed to be a meeting place. Men of my father's generation gathered out front to visit with one another. My father told me many of them still had family in China. In 1923, the Canadian government had passed a law that wouldn't let any more Chinese into the country, and a lot of the men who were already here had to leave their wives and children behind. After the Second World War, the government changed its mind and allowed the families to come over, but some of them were too old, like Uncle Yat's wife, and the Communists made it hard for them to leave China. The old-timers in Canada, the *lo wah kew,* as Father called them, had grown used to a life suspended between a country that offered only hardship and a homeland they no longer knew. I was struck by how much they all reminded me of my father and of Uncle Yat, partly because they seemed around the same age, all dressed in white shirts and dark pants worn thin, but mostly it was a way they had about them, a resignation to their lives in the new world.

My father had always talked about how important it was to endure, to *hek fuh*, to swallow bitterness, yet he often told me the story of a Chinaman in a restaurant up north somewhere who was being bullied by a *lo fon*. "But, Su-Jen, the *lo fon* didn't know that the Chinaman knew *kung fu*. Even though the Chinaman was as skinny as a toothpick, he picked up the *lo fon* who was twice his size and threw him out the front door. The *lo fon* landed so hard on a garbage pail that he squashed it flat." My father slapped his hand on the table, emphasizing the fate of the garbage pail. "Nobody in the town ever called him a Chinky Chinky Chinaman again." Whenever my father finished this story he laughed with delight and triumph, but I knew that he wasn't heroic like the man in the story. He was like the other old men I saw in Chinatown, who only understood hard work and sacrifice. I was surprised he knew so many of the *lo wah kew*, but I guessed that over the years he had met people on the boat and in the small towns where he had worked before. In spite of his shyness I could tell that he was pleased to see these people, to be talking in his own language.

I followed my mother, Aunt Hai-Lan, and my brother to the fresh produce section of the China Trading Store while my father and Uncle Jong visited with the *lo wah kew*. The men in the shop seemed eager to serve my mother. They joked with her and asked when she was moving to the big city. She tilted her head and smiled back the way she smiled at my brother when she thought no one was looking.

While Elder Brother picked through the vegetables, my mother and Aunt Hai-Lan slipped over to the medicinal herb section at the back of the store. The herbalist was a tall man with slender, wrinkled hands who stood behind a narrow glass cabinet. He had large, fleshy earlobes, shaped like pears, and I wondered if he would live a long life. The shelves inside the glass case were filled with wooden trays containing dried seeds, roots, leaves, and even dried reptiles and insects. The two that fascinated me the most were the tiny gecko and the seahorse. The gecko was grey and had a tough, leathery appearance, like a dried oyster. The fragile seahorse seemed to be made up of wispy sheets of charred paper, so delicate that one strong blow of breath and it would be gone.

My mother whispered something to Hai-Lan as they waited for the herbalist. Aunt Hai-Lan's eyes widened and her mouth dropped open. "At his age!" she said, then added in a concerned tone, "Lai-Jing, you must be more careful. You will not always be able to fix it." My mother lowered her head and whispered something more.

The herbalist approached them and asked my mother what she wanted. She hesitated for a moment, turned to me and said, "Su-Jen, here's some money. Go and pick out a bag of *moys* for yourself." I walked away thinking she must have forgotten that last week I had bought a package from Pock Mark, still unopened.

I stood at the shelf of dried fruit and watched my mother lean over the glass counter and say something quietly to the herbalist. The herbalist remained expressionless as he seemed to ask her questions. She hesitated for a moment, then made a gesture with her hand. The herbalist nodded, turned around, and opened several drawers. After scooping out different ingredients, he weighed each of them on a handheld scale and wrapped them together in a fold of white paper. My mother paid him, and quickly put the small package in her purse.

I was so preoccupied watching my mother that at first I didn't see the man and woman next to me. She was round-faced and Chinese, but the man was tall, with bony features and fair skin. I could tell by the way they spoke to each other, the way they stood so close, they were a couple. What sort of person was this Chinese woman to be intimately involved with a *lo fon* man? Whenever my parents spoke about a Chinese man taking a *gwei poh,* a white ghost woman, it was in hushed, disapproving tones, as if the woman was somehow beneath us in value. I had never seen a *gwei poh,* but I imagined such a woman dressed in revealing clothes, wore heavy makeup on her face, and lured the unsuspecting Chinese man away from his hard work. But a Chinese woman with a white man? It was something I had never considered. And this woman looked perfectly ordinary. If she had been alone or with a Chinese man I would not have noticed her. But this white man stood out, his skin, his height in contrast to everyone in the store. I couldn't help staring at him, the blood rushing to my face. Was this how I stood out in Irvine?

As I stood in line to pay for my *moys,* I turned around and saw him behind another person. He caught my eye and held up his package of *moys*. They were the same as mine. When he smiled, I turned away.

From the road I could see the round Irvine water tower reaching into the sky, the town's name emblazoned in large black letters on its sides. For a small community like Irvine, it always seemed like a bold declaration. In the past whenever I had returned on the bus with my mother, I found comfort in seeing it, in knowing that I was home. But after spending the day with my family in Chinatown, seeing their ease and happiness among Chinese people, I wondered if anyone else in my family felt as I did about anything.

As soon as we got home my mother rushed upstairs and changed out of her city clothes into one of her flower-print dresses. When she came down to the kitchen she filled a pot with water and put in some pork and chicken bones, chunks of ginger, and a small handful of dried pink shrimp. Into another pot of water I saw her empty the contents of the white envelope from the herbalist. My brother was watching her, but she ignored him.

Over supper that night, my father mused happily that perhaps we could close the restaurant every few months for a visit to Chinatown in the new car. My mother talked about how much she enjoyed walking around the busy streets and being with Aunt Hai-Lan. I felt I was the only one who was relieved to be back in Irvine. Then I remembered the *lo fon* man in the Chinese grocery store and it was as if a shadow crept over my thoughts.

My parents seemed to bicker all the time now. In the months leading up to the arrival of the mail-order bride, my brother's bitterness grew. He often went out for drives, returning before the supper hour. He never said where he was going, but I eventually stopped worrying that he wouldn't come back.

The only time there was any feeling of happiness was during the Sunday trips to Toronto that we began to make every so often. We would drive to the city for lunch, returning in the afternoon. Sometimes my mother would stay for a night of gossip and mah-jong with Aunt Hai-Lan and her friends. I could picture them, sliding the tiles on the surface of the game table, stopping only to flip and rearrange the ivory blocks or to crack red melon seeds between their teeth, sucking out the flesh and flicking the shells into a bowl. Their chatter was constant. At the restaurant, my mother laughed occasionally, but at Aunt Hai-Lan's it had a different sound. Sometimes loud and raucous, but never edged with bitterness or sarcasm, her laughter was spontaneous, tumbling out like notes in a song. She belonged.

Spring eased gently into summer that year. I was now eleven years old and felt a new sort of freedom. I passed entire afternoons at the park and the playgrounds around the school, without adult supervision. I spent many days with friends at Irvine Lake. I told my mother that I stayed on the beach watching my friends and never went near the water. I suppose she had no choice but to believe me.

But if my parents had known how far I ventured from Irvine on my bicycle, they would have been much more alarmed than by the thought of me playing at the lake. Charlotte and I explored the countryside as often as we could, each time venturing farther and farther, even sneaking onto properties with No Trespassing signs that seemed to reel Charlotte in like bait at the end of a fishing line.

In the middle of the summer Charlotte and I rode farther than we had ever been before. The land around Irvine was flat with a few hills, long and slow in their rise and fall. We came upon a dirt road that descended at a steep pitch, barely levelling out before rising again. On one side of the road were massive boulders covered with green velvet moss; on the other side, a farmer's field. It was late in the day and I was tired and hot. I wanted to turn back, but Charlotte's eyes gleamed with sudden energy. She hopped on her bike and took off down the hill, expecting me, I was sure, to follow. I called after her, my words likely drowned out by the air whistling in her ears. I was tempted to turn around and ride home alone, but the thrill of watching her flight beckoned me. She waved at me from the bottom, urging me to join her. I steadied my feet on the pedals and started down the slope. At first I was cautious, using my brakes to slow my speed, but gradually I released them and felt myself soar as I sped faster and faster. When I reached the bottom, my arms were trembling. I had never felt such exhilaration. I came to a stop, laughing helplessly, unable to speak. Charlotte smiled from the side of the road where she had watched my descent.

I wheeled my bike over and laid it down next to hers. I sat on the ground to catch my breath, but Charlotte stepped off the side of the road onto what appeared to be a path. It started between two boulders and followed a line of electrical poles into the woods. She seemed to know where she was going and called for me to follow. I shook my head and moved over to cool off in the shade.

Charlotte scrambled up the path and disappeared behind trees and rocks. I expected her to return right away, to tell me what she had discovered, but when some time had passed and she still hadn't come back, I grew worried, and I decided to seek her out. I climbed up the rocky incline that started by the edge of the road and found myself surrounded by more huge boulders that looked like a giant's teeth pushing out of the ground. Twisted cedars grew on top of them, wrapping their roots around the rocks to reach the thin soil underneath. I stood mesmerized by the beauty of the place, both frightened and enchanted. I touched the moss that covered one of the stones. My fingertips sank into the soft dampness. I called out Charlotte's name. There was no answer. I walked farther and saw tall, leafy trees all around me. I called for her again. My heart was pounding.

This time there was a distant answer. "Over here, Annie!" I followed the voice, climbing higher and higher until I came to what appeared to be a precipice, overlooking farmers' fields below. Charlotte was nowhere to be seen. I walked as close to the edge as I dared and looked down. The cliff followed a meandering line and in some places it jutted out and cut in again, like the profile of a person with a nose, mouth, and chin. "Charlotte?" I called again. "Where are you?" This time her voice sounded closer. I looked all around me but still couldn't see her. "Down here. Climb down here." I walked a few steps toward the sound and saw a place where the cliff separated into deep cracks leading far below. I crouched and looked in between the rocks and saw Charlotte partway down, grinning up at me.

"I found a cave. Come down. See, there're places to put your hands and feet." She pointed at grooves in the rocks that formed a natural ladder. I started to lower myself into the crevice, noticing that it felt much cooler between the rocks. Charlotte was waiting for me when I reached the bottom. The crevice was wider there, opening up to a rocky ledge at the side of the cliff. We went out on the ledge and I followed Charlotte for a few steps until she took me into a cave, an open space with a smooth floor and concave walls, a round room in the middle of the cliff. I sat and leaned against the wall and caught my breath. I felt the quiet all around me.

"I thought this place looked familiar. I recognized the boulders by the road," Charlotte said, her voice breaking the stillness. "I've been here in the car, with my mum. She told me that she used to come here as a teenager, and then to be alone with my dad before they were married. She said that it was her favourite place to hide."

Charlotte and I returned to the ledge outside the cave, sitting with our backs against the rocks. She lit one of the cigarettes that she had stolen from her mother. I looked down at the treetops and beyond to the valley of grassy fields stretching out to meet the hills on the other side. The air was filled with the gentle rustle of leaves. It had been a long time since I had felt such peace.

It was almost seven in the evening by the time we got back to Irvine. I knew my parents would be worried and angry. I had never returned from an outing this late and I knew if my parents found out how far I had been they would forbid me from spending time with Charlotte again. I parked my bicycle in the back hall behind the entrance to the kitchen and walked around to the front of the restaurant. I had decided that it would be better to see my father first. I was relieved to see the dining room full – they would be too busy to bother with me.

My father was hurrying to serve one of the booths along the wall. When he saw me he looked relieved, then stern. "Where have you been?" he called. He put down the dishes and walked toward me. "What happened to you?"

I was suddenly aware of how dirty I must have looked from my ride in the country and from crawling around on the rocks. "I was in the park," I said, avoiding his eyes. "I didn't know how late it was getting. I'm sorry." I wasn't lying completely. Charlotte and I had been in the park before going into the countryside. There was no need for anyone to know anything more.

My father shook his head. "You are home too late. Your mother has not stopped looking at the clock. Go and tell her you're here."

I went into the kitchen and found my mother at the chopping block slicing vegetables. "You're late coming home," she said, raising her voice above the drone of the exhaust fan. "You need to watch the time more carefully." I glanced at my brother – he faced the stove, his arm and shoulder moving back and forth as he tossed ingredients around in the wok, the metal spatula hitting the sides in a steady mechanical rhythm. I was expecting her to follow with angry questions, but she said nothing. I quickly went upstairs to wash before she changed her mind.

In the bathroom, as the sink filled with water, I stared at my reflection in the mirror. I needed to be more careful in the future. If I was late again I knew I would have to have a story ready. But tonight my mother seemed preoccupied and had not asked where I had been. I told myself I should be relieved.

MY FATHER STARTED the day by pouring boiling water into a teapot with tea leaves. As the day wore on, he would add more of each. The outside of the pot was white with a stained-brown spout, but inside it was as black as charcoal. When my brother first arrived, my father used to sit across from him at the back table and would talk about stories from the newspaper, trying to engage him in conversation. During lulls in the business, my father now perched on a stool at the front of the dining room behind the glass case that held the cigarettes. He was there when I came home from school or from being with Charlotte.

My brother worked with my mother at the opposite end of the building, in the kitchen, behind the wooden swinging door. When they came into the dining room, one usually sat at the back table and the other in the booth under the calendar. As I looked at my mother, my father, and my brother each staked out in their separate territory of the dining room, I asked myself how long had they read from the same script, understanding the unspoken boundaries.

❧

FOR THE REST OF the summer, Charlotte and I rode our bikes to our secret hideaway several times a week. We walked in the woods and climbed down the cliff face, exploring between other fissures in the boulders but always returning to our cave. Often we sat in the sun on the ledge outside the entrance and read or talked. Sometimes we sat in silence while Charlotte drew in her sketch pad and I read my books. I loved the sound of wind through leaves and the sight of treetops swaying below. I wanted so badly to tell Charlotte about my mother and my brother, but each time I tried, nothing came out of my mouth. She would look at me in that unblinking way of hers and return to her drawing.

Once, I asked Charlotte if I was her best friend. She turned to me and gave a little laugh. "Sure you are, Annie," she said, touching me on the arm. "How come you're asking?"

"I don't know," I answered. There was no doubt in my mind that Charlotte was my closest friend and would be forever. I could not imagine life without her. But deep down, I knew I was not as good a friend as I wanted to be. Best friends shared their secrets. I held mine inside, unable to let go.

Charlotte gave me a look. "Annie Chou, you're a funny girl," she said.

Charlotte and I were inside Sniders' leafing through comics and magazines the week before school began. Standing at the far end of the counter was a girl I had never seen before. She had a look about her that made me think she was from the city. Her hair was a whitish blonde, teased and puffy on top and flipped up at the ends. She had round breasts that pushed out from a tight, pale blue sweater. Although Charlotte was also beginning to show, her body did not have the same maturity. Several girls from my class were beginning to develop. I had seen Norma Benson in Reids' walking with her shoulders hunched and dressed in loose-fitting clothes. She seemed embarrassed by the full breasts that had popped up over the summer. I felt sorry for Norma, yet at the same time it seemed unfair that she should have so much while someone like me still had almost nothing. I saw a couple of boys in the store steal furtive glances at her, then whisper and make rude gestures with their hands.

The new girl seemed at ease with her curvy body, standing casually with one foot in front of the other, her hip thrust out, her short skirt and snug sweater. I knew the boys would never tease her. They might look, but they wouldn't dare flirt.

The girl approached us and introduced herself as Wendy, telling us that she and her mother had just moved into an apartment above a store on Main Street. Even though Charlotte appeared engrossed in her magazine and answered with only a casual "Oh?" when the girl first spoke to us, I knew they were sizing each other up.

Wendy seemed to talk directly to Charlotte, with only a few glances in my direction. There was something in the tone of her voice, the way she shrugged her shoulders, that suggested to me a worldliness and experience the rest of us, maybe Charlotte even, lacked. I was surprised to find out that, like us, she was going into Grade Six.

Wendy looked at the magazine that Charlotte was reading and saw the photograph of beautiful Elizabeth Taylor. She said to Charlotte, "My mother cut Elizabeth Taylor's hair, you know."

"Really?" I said, impressed.

"Is that so?" said Charlotte, clearly skeptical.

"It's the truth," Wendy bragged. "At the hairdressing salon she used to work at, in Toronto. My mother got her autograph."

"So what was Elizabeth Taylor doing in Toronto?" asked Charlotte.

"Some kind of movie-star business," replied Wendy. "How should I know?"

"If your mother was good enough to cut Elizabeth Taylor's hair, then how come you moved from Toronto to live here?" Charlotte was having none of it.

"The other ladies at the hair salon where my mum worked were jealous because she's so much better than them. She brought in all kinds of extra business, you know, but the boss wouldn't pay her any more money. So she quit and got a job here."

"Hmm . . . ," said Charlotte slowly. "That autograph from Elizabeth Taylor, can you show it to us?"

"I'd love to," said Wendy with a cool smile. "But we lost it when we moved."

Charlotte's eyes narrowed. I could tell there was something about Wendy that interested her. Charlotte had never really bothered with the other kids at school. She said they bored her, and in turn, they thought she was strange. Clearly Wendy was different.

Later, as Charlotte and I walked back to her house, I asked her if she really thought Wendy's mother had cut Elizabeth Taylor's hair.

Charlotte stopped walking. "Annie!" she said. "You actually believed her! You're so gullible." I stared at her for a second.

"Well," I said, trying to cover up my mistake. "I just wanted to know if *you* believed her."

"Sure, Annie," muttered Charlotte, the sarcasm in her voice like a slap.

We sat in Charlotte's bedroom and she read out loud from one of the love comics, but I wasn't in the mood to laugh. I was annoyed that I had been taken in by Wendy while Charlotte had seen through her. I felt stupid and Charlotte calling me gullible only added to it. She always seemed to know what was going on ahead of me, and recently she'd started using all these new, adult-sounding words. It wasn't that I didn't understand them, my difficulty was knowing when to use them, to make them sound as if they belonged to me. The other day Charlotte had described herself as feeling wretched. I knew that if I tried to talk like that it would be like playing dress-up, the words too big, awkward, like someone else's shoes.

At four o'clock in the afternoon there were only a few people in the dining room: customers snacking on pie, or breaking for coffee and cigarettes. The supper business would not begin for at least another hour. I was home from Charlotte's and was standing for a moment at the lunch counter, flipping through a *Life* magazine that had a feature about the Kennedys. My father came and stood beside me and together we looked at the pictures. He said to me that he thought the Americans had made a mistake, choosing such a young man to look after their country. I told him that a new girl had moved into town. He seemed to like these unplanned moments. Nothing much was ever said, but it was our time together. He looked up and saw a customer standing at the cash register. Before he hurried off, he gave my arm a squeeze. I walked toward the kitchen to go upstairs and heard a sharp exchange of voices as I opened the swinging door. My mother was at the work counter with her back to me. "You don't have to send so much money," she said. "Not yet." Lee-Kung looked up from battering pieces of fish. I had interrupted something.

My mother glanced over her shoulder. "Su-Jen," she said, "get something to eat, you must be hungry."

"Later," I said, pushing past her. I ran upstairs and slammed my magazine on the homework table. I was angry with my mother and Lee-Kung for arguing over his mail-order bride. They never seemed to talk about her except to fight. And I was angry with Charlotte even though she hadn't done anything wrong.

By the end of the first day of school it seemed as if everyone knew Wendy. She was the girl from the big city. Everyone was impressed by her and gathered around her in the schoolyard, vying for her attention. The only person who didn't appear impressed was Charlotte. She didn't giggle over Wendy as the other girls did. Maybe that was why Wendy gravitated toward her.

One day Wendy invited Charlotte to come over after school. Charlotte agreed to go, but only if I came too. Wendy lived with her mother above Gildners' Jewellery and Watch Repair, just a few stores down from the Dragon Café. Mr. Gildner was one of my favourite merchants on the street. Every morning he made the forty-five-mile drive to Irvine from his home in Toronto and every afternoon at three o'clock he put a sign on his door that read, *I'm having coffee with the Dragon. Back in ten minutes.* When I saw him in his store, Mr. Gildner was usually bent over behind the counter with one eye squinted around a glass lens that resembled a miniature telescope, examining the inner workings of a watch. He made me think of the shoemaker in *The Shoemaker and the Elves,* a small, dark man with twinkling eyes and a quick smile. Once, Mr. Gildner had pried opened the back of an expensive Swiss watch. I had stared in amazement at the tiny shining brass pendulum, the miniature gears, and little red rubies the size of pencil points. He often let Charlotte and me try on rings and bracelets. He liked to joke with us, teasing us about boys.

It was Wendy's mother, Rose, who would later introduce me to that expression *honey attracts more flies than vinegar*. She had sensed right away that Mr. Gildner was a soft touch, and had convinced him to repaint the entire place. Wendy also told us that Mr. Gildner was a Jew. I didn't understand why she spoke in such a secretive tone, as if it was something to be hidden. That was why he was so rich, she told us.

We walked home with Wendy and stood back while she unlocked the door to the apartment. The restaurant was always open when I returned, and the houses that I visited were never locked. Wendy's door opened onto a staircase. We followed her to the second floor.

Wendy poured us each a glass of orange Freshie and took us into the living room. There was a turquoise couch with plump cushions and matching end tables. Each table held a lamp with a pleated shade made of pale yellow chiffon, decorated along the bottom rim with a row of dangling teardrop pearls. On the coffee table were two small white porcelain figurines: a torso of a woman with no arms, and a naked man with one arm bent at the elbow and the other hanging at his side. In between them was a pink glass ashtray in the shape of a swan. I had never seen a living room like this one. I had been to Jonette's and Darlene's houses and had sat in their living rooms. They were pleasant and more comfortable than anything I knew in my own home, but they paled in comparison to this. I knew that both my parents would see buying things like glass and porcelain figurines as wasteful, something you might do only if you were rich. They would disapprove of the way Wendy's mother spent money on these furnishings when she could only afford to rent rather than buy a house. I knew we weren't rich, but at least we owned our restaurant.

I found myself staring at the statue of the naked man, and felt a flush of heat in my cheeks. Charlotte also noticed the statues right away. She exchanged a glance with Wendy and giggled. Wendy told us that her mother called the lady Venus and the man David. During the entire walk from school Charlotte and

Wendy had been talking about the boys in our class. Once again they started: who was the best-looking, who was the most fun, and why. Then they looked at the porcelain David and started to laugh. When I asked what was so funny, they laughed again. Charlotte put her arm around me and said, "Nothing, Annie, nothing."

One night Wendy and her mother came into the restaurant for supper. Before sitting down at their booth, Wendy introduced us. In my eyes, Rose Jenkins was the most glamorous woman in Irvine. She spoke with an English accent, her lipstick was reddish orange, and her eyes were lined in black, her bright red hair was puffy on top, and swept up into a perfect French roll. She said she had a job working at Myrna's Cut and Curl.

On her second visit to the restaurant, Mrs. Jenkins waited alone at the lunch counter for a takeout order. In between puffs on her cigarette, she told me that Wendy's father had been killed in a car accident when Wendy was only a baby. They had packed up shortly after his death and come to Canada to start a new life. They had lived in Toronto and some other small towns, but liked Irvine best, she told me. She winked and insisted that I call her Rosie. I was in awe of this woman who waved her cigarette, jangling the bracelets on her arms, who was so brave, taking her life into her own hands.

If Rose was different from the other mothers I knew, she was a world apart from my own. I could tell that my mother was still a beautiful woman with her flawless complexion, dark eyes, and shiny hair, but I was beginning to see her as someone who had no style. The dresses she made on the treadle sewing machine in the foyer were all a variation of a shirtwaist with a flared skirt: light wool in the winter and flower prints in the summer. Rose was vibrant, all colour and glossy red lips and a saucy attitude. After she left, I went to the bedroom and looked in the warped mirror above the wooden bureau. With one hand on my chest and the other waving an imaginary cigarette, I mimicked her slanted vowels and crisp consonants. Rose walked with a girlish sway of her hips, a walk I liked to imitate whenever I found myself alone.

Another time, after Rose had left the restaurant with takeout food, my mother said, "That woman is like a many-mouthed bird, *dee-lee-dil-lil,* doesn't know when to shut up, going on and on about herself."

"How do you know?" I said. "You can't understand."

My mother shook her head. "I know what she's saying just by the way she talks."

&

THAT AUTUMN CHARLOTTE and I didn't bicycle out to the cave very often. Instead, we began to spend more time with Wendy at her apartment. I liked it best when Rose was home. She told us funny stories about the customers and let us experiment with her makeup. But when I was alone with Wendy and

Charlotte, they would whisper and giggle, claiming I wouldn't understand. It was a side of Charlotte I had never seen.

Late in the term, a new music teacher arrived. Mr. Cameron stood out from the other male teachers at our school. Obvious things like his expensive clothes set him apart, but it was more than that. His sense of humour seemed sharper and wittier, he was interested in books, music, and art. He was willing to talk about himself in a way that the other teachers never did. He described a summer trip to Europe, and talked about having dinner at a restaurant in Toronto. In Irvine, dinner was what we ate at noon.

In music class, even though we continued to sing some of the same favourites like "Donkey Riding," "Drink to Me Only with Thine Eyes," and "The Red River Valley," Mr. Cameron also played the occasional rock 'n' roll song on the piano. At the same time he was more serious about music than our previous teacher. Mrs. Whitehall had allowed us to sing sitting in our seats, but Mr. Cameron made us stand tall. He used a pitch pipe and reminded us to keep the note in our heads.

Mr. Cameron wasn't married and I often wondered why. Next to my brother he was the most handsome man I had ever seen. With his thick brown hair, strong jaw, and white square teeth, he looked almost as handsome as Ricky Nelson. I noticed how brightly the female teachers smiled when he joined them for recess duty. The senior girls giggled and talked about him in hushed voices. Wendy even wondered to Charlotte what it would be like to go on a date with him. Charlotte shrugged her shoulders as if she hadn't thought about it, but I knew that wasn't true. I could tell by the change in her voice when she and Wendy whispered about him. One day he had noticed Charlotte reading *Alice in Wonderland*. She told him that her favourite character was the Cheshire Cat. He said to her, "Ah, that's because you have the smile that everyone remembers." It was the first time I'd ever seen Charlotte blush.

Mr. Cameron was the first teacher to take a real interest in Charlotte's drawing. One day he brought his own sketches to school to show her after class. I went with Charlotte to the music room to look at his work, which was mostly landscapes and still lives. The compositions were beautiful, the sort of thing that might eventually be framed and placed on a wall. I told him they were wonderful, how much I liked them.

"You're very kind, Annie," he said. "Charlotte, here, is the one with real talent. I'm what you call an amateur. You see, what Charlotte has, you can't teach."

I wondered if I had talent. I thought about my poems, my recent attempts at writing. I wouldn't dare show them to Mr. Cameron. Even the thought of it made my heart race.

When Wendy teased Charlotte about Mr. Cameron, Charlotte gave her a sly look. "Are you jealous?" she asked.

In February, Mr. Cameron announced that the school was going to put on a musical called *Sunflower Sal*. He said that it was about a beautiful girl whose mother died when she was a baby. Then her father died when she was a teenager, leaving her to live with a tyrannical stepmother and horrible stepsisters. At the end of the story, Sunflower Sal ended up rich because she inherited a farm in Alberta that happened to have an oil well. With auditions scheduled in two weeks, the atmosphere at Alexander Chiddie vibrated with excitement. Every night after supper I shut myself in my room and practised Sal's solos, pretending to suffer the scoldings of my stepmother. I wanted the lead more than anything else.

All the girls in my class, even Hilary Beeston, were gathered in the school gym waiting to try out for the play.

"Are you hoping to get a part, Annie?" Jonette asked.

I hesitated for a moment. I wanted to play Sunflower Sal like everyone else, but the way she asked made me too embarrassed to say so.

"I don't think there are any Chinese girls in the play," said Hilary.

"There might be Chinese people in the town," I said.

"I suppose," said Hilary, crossing her arms, "but I've never heard of a musical with a Chinese person."

"Well maybe she could take a small role," said Jonette.

"But definitely not the lead," said Darlene. "Sunflower Sal has blonde hair and has to look like her parents who die."

"Well, maybe she's adopted," interrupted Charlotte. "So what?"

But Hilary had made her point. When Mr. Cameron asked if I was going to try out, I replied that I was only there to watch my friends and would like to join the choir instead. I sat through most of the auditions, willing myself to take a turn onstage and sing. Instead I left early and went home alone. The worst of the winter was over and the snow now looked like sugar rather than powder. I thought about what Hilary had said, and I felt the heat of embarrassment rush through me again.

It was no surprise to anyone when Mr. Cameron called Wendy to the front of the class and announced that she would be playing the role of Sunflower Sal. All morning I had listened to talk about the auditions, about Wendy's singing and how good she had been. With Mr. Cameron's arm around her, she beamed at everyone in the room. I turned and caught a glimpse of Charlotte, her face in a scowl, rifling furiously through pages in her binder.

Later I stood between Charlotte and Wendy as we leaned against the railing of the bridge at Willow Creek. Since music class Charlotte had been acting strange. She seemed angry with Wendy, and their usual whispering had disappeared.

Once again I was a wall between two people fighting. I stared over the bridge at the narrow ribbon of water that had managed to break through the ice during the recent thaw, imagining how, in another few months, it would be roaring under the bridge. That was when the creek seemed most alive with water demons. The lake, with its placid, peaceful surface, never frightened me in the same way. No one outside my family knew about the fortune teller's book, about my mother's warnings. I knew my friends would think that believing in predictions and curses was crazy. People drowned because of the water current, the undertow, the temperature of the water, not because of demons pulling them in. Even though I knew they were right, I looked at the cracks in the ice and wondered if the demons were rousing from their sleep.

Charlotte pulled herself from the railing and we started toward town. Wendy repeated over and over what Mr. Cameron had said, that she was perfect for the role of Sunflower Sal. As we were nearing the centre of town Charlotte said in a flat voice, "*Sunflower Sal*'s a pretty dumb play."

"Who asked you?" said Wendy.

"The songs are pretty good," I said, but they both ignored me.

"If you stop and think about it, it's really stupid," said Charlotte. "It's obviously copied from *Cinderella*. It's not even funny."

"Is somebody else jealous now? Did teacher's pet expect to get the lead?" Wendy jeered.

"Even if I were offered a role, I'm not sure I'd take it," Charlotte said with her nose in the air.

"Come off it, Charlotte. Can I help it if I have the best voice?" said Wendy.

"You do have to have a good voice for the lead role, Charlotte." I regretted the words as soon as they left my mouth. Charlotte glared at me.

"See, Annie agrees with me," Wendy jumped in. "Just because you think you're Mr. Cameron's favourite doesn't mean you get the lead. You always act so superior, Charlotte, but this time you're no better than anyone else."

A dark silence hung over us after that. No one said anything more until we were about to cross the road toward Wendy's apartment. That morning Wendy had invited Charlotte and me to her house for supper, but as we stood on the curb, Charlotte suddenly announced that she didn't feel like going to Wendy's.

"Fine, don't come," said Wendy. "But you're still coming, aren't you, Annie?" She linked her arm through mine. I looked back and forth at the two of them, both waiting expectantly. When I didn't say anything for a moment, Charlotte gave an angry huff.

"Suit yourself, Annie," she said and turned on her heel and marched off down Main Street.

Wendy pulled me across the road. "Charlotte!" I called, but she didn't seem to hear me.

Outside the Dragon Café, I hesitated at the door. "Wendy, I'm not feeling very well. I don't think I'm going to come for supper."

Wendy rolled her eyes. "You're such a baby," she said and left me standing there.

That evening I rushed through dinner. I couldn't stop thinking about Charlotte and how bad I felt that Wendy had been so mean to her. As soon as I finished helping my mother clear the table, I told her I had to return a book to Charlotte. My mother was about to question me and probably suggest that I wait until school the next day. But before she could protest, the phone in the kitchen rang, distracting her. As I was leaving I heard my brother call to my father, "Quick, pick up the phone."

I ran around the corner to the Heighington house. When I knocked on the side door, Mrs. Heighington told me Charlotte had gone to pick up her brothers at a friend's house and wouldn't be back until later. "Oh," I said, disappointed. "Will you tell her I stopped by?"

Mrs. Heighington smiled down at me. "I will, Annie. Goodnight." I walked home slowly.

My father was waiting when I came in the door. I had seen him watching for me through the front window.

"Su-Jen," he said, "I have sad news." His face was ashen; his eyes sagged and the lines in his face looked even deeper than usual. He seemed so alone. I suddenly remembered the phone call just before I left and the urgency in my brother's voice. I rushed around the counter and put my arms around my father.

"It's Uncle Yat," I whispered. "It's Uncle Yat."

"He's gone," said my father. "For fifty years, my friend for fifty years."

We held each other for a long time. My father had lost his best and only friend. Even though he hadn't seen Uncle Yat since he left Irvine, they still played a large role in each other's lives. In their letters they shared news about their families, their sons, and their poetry. Several years ago Uncle Yat had expressed great disappointment that his son had taken a French-Canadian girl for a wife. But more recently he had told my father how fortunate he felt, how well his daughter-in-law cared for him, how proud he was of his new grandson. I couldn't help but detect a note of envy in my father's voice when he told me about Uncle Yat's good luck. The gods were never fair. My father, too, was a kind, hard-working man.

"I have to go to Ottawa, just for a few days," he said. His voice was tired and strained. "Su-Jen, you look after things, okay?" Without my father saying so, I knew for certain what I had suspected: that he, too, knew about my mother and Lee-Kung. In the dark corners of our hearts we now shared the same secret and understood it was something never to be given voice.

While I was at school the next afternoon, Father took a bus to Toronto, then another to Ottawa. At supper that night my mother and Lee-Kung talked about the customers, the weather, and the death of Uncle Yat. From the outside, it seemed as if nothing had changed. But I saw otherwise. There was something about my mother that seemed softer, her body more relaxed and her voice less strained. My brother didn't jiggle his leg as much as usual and when they spoke they looked directly at each other. I found it hard to be at the same table with them as they talked so calmly. For me, what was unspeakable drowned out what was being said. My eyes barely left the rice in my bowl.

There were only a few evening customers sitting in the wooden booths at the front of the dining room. Someone had put a dime in the jukebox and Elvis started to sing "Can't Help Falling in

Love." I stood in front of the sink behind the lunch counter, thinking about Charlotte and washing the glasses from the supper business. She had ignored me all day at school, even though I had told her that I didn't go to Wendy's for supper. She had said it made no difference to her, that real friends stood up for each other, and then she had asked me if I knew who my real friends were. When school was over Charlotte had left by herself and I had stayed for choir rehearsal. After practice I had started to walk home with Wendy, but in the schoolyard we ran into Charlie Williams, a boy in Grade Eight. The two of them had teased and flirted with each other as if I weren't there. I had finally left without saying goodbye.

A glass slipped out of my hand and broke in the sink. I wasted an extra half-hour draining the water and picking out the broken pieces.

My mother said to me, "Su-Jen, you must be more careful."

"What's the big deal?" I shot back. "It's just a glass."

"It costs money, that's what," She glowered at me as she spoke.

That night my mother never bothered coming to our bedroom. She didn't lie down beside me, waiting for me to fall asleep.

In the middle of the night I got up and stood at the door of my brother's bedroom. I knew I shouldn't, but I pressed my ear against it. I wanted to rush in and tear them apart, to kick them and kick them.

❧

THE NEXT DAY I stayed at school after choir rehearsal to watch Mr. Cameron work with the solo performers. He played the opening bars on the upright piano, and signalled to Wendy with a nod of his head as he walked to the back of the auditorium. She began to sing:

Mopping the floors, wiping the doors,
I'll never be done; it's more, more, more,
Moon above, oh moon above,
When will I find my own true love?

Wendy stood with her hands clasped in front as she finished her song. She hadn't said anything about the way she and Charlie Williams had ignored me the previous afternoon. I wondered if she even remembered that I had been there. Earlier in the day she had spent both recesses walking around the schoolyard with the older girls.

That morning while everyone was waiting for the bell to ring, I had found Charlotte in a far corner of the schoolyard sketching in her book. I tried to approach her, but she remained aloof, coolly saying hello, not putting down her pencil to talk. I wanted to tell her how much I missed her, that I wanted to be friends with her, not Wendy, but I didn't know how to make her listen.

"That's coming along, Wendy," Mr. Cameron called from the back. "The words will have to be completely memorized by next week." His words jolted me out of my thoughts.

Mr. Cameron walked back to the stage and spoke to Keith Langley, the male lead. "You're going to have to project more.

Your voice needs to hit the back of the auditorium. Like this." With his arms extended, Mr. Cameron leaned toward Wendy and sang.

Sunflower Sal,
You're my kind of gal,
When I look at you,
My heart feels so true.

When Mr. Cameron finished, we heard someone clap and call out, "Bravo! Bravo!" We all turned and saw Wendy's mother standing in the doorway.

Rose put her coat over her arm and came into the room, her high heels clicking against the hardwood floor. Even though she said that she had left work early to take Wendy out for a treat of fish and chips, it was clear to me that her real purpose was to see Mr. Cameron for herself. From the way she tossed her hair and smiled, I wondered if she was looking for a date. My parents would never approve of a woman being so forward with her intentions. But I also couldn't imagine Rose contacting a matchmaker and writing back and forth to someone to find a husband. Just thinking about it made me smile to myself.

All day the wind had been gathering strength. I hugged my books and binder closer to my chest. I walked into the Dragon Café and saw only a few customers finishing their meals in the booths and one at the lunch counter. I wondered why my mother wasn't in the dining room and went to look for her in the kitchen, but hesitated at the door and opened it a crack instead. My mother and Lee-Kung were standing together on the other side of the work counter behind the chopping block. His arms were around her and she was crying into his shoulder. I saw her look up at him. I couldn't make out what they were saying, but I watched my brother brush some loose strands of hair from her face. He was trying to tell her something; she shook her head and pressed her face into his shoulder again. He held her for a moment longer. Finally, she pushed herself away and walked toward the door to the dining room. My brother stood watching, still as a statue. I rushed to the back booth and sat down, staring straight ahead. For a moment my mother looked surprised to see me, then quickly recovered and told me to get something to eat.

For dinner, Lee-Kung made my favourite foods: chicken steamed with dried mushrooms, fish stir-fried with Chinese broccoli, and oxtail and carrot soup. Refusing to acknowledge their efforts I ate very little and finished as quickly as I could, claiming that I had a lot of homework.

As I ran up the flight of stairs, I felt like knocking over all those boxes filled with cooking oil, chocolate syrup, and soya sauce. I sat down at my homework table and stared for a long time at the wall and remembered for some reason the egg-shaped impressions left by Charlotte's grandparents in the pillows that I had seen in their room. That my parents ever shared a bed was unimaginable. In our house it was my mother and Elder Brother who slept together in the night. I had again caught them unawares. Their anguish, their tenderness were unbearable. I desperately wanted to cry, but my eyes remained dry.

When I was a small child my mother was my entire world. I remembered leaning into the softness of her body, her love, constant and secure, wrapped around me like a warm blanket. Her love for me was still there. But now it seemed either far away, or sharp and oppressive, jabbing at me through her scoldings and fussings. At times I wanted to be free of my mother, other times I just wanted us to be a family like everyone else. I could hardly wait for the next day, for Father to return.

All the way home from school the following day after rehearsal, I prayed that my father would be waiting for me at the Dragon Café. When I looked in the window of the restaurant and saw him through the branches of the jade plant, in his usual place behind the cash register, I rushed in the door and around the counter and threw my arms around him, almost knocking him off his stool.

"Ah, Su-Jen, Su-Jen," he said, hugging me in my heavy winter coat. "My daughter, Su-Jen." His voice was gentle and soothing. When I finally stepped back I was weak with relief. I realized then I had been afraid he might not return.

Later I sat down for supper beside my mother, across from Father and Elder Brother. It was barely discernible, but now that my father was home, I noticed a slight shift in my mother's and brother's behaviour to where it was before: a stiffness in their backs, a carefulness in their voices, and their eyes no longer meeting. But the conversation remained the same: food, weather, customers. Then Father spoke about the funeral and the two nights that he had spent with Uncle Yat's son and his family.

"Uncle Yat was a lucky man. He had a good daughter-in-law, especially for a *gwei poh*. She even cooks Chinese food. And his grandson is *ho lek,* very smart."

"It's always sad to lose someone," said my mother, "even when he's lived a long life."

"Uncle Yat died a happy man," Father said. "In one of his letters he wrote that even if his daughter-in-law were Chinese she would not have been able to take better care of him."

&

AS REHEARSALS FOR THE PLAY went on, Rose Jenkins started coming twice a week to help cast members learn their lines. She would always arrive a little breathless and wave at Mr. Cameron while she patted her hair into place.

Mrs. Heighington also began to join us. Mr. Cameron had asked her to play the piano so that he could conduct the choir. I had not seen her very much in the past while and I hadn't realized how much I'd missed her until her first rehearsal, when she came pushing her youngest daughter in a stroller. She had seen me standing in the choir and had given me a wink.

One afternoon Mrs. Heighington brought Charlotte with her to mind the toddler. She sat at the back of the auditorium drawing in her sketch pad and entertaining her little sister. Mrs. Heighington played the piano and the choir practised our songs again and again. During the break I followed Mr. Cameron as he walked over to talk to Charlotte. She looked up and said to him, "So here comes the star of the choir! Isn't that right, Mr. Cameron?" When he looked down at her sketch pad, she crossed her eyes at me and I broke into a wide grin.

After the rehearsal Mrs. Heighington asked me back to their house. Although Charlotte didn't say anything, I eagerly accepted her mother's invitation, hoping that finally I might make things right.

I sat down at the Heighingtons' kitchen table, looked at the stacks of books, the dirty dishes, and breathed in the sweetish scent of rotting apples. I had missed this house so much: its clutter, its warmth. Charlotte put on the kettle. "You want some tea, Annie?" she said, setting out a plate of Fig Newtons.

Mrs. Heighington lit a cigarette and put her feet up on a chair. She looked back and forth at the two of us and said, "It looks like all the kids are having a good time at rehearsals. It's going to be quite a show."

"I always thought it was a little bit dumb," I said.

Mrs. Heighington smiled and said, "Yes, there are a lot of jokes for adults. Mr. Cameron is doing a good job. I really like him." She saw the surprised look on my face and her smile grew bigger. "He's great fun, you know."

"A lot of the lady teachers like him," I said carefully.

"I think Wendy's mum likes him too," said Charlotte, glancing in my direction, a sly look on her face. I giggled back at her.

"I know," said Mrs. Heighington, shaking her head. "Poor woman, she's wasting her time. He's not the marrying kind."

"I bet he's a ladies' man," said Charlotte, her mouth full.

Mrs. Heighington laughed. "Hmm, I don't think so. Let's just say he's not the marrying kind. Trust me, I know. Someday you'll understand." Her voice became wistful. "I fell for a guy like that once."

Charlotte became alert. "You never told me that," she said.

"It was a long time ago. In my second year of university. I ended up with a broken heart." Mrs. Heighington sucked on her cigarette, a haze of smoke around her head. She smiled and spoke with a kind of false cheerfulness. "But I came home for the summer and, lucky girl that I was, ended up marrying your darling father and never went back." She reached over and patted Charlotte on the shoulder.

I hated it when people spoke like that, even Mrs. Heighington. It was that adult way of telling the truth so that we wouldn't understand.

I had to go home soon for supper, so Charlotte walked me to the vestibule where I'd left my coat. It was quiet except for the rustle of cloth as I did up my buttons. "Charlotte . . . ," I finally said, looking at her, ready to apologize for what had happened.

"Forget it, Annie," she interrupted. "It's okay." Then she hugged me tight and promised we'd get out on our bikes when the snow was gone.

I walked into the Dragon Café to find my father grinning behind the cash register. It seemed that Mai-Yee, my brother's mail-order bride, had passed the test for *fuh loh.* "Finally, your brother can apply to the government to bring her over and get married. If everything goes well, she should be here sometime in September or October," he said. I smiled back at my father, unable to contain my relief. I think we both believed it was the answer to all that was wrong in our lives. What I hadn't expected was to find myself worried about my mother.

I went into the kitchen to go to the apartment and saw Lee-Kung leaning against the stainless-steel counter, smoking a cigarette, flicking the ashes in the garbage can.

"Where's *Mah*?" I asked.

"Upstairs," he answered without looking at me. He released a heavy stream of smoke.

I rushed up the steep wooden stairs to the apartment. The door to our bedroom was closed. When I opened it, I saw her sitting with her legs folded under her on the tiny space of floor. She had the green silk cloth that her mother had given her on her lap. In front of her was an open book filled with Chinese characters. Holding a bundle of small sticks in one hand, she was laying them out one by one in a pattern on the floor. She looked up at me with an expression so bleak that my words left me. The smell of burning incense followed me as I closed the door and returned downstairs.

That evening my father talked excitedly about the arrival of the mail-order bride, while my brother rushed through his meal. My mother sat beside me, her face pale and drawn. I had never seen her look so sad. I decided to tell my family about the musical at school and that all the parents were invited. Even though my parents had never been to the school for any of my school concerts or for parent-teacher interviews, I asked them to come. My father told me how proud he was that I was doing these things for my school. My mother smiled and shook her head, saying she wouldn't understand a word and wouldn't be able to talk to anyone.

It was one of those days of perfect weather in early May. The sky was bluer and the sun was brighter. I dashed across the road to go into Reids' and ran into Rose Jenkins, who was looking in the window of the store. Just as we were about to go inside, we heard a soft honk from a car. I turned and saw Mr. Cameron in his dark glasses waving at us from his convertible. Riding in the passenger side was a good-looking young man, also in dark glasses, one arm stretched languidly behind the front bench, the other arm resting casually on the passenger door, a cigarette between his fingers. I could see the ripple of muscle underneath the white cotton jersey of his tennis shirt. The two of them were like Tod and Buzz driving around in their convertible on the television show *Route 66*. The sky-blue car, their tanned faces, smiles of perfect teeth, expensive sunglasses, their elusive confidence and ease. Watching them, it was so obvious they didn't belong in

Irvine. Mr. Cameron and his friend reminded me of the pictures I'd seen of the Kennedys on vacation, living their lives bathed in sunlight. I waved back at Mr. Cameron and watched them turn the corner. I glanced at Rose. She stood with her mouth slightly open, looking in the direction of the vanished car. She swallowed and muttered something under her breath, something that sounded like "Well I'll be damned." I stared where she stared, but I only saw an empty road.

The night before the musical opened, I stayed late at school to help Miss Skinner, a Grade Seven teacher, fold the programs. She was a teacher no one particularly liked, known to be strict and mean. I didn't mind helping out, but I rushed through the chore, embarrassed to be there with Marion Pike, who had also volunteered.

I walked down the quiet halls, past empty classrooms and darkened doorways. I stopped outside the auditorium and pulled on the door. Finding it unlocked, I stepped inside and looked at the wooden chairs arranged in horizontal rows, ready for tomorrow. I climbed up on the stage and stood for a moment in the centre. Last week I had stayed late for two nights, to help paint the scenery. One of the screens had been painted to look like the outside of a house. It had a window cut out so Sunflower Sal could lean through during one of her solos. I tiptoed over to the fake wall and poked my head through the window, looking out at my audience of chairs. I knew every song. I sang them under my breath when I walked home from school and at the top of my lungs when I was alone upstairs at the restaurant. The auditorium echoed with my steps. I leaped off the edge of the stage, grabbed my jacket and my books, leaving before anyone came in and caught me.

The musical was a big success. The weeks of preparation had paid off. All three nights I stood in the front row of the choir between Jonette and Darlene. Rose sat as close as she could to the stage and cried, smudging her mascara and eyeliner, during Wendy's solos and again when Wendy took her bow from centre stage at curtain call. On the night of the last performance, Mr. Cameron thanked everyone who had helped and presented Rose and Mrs. Heighington with bouquets of red roses.

A crowd of people gathered outside the change room to wait for the performers. When Wendy came out, her mother had roses in one hand, a bunch of white daisies for her daughter in the other. Wendy smiled and accepted the flowers; she beamed as others in the crowd joined Rose in applauding her again. She was a star basking in the praise and attention of her fans.

For a moment, the way Wendy stood, with her flowers held in both hands, reminded me of a bride. I found myself wondering what kind of flowers my brother's mail-order bride would be holding at the wedding. Would she dress in white and walk down the aisle of a church? With the excitement of the play that evening I had for a short time forgotten about my family's unhappiness.

ONCE THE PLAY was over, Wendy started to spend most evenings and Saturday afternoons in the Dragon Café hanging out with the boys who had failed Grade Eight, the ones with the thickly greased hair combed into a ducktail and packs of cigarettes tucked in the sleeve of their white T-shirts. She usually said hi when she came in, but aside from that never bothered to talk to me. When my mother saw Wendy in her tight clothes with her red lips and blue eyeshadow, she said, "*Eii-yah!* Look at her. With all that paint, her face looks like a monkey's shit bottom." Then she turned to me and scolded, "Don't you smear that stuff all over your face."

"What's wrong with wearing makeup?" I asked.

"There's nothing wrong with a little," she said. "But that much just makes you look *yeu yah,* sleazy. Nice girls don't look like that."

"Not sleazy," I said, feeling a rush of heat, "like you."

My mother went still. "What did you say?"

A part of me wanted to push further, but I lost the nerve. "Nothing," I said just under my breath. "Nothing."

Wendy and her friends sat in the two front booths of the dining room. The boys swaggered and the girls swivelled their hips as they sauntered to the jukebox to pick out songs. They flirted, giggled, and boasted. My parents referred to them as the *kai gwei* boys and girls. *Kai* was one of those funny Chinese words. If you were a *kai* two- or three-year-old, it meant that you were bright and cheeky. But to be a *kai* teenager was bad; it meant that you were mouthy and disobedient. Good Chinese girls were quiet, obedient, and always deferred to their elders. I watched from the sidelines, intrigued and unnerved by the dark sexual undercurrents in their laughter and talk.

My parents disapproved of the *kai* boys and girls; they saw them as people who would never amount to anything. Boys like that ended up working in the tannery and the girls got pregnant in high school. My mother would be alarmed by my fascination with them. Both my parents expected me to become a high-class person, a professional, someone with a university degree. Whatever reservations my mother might have had about Charlotte, the girl with the devil eyes, they appeared minor compared to how she felt about Wendy.

As I leaned against the end of the lunch counter, pretending to read the local paper but secretly watching Wendy, I thought about Charlotte and how I had almost lost our friendship. I promised myself that I wouldn't be so foolish again.

On the Saturday before school ended, Charlotte and I planned to cycle out to our secret cave. I hadn't been there since the fall and wondered if she had been on her own. After breakfast, I put some food and pop in a brown paper bag. The restaurant was quiet and dark; the blinds in the dining room were drawn. Everyone was upstairs, still sleeping. It was past nine o'clock when I wheeled my bicycle from the hall into the backyard. In another hour my brother would begin work in the kitchen and my father would unlock the front doors.

When I got to the Heighingtons', Charlotte was alone in the kitchen stirring a pot in front of the stove. The mess was worse than usual, dirty dishes piled in the sink, toys scattered on the floor, and books left everywhere. I looked around and asked where her mother was.

"She's reading in the living room," said Charlotte. "She's on strike. That's why I'm making the oatmeal."

"She's on what?" I asked.

"A strike," said Charlotte, still stirring. "Every year she stops working for a week so she can read *Anna Karenina*."

"What's Anna Kernana?"

"*Anna Karenina*. A Russian book about a married woman who runs away with her lover. It always makes her cry. You want some tea before we go?" Only Charlotte would say a word like *lover*.

She poured two cups of tea and added lots of sugar. "Let's take this upstairs," she said. "I've got something to show you in my room."

I followed Charlotte out of the kitchen and into the dining room. Stacked against the wall were several laundry baskets filled with clothes. As we passed the grandmother's bedroom I could hear snoring through the door. In the living room Mr. Heighington was watching Saturday-morning cartoons with his sons. There was a vase filled with flowers on the old piano. Mrs. Heighington was sitting in an armchair by the window, the dog lying on the floor in front of her. She had her feet on a stool, a book in her lap, and a cigarette in one hand. Thin plumes of smoke hung in the air. "Hi, Annie," she said over the noise of the tv. "I heard the news about Mr. Cameron taking a new job in Toronto. He'll be much happier in the city. We were lucky to have him though." All the girls at school had been heartbroken when we'd found out.

"He does seem like a big-city type, doesn't he?" I said.

"Well, Irvine's so boring," said Charlotte. "I can't blame him for wanting to work in the city. I'm getting out of here as soon as I can."

"I used to think that too," Mrs. Heighington said. "After university I was going to travel, see the world. More than anything else I wanted to see the pyramids. But life has a habit of getting in the way, and you just have to do the best you can." She gave us a half-smile and went back to her book.

When we got upstairs, I saw that Charlotte had decorated the walls of her room with new drawings. Replacing the horses were sketches of naked men and women. "What do you think?" she asked.

Speechless, I walked around her room examining the pictures. I had never seen drawings like these, showing every part of the body. Where had Charlotte seen things like this? I was stunned by her drawings of naked women lying down or facing away, and yet they were elegant and beautiful. One drawing was of a man with his hands behind his back, and his eyes looking at the sky. His expression was of pain and sorrow. I felt breathless. In the corners of some of the sketches were odd little creatures that looked human but with horns and wings. "Did you do all these?"

Charlotte pointed to a large black book on her dresser. She picked it up and brought it to her bed, opening it. "I copied a lot of them from this book. It's full of old paintings by people like Michelangelo and Leonardo da Vinci."

Looking at the different reproductions of paintings and sculptures I could see where Charlotte had found her inspiration: the young man with his finger pointing in the air, the beautiful woman seeming to rise from the sea, her hair streaming down her body.

Charlotte interrupted my gazing and said, "Let me show you something really strange." She turned back several pages and showed me a painting with people writhing all over the page, contorted into awkward positions.

"What are they doing?" I asked. "It looks disgusting," I added, pretending not to know.

Charlotte glanced at me quickly.

Mrs. Heighington appeared in the doorway. "It's a painting of hell by Hieronymus Bosch," she said. "And those people are overcome with lust."

The look on my face must have amused her. She smiled as she came into the room and added, "Don't pay any attention to me, Annie. I'm just teasing. This is a book of famous paintings and sculpture from ancient to modern times. It was given to me shortly before I was married, when I was a romantic, impetuous youth." Mrs. Heighington sat down beside me and placed the book on her lap. "Let me show you some paintings by my favourite artist." She turned a few pages before coming to the painting that Charlotte had shown to me earlier: a female nude standing on a seashell, on her right a woman about to wrap her in a cloak and on her left an angel with another in his arms, both blowing the nude to shore. "This is the *Birth of Venus,* Annie, by Botticelli. My father used to say that I looked like I'd just stepped out of a Botticelli painting. That was when I was much younger, of course."

"*Mo–ther!*" whined Charlotte.

"I know, I know, you've heard it all before," said Mrs. Heighington.

I looked at Mrs. Heighington, past her papery skin and dark, hollow eyes, and remembered again the lovely young woman in that photograph. I looked back at the painting. "She's beautiful," I said, ignoring Charlotte. "Have you ever seen it?"

"No, Annie, but I've always wanted to. Maybe one day you'll go to Italy and see it for me." She gave my shoulder a squeeze and left the room to see if Charlotte's little sister was awake.

When Charlotte and I started out on our bikes, the air was cool and fresh, but by mid-morning, with the sun beating down and the heat in the asphalt road radiating back on us, we were glad to sail down the hill to the path at the side of the road. I had missed the thrill of the descent.

We propped our bikes against an electrical pole and took the food from our baskets. Charlotte grabbed her sketch pad and we scrambled up the rocky incline into the woods.

I followed Charlotte along the path through the cedar trees and between the moss-covered boulders, feeling the soft bed of cedar and pine needles beneath my feet. I looked at the sky through the green of the trees.

We climbed down the crevice and eased ourselves carefully along the ledge to the secret cave. The air inside was cool and damp. We later found a sunny spot on the cliff, where Charlotte drew for most of the afternoon while I read, my mind wandering back to what she had shown me. I had thought of bringing some of my poems to share with her while she sketched, but at the last minute I had changed my mind. I looked over Charlotte's shoulder and watched her work. She had drawn the treetops, but peeking through the branches were the same little winged creatures with horns I had seen in the corners of her pictures that morning. It was hard not to stare at them. The skin on my neck tingled and I wrapped my arms around myself.

I would come to see that with Charlotte there was something deep and mysterious that set her apart from me and everyone else. What I didn't know then was how cruel the gods could be and how they would entwine her fate with mine.

I LOOKED UP FROM serving a customer at the lunch counter and saw my father's excited expression, his light footsteps, as he rushed in the door, waving a letter in his hand. I guessed that something from Mai-Yee had arrived and I hurried into the kitchen after him.

"A letter from Mai-Yee," Father announced. "Open it, open it."

Lee-Kung was making a clubhouse sandwich. "Just a minute," he said, without looking at Father, "let me finish." He sliced the sandwich into four triangles and placed them on a plate along with a dill pickle, then wiped his hands and took the letter. My father handed me the plate. "Su-Jen," he said, "take this out. It's for the uncle in the booth by the window. You know which one, he always orders the same thing."

I hesitated for a moment, then picked up the dish. As I turned to leave I glanced at my mother standing at the end of the counter closest to the upstairs entrance. She kept her head down as she sorted a bag of bean sprouts, putting the good stems in a bowl and the wilted ones in the garbage.

Mai-Yee would be here in just over a month, on September fifth, the day after school started. Father had been talking for days about who should be invited to the wedding banquet, people he hadn't seen in many years. When he asked Lee-Kung who he wanted to invite, my brother replied, "Only a few friends from Owen Sound. The rest makes no difference to me." Father let the remark pass, the air heavy with Lee-Kung's sullenness.

From that point on, I spent most nights alone in bed. My mother seemed to have left all caution behind, relying only on our closed bedroom door and my silence to keep her secrets.

Father wrote Uncle Jong in Toronto, asking him to make arrangements for a wedding, for the second Sunday in September at the Chinese Presbyterian Church where Aunt Hai-Lan worshipped, and to arrange for the reception afterwards at the Shanghai Restaurant. Uncle Jong had the wedding invitations printed for us in Toronto. I had seen *lo fon* wedding invitations before in some of my bridal magazines, white, with curling script, and a sheet of translucent tissue paper for an insert. But the invitations for Lee-Kung were deep red, decorated with a golden dragon and phoenix dancing on either side of the Chinese character for double happiness. What chance did Lee-Kung and his bride have for happiness, much less double happiness? Once the invitations arrived from Toronto, Lee-Kung stayed up with Father and stuffed them into envelopes.

For the first time, I became angry with my father. He was an honourable man who had sacrificed everything for his family, never taking a holiday, never spending a penny on himself, working hard all his life to save money for things like the mail-order bride, the wedding celebrations, and for my future university schooling, but I did not understand how he could say nothing, never confront my mother or Elder Brother, be wilfully blind to the betrayal by his wife and his son of everything that was important to him.

Over supper one night toward the end of the summer, my mother announced we could not have a new bride in our home when it looked so shabby. "We need to paint the upstairs. I wouldn't want anyone to see how I've had to live," my mother said.

"There's nothing wrong with the way we live," said Father. "We don't lack for anything."

"You've lived like this for so long you don't know any better," said my mother, shaking her head. "You think deprivation is normal. Su-Jen does her homework in a dark corner surrounded by boxes. We don't even have a chair with a cushion. Some animals in this country live better than we do."

"Of course, I'm just a lowly country boy who doesn't know any better," Father sniped back.

"It's not just the upstairs, it's the restaurant, the town. Day in, day out, it's work and more work. Nothing ever changes. You begin to feel like the walking dead. Somebody should tell the poor girl what she's getting into. At least she has a choice. I had to marry you to save my son and now my son is dead. I don't even know why I thought painting would make a difference."

My mother's words were as sharp as knives. My parents rarely talked about their dead sons, and now my mother was using hers as a weapon. My father's face was white and his mouth pinched. I couldn't bear seeing him in such pain. Something within me gave way. I clenched the edge of the seat and screamed, "Stop it. Stop this fighting!" My parents and my brother stared at me, stricken, their mouths gaping in shock. I caught myself just in time, before the words I really wanted to say about my brother and the deep secrets we all pretended we did not know escaped my lips. My mother was right, the new bride should be told the truth about how things are, but my mother would only tell part of the truth, whereas I would tell it all. I wanted to run from the room, but I stayed rooted in my spot. My brother and I locked eyes.

My father barked at me, "Su-Jen!" I could tell that he wanted to say more. My behaviour was inexcusable for a proper Chinese girl. But he sighed and shook his head. My mother looked at me as if I were a stranger. She picked up her chopsticks and resumed eating. No one said anything more for the rest of the meal. I blinked back tears and forced myself to swallow another mouthful of rice.

It seemed to me that even in death, the first-born sons of each of my parents had a grip on my family, the shadow of their presence always felt. Later that night, I went downstairs to find my father alone in the restaurant. He was sitting at the back table, his accounting books and abacus in front of him. "Su-Jen, what are you doing out of bed?" he said when he saw me standing in the kitchen doorway. I went to sit across from him and asked him to tell me about his first son. My father looked at me sadly and said yes, it was time for me to know.

"When I left China in 1930 a few months after Lee-Kung was born, my first son, Wei-Mun, was only six years old. I did not want to leave, but the business I had started in Hoi Ping had failed so I had to go back to Canada to make more money for the family. Not long after I arrived, I received a letter from my wife. Our oldest son had died very quickly of a fever. There were only herbalists in the village, no doctors to help him. If he had been in Canada, maybe there would have been better medicine. He was not lucky like you, Su-Jen, to be living here."

I imagined my father alone, learning the news of his son's death. "Did you go home then, to be with your family?" I asked.

"I'd just spent all that money to return to Canada, to spend more to go and come back again made no sense. Every year I meant to go home, then war began and I couldn't go back even when my wife died. I didn't return until 1947. By then Lee-Kung was seventeen and his mother had been dead for almost five years. When I saw him he was living with his uncle. He had become a young man I barely knew. Those early years in Canada were very hard, *ho ti leung*. We were all far from our families and we did work that no else would do. The *lo fons* kept pets who lived better than we did. They called us names they would never call their animals. Remember, Su-Jen, no one can take away what you have in your head. You are lucky to be speaking English as if you were born here and to have a chance at a good education. One day you will live just as well as some of the *lo fons* here, if not better. You won't have to be like me, to have to ask others for help, to spend a life working with your head down."

A part of me had always known that when I grew up I would not make my living in the restaurant business, that my parents had high hopes for me. Yet even when I felt hurt or angry, I could not imagine a life away from my family, away from our home at the Dragon Café, away from the town of Irvine.

"I wish I had known my other brother too, *Mah*'s son," I said quietly. There was a long silence. I thought I had said something wrong.

"He was a very handsome boy, looked like his mother. And smart," my father finally said. "When I met him, he was already reading and writing at an advanced level for his age. Your brother was a very special child. It's true, what your mother said, we married for him."

For a while neither one of us spoke, then he continued, "After he died, your mother could not forgive me. I had taken him down to the river to swim as we did every morning. Shing-Kam loved the water. He was like a fish, he was so at home," Father smiled at me in that sad way of his. "That morning he swam out too far. I had warned him about the currents, but he was a wilful boy and did not listen. When I saw him thrashing in the water, I knew he must have been caught in an eddy. I could not get to him in time. How quickly it all happened. Later that day one of the villagers found his body farther downstream. So you see, Su-Jen, I understand why your mother is angry with me. She still believes, like I do, that it was my fault." These words were whispered, barely audible. My father's head was bowed, as if too heavy to lift.

"No, *Ba Ba!*" I reached across the table and took his hand. "You couldn't help it. It wasn't your fault." In my mind I could hear my mother screaming, see her tearing at her hair.

In the days that followed I thought about my brother who had drowned. I now understood why my mother was so obsessed with my water curse. I wondered how I compared to my brother, how I could possibly live up to someone so perfect, who didn't live long enough to do anything bad. But more than anything else, I thought about my father, how he carried the responsibility of the death of my mother's son. All these things he suffered silently inside him. How could my mother be so blind to his burden?

In the end, my father relented to my mother's complaints about our shabby apartment and agreed to have it painted. Later he even suggested buying new furniture for the bedroom. He asked me to help Elder Brother choose some paint at Swackhammers' Hardware.

In a dusty back corner, Mr. Swackhammer stacked pails of paint that had been opened and returned, but not used. For as long as I could remember, that pyramid of cans with peeling faded labels had stood like a sculpture overlooking the store. I felt awkward being with my brother. Lee-Kung examined the strokes that had been brushed across the lid of each can, indicating the colour inside. There wasn't much choice of colour in the returned paint. But my brother didn't seem to care, his only concern was price. He nodded curtly when I found three pails that were the same. Watching him, I was suddenly aware of how haggard he seemed. His face was still handsome, but there were lines around his eyes. The energy that he had had when he first arrived in Irvine seemed diminished and replaced by weariness. I felt a slight shift in the anger that sat like a stone in the pit of my stomach.

Beginning that night my father closed the restaurant early several evenings in a row to allow Lee-Kung time to paint the upstairs. Father had decided that Lee-Kung and Mai-Yee should have the front room, where he had been sleeping. Father would move into Lee-Kung's room since it was the smallest.

Lee-Kung quickly painted the foyer and the front room. Since there was no time for a proper job, he went right over the chipped woodwork and the old flaking paint, not bothering with the other two bedrooms. The ceiling and walls of the front bedroom, the foyer, the bathroom, the staircase, and even the window frames and baseboards turned from a dingy grey-green to a horrible pink. After that, whenever I went upstairs I felt as if I were walking inside a giant mouth, like Jonah trapped inside a whale.

&

WENDY SAT AT THE lunch counter waiting for Saturday-night takeout food. She seemed uncomfortable, her eyes watchful, as if she were looking for someone. When I came out with her order, she leaned over the counter, gesturing to me to come closer. She looked around again at the other customers. "Can you keep a secret?" she whispered to me. I nodded, wary of what she wanted to draw me into.

"My mum and I are going away tomorrow," she said behind a cupped hand.

I looked at her in surprise. "Where are you going?"

Wendy placed a finger over her lips. "We're moving to Urquhart. My mum has a friend there and we'll stay with him until we find a place to live. I might have to start school there. But don't tell anyone. It's a secret."

"Why is it a secret?" I said, not really caring to know.

"My mum doesn't want to tell Mr. Gildner until we've moved out. He really likes her and she doesn't want to upset him," Wendy whispered. She put a brown paper bag with something inside on the counter. "My mum wants to give these to you," she said. "They're David and Venus. She knows you've always liked them."

I said goodbye to Wendy and told her that I'd miss her, even though I knew I wouldn't. Already I was worried about what my mother might say about having a statue of a naked man in my bedroom. I hid them in the bottom of my drawer under some sweaters, and only looked at them when I was alone. I kept my mouth shut when customers like Mr. Swackhammer complained how Rose Jenkins and her daughter had disappeared without paying their credit.

Charlotte didn't seem upset when I later told her that Wendy and Rose had left town. Instead, she laughed at their sneakiness and said she was glad we wouldn't have to put up with Wendy at school that year. We spent our remaining days of summer freedom riding our bikes around the countryside, wandering the cliffs and hanging around at our cave.

One day, a week before Mai-Yee arrived, I parked my bicycle in the back entrance behind the kitchen and came around to the front, where I found my father poring over the Eaton's catalogue. He looked up as I walked in. "Su-Jen, which one do you think is the best for Lee-Kung and Mai-Yee?" he asked, pointing to the pictures. "We need to order a bed and a chest of drawers."

I examined the choices on the page. Did Lee-Kung want a bed with a padded headboard, or one with a shelf for a radio? When I asked which Elder Brother liked, my father sighed. "He said he doesn't care. What about these two? They cost the least."

"You might as well get the one without the space for a radio. It's the cheaper of the two, and he doesn't listen to the radio anyway," I said.

"That makes sense," Father replied. He shook his head and added, "I didn't know that space was for a radio. Good thing you know about these *lo fon* things. You must come with me to the Eaton's order office."

Although Father had struggled and managed in the *lo fon* world with his broken English for many years, increasingly he relied on me to smooth the way. A few months earlier I had gone with him to the post office to fill out a money order to China to pay for visits to the graves of dead relatives. Whenever I translated for him I could see the pride in his eyes as he listened.

At the order office we also picked out a double mattress, two chests of drawers, four sheets, four pillowcases, two pillows, a blanket, a brown sofa, and a maple veneer coffee table. I filled out the form, tore out the customer's carbon copy, and gave the lady behind the counter a delivery date.

When I was a child living in Irvine, I had wanted so much to have what other children had: piano lessons, to be sent to camp, to be taken on a holiday, all things that cost money. I thought my parents gave me so little. It has taken many years for me to realize how wrong I was, to understand the depth of their sacrifices.

At the time I was blind to how they tried to protect me in what must have been for them an alien world. Over the last year I had been helping more and more in the restaurant. My parents now expected me to wait on tables during the weekend and to manage the cash register. On Friday and Saturday nights I was sometimes up past eleven, helping in the dining room. Our restaurant was open later than any of the others in Irvine. I hated seeing those men who reeked of alcohol after a night of drinking in the Irvine Hotel stumble into the café to order chow meins, egg foo youngs, and plates of egg rolls. Sometimes I caught them as they talked about ordering chink food. They laughed among themselves and referred to my father as Hop Sing, the Chinese houseboy in *Bonanza,* while they leered at my mother. I once heard one of them say something about it not being fair, that an old chink should be married to such a dish, that he probably didn't use it any more. Then they started snorting and laughing. My mother always muttered under her breath, "Here come those *sei doo mow gweis,* those dead drunken ghosts." But she smiled and took their orders anyway. If they seemed especially drunk, neither of my parents would allow me to serve at their table.

A few days after our trip to the Eaton's order office, the store's delivery truck parked on Main Street outside the Dragon Café; Father directed them around to the back of the restaurant. He had stayed up the previous night to clear the stairs of boxes and jars. With sweat dripping down their faces, the two men manoeuvred the pieces from the bedroom suite, the double mattress, the sofa, and the coffee table through the narrow hall, then *Jesus Christ*ed it up the steep flight of stairs.

My mother watched for a few moments from the open kitchen door; she shook her head and turned away. "They could line that room with gold and it won't make any difference."

Later in the afternoon my mother and I were drying a stack of plates in the kitchen and I heard the car door slam. She stopped for a moment and said, "I wish I knew how to drive. Sometimes I'd like to get away. Be by myself." Her eyes looked sad.

"Life will be so much better for your generation, Su-Jen. You'll have an education, a good job, learn how to drive, be able to make your own decisions. Women like me were born at a bad time. Lee-Kung's poor mother couldn't stand it any more." She hesitated before speaking again. "You must not tell your father, but Lee-Kung told me that his mother was so unhappy, she hung herself from a tree." She turned and shook her head sadly.

My stomach lurched. "But I thought she died of a fever. That's what *Ba Ba* told me."

"That's what your father still thinks. That was what the village schoolteacher told him in his letter. But your brother told me that he cut her down from a tree all by himself even though he was only a boy. Then he and his grandmother buried her. It was a great shame on the family and they did not want anyone to know. For a long time nobody knew the truth except your brother." My mother looked at me again. "All the people in your family have had hard lives. Except you, Su-Jen."

Listening to my mother I knew she was right. I should be grateful, but at the same time it seemed that everything rested on me, that all the good things in my life and future seemed to be built on not just someone's efforts but someone's sacrifice, someone's misfortune.

When my brother got back from his drive, Father didn't scold him for being gone so long, even though the supper hour had already started. I looked at my brother, his arm moving in a steady rhythm as he stood in front of the wok, and I felt a swelling in my throat.

The day before Mai-Yee's arrival I walked home from school with Charlotte, Jonette, and Darlene. I told them about my brother's mail-order bride and that the next day I would be away from school in the afternoon. Everyone stopped talking. Jonette stared at me, her mouth open. "His *what*? You mean he hasn't met her?" she asked. I explained again. She and Darlene looked at each other, eyebrows raised. "That's kind of weird, don't you think?" she said. Her remark caught me off guard.

"Well, it's different," said Darlene. With her head slightly tilted she asked with a sugary smile, "Annie, are you going to be a mail-order bride someday?"

"She'll have to, if she's going to marry somebody Chinese, or else move to Toronto. You won't get a Chinese boyfriend in Irvine," said Jonette before I could respond.

"Who said I had to have a Chinese boyfriend? I can marry anybody I want," I said, sounding more confident than I felt. "Anyway, I wouldn't put up with something as old-fashioned as an arranged marriage. I hate to think who I'd end up with if my mother picked out my husband. Brother! I'd rather be an old maid."

Darlene looked at me with a blank expression, then giggled. How could they think that I might be a part of a custom that was so unromantic, so not Canadian? I hated being thought of as different. I thought about my secret crush on Larry Granger, the best-looking boy in the class. Would I ever be brave enough to have a *lo fon* boyfriend? Would he ever like a Chinese girl?

Charlotte slowed down, and was quiet for a while. Then she said, with a thoughtful expression on her face, "It'd be hard, wouldn't it? To marry someone you didn't know."

"Well, he has been writing her," I said.

"It's not the same as talking," said Charlotte. "I mean, he hasn't even met her."

"It's not something I'm doing, that's for sure. I don't care how romantic the letters get," I said, kicking at the dirt.

Hardly a word was spoken at the dinner table that evening. Yet my mother seemed high-strung and worried. As soon as she saw that Father's or Lee-Kung's rice bowl was empty, she leaped up from the table and refilled it. She dropped my bowl when she cleared the table and rushed into the kitchen for a broom to sweep up the shards. I was glad that it was Tuesday, the local library was open and I could escape.

I woke in the middle of the night. Unable to get back to sleep, I got up and went to stand on the fire escape. There was no moon and the sky was a dark, foreboding grey. The only light was from the street lamps at either end of the alley. I tried to see into the backyards that had intrigued me as a younger child, but there was only darkness. I stared for what felt like a long time at the empty alley below. I took a deep breath and stepped over to my brother's window. Peeking through a gap in the curtains, I saw my brother sitting on the bed, his head in his hands. My mother stood weeping at the dresser, her back to him. I remembered that night when I first saw them together, how my body had trembled and my heart had raced. Why was I looking now? The next day Mai-Yee would arrive and I was expected to go to the airport and welcome the mail-order bride, to smile as if there was nothing wrong. And yet I knew that once again our small universe would change. I felt the cold iron slats of the landing press into my feet and I shivered in the night air. I turned and walked back into the dark bedroom, to wait for the morning to come.

&

MAI-YEE ARRIVED ON A cool end-of-summer day. On the way to the airport my mother sat next to my brother in the front seat and I sat in the back behind her. I noticed Elder Brother's knuckles were white as he gripped the steering wheel. Every so often he put one hand on the back of his neck, massaging it. My mother sat quietly looking out the window, her face pale.

We waited as the passengers came through the arrival door at the airport. I recognized Mai-Yee right away from her photograph. She walked more slowly than the other passengers, her hand clutched around the shoulder strap of her beige purse, an anxious, searching expression on her face.

My mother stood with me as my brother rushed forward to shake hands and take her bags. Mai-Yee seemed both relieved and nervous as my brother introduced my mother and me. She spoke to us in our Four Counties dialect. My mother nodded. Mai-Yee was actually prettier than her picture. She was dressed in a fashionable light-pink pleated skirt and a short matching jacket. A gold chain with a heavy jade pendant peeked from underneath the collar of her white blouse. Her hair had been permed into large, soft curls. I glanced at my mother. She was wearing a wool cardigan over a flower-print dress that she had made herself, her style of dress unchanged from when we first arrived in Irvine.

Lee-Kung took Mai-Yee's large blue suitcase, and I picked up one of her smaller bags. At the parking lot he put her luggage in the trunk of the car. My mother told me to sit in the front seat. She would sit in the back with my brother's future bride.

During the ride home my mother and my brother tried to make conversation with Mai-Yee. My brother asked her about her flight. She replied that it was uneventful and asked if it was very far to Irvine. My mother inquired if there were many Chinese people on the flight, and Mai-Yee answered that there were lots, but she had no chance to speak to them. She had sat by a window and next to a *lo fon* woman. All the way home I remained silent. I didn't know what to say to this stranger who would in another few days be married to my brother.

I saw my father peer through the restaurant window, over the bladelike leaves of sanseverias, and I recalled the first time I saw the Dragon Café, Uncle Yat where my father now stood. He held the door open as we filed through. Gripping the suitcase,

Lee-Kung led the way, followed by Mai-Yee, me, and my mother. Mai-Yee glanced, just as I had done, at the long row of booths along one wall, the Formica counter across from it, the free-standing tables farther along the same side, and at the flirtatious movie star on the wall calendar.

Lee-Kung took Mai-Yee through the kitchen, past the draining board stacked with dirty dishes and pails of garbage underneath, then into the hall behind. He yanked open the door leading to the upstairs. Holding the suitcase in front of him, Lee-Kung trudged up the stairs. Mai-Yee held on to the banister as she delicately negotiated the steps, taking care not to knock over the bottles and boxes. I followed behind with one of her smaller cases. Every so often my brother stopped, turning around to check our progress, just as my father had done for my mother and me.

Earlier in the afternoon my mother had gone into Father's old room and put fresh sheets on his single bed for Mai-Yee. The new furniture that was meant for her and Lee-Kung after they were married had been set up and pushed against the wall. My brother took the cushions from the sofa and put them on the floor of his room. Until he and Mai-Yee were married, he would sleep on the floor while Father slept in his bed.

Lee-Kung put Mai-Yee's suitcase down next to the single bed. He stood awkwardly for a moment, then said, "Well . . . you might as well unpack. The chest of drawers is for you." Mai-Yee nodded, her hands clasped in a knot.

"Do you want any help?" I asked.

Mai-Yee shook her head. "Thank you, thank you. I can manage."

After another moment of silence, Lee-Kung said, "Come downstairs with us for some tea."

Mai-Yee followed us back into the hallway and down the stairs, her eyes widening as she looked around at the deep-pink walls and ceilings. I wished Elder Brother had chosen a different colour, spent the extra money.

After doing some homework, I went downstairs again before supper and found Father sitting in the back booth with Mai-Yee. Her hands were on the table, her fingers fidgeting. He was asking her about her flight, her stopover in Vancouver, about living conditions in Hong Kong. He told me that tomorrow the photographer from the *Irvine Examiner* would be coming to take Mai-Yee's picture.

For supper, Lee-Kung had cooked a whole fish steamed with garlic, ginger, and green scallions, crispy-skin chicken, stir-fried greens and red peppers with cloud-ear mushrooms, and fuzzy melon soup made from a broth of pork bones, carrots, and sliced ginger. I wondered if my father had also noticed that Lee-Kung had chosen dishes that would please my mother. Mai-Yee beamed when she saw the food on the table. She said the food on the airplane had been terrible, the meat cold and slippery, and the fruit served in a thick, too-sweet syrup. After finishing one bowl of rice, she had another, all the while exclaiming how delicious everything tasted. My mother barely finished half a bowl of rice.

Afterwards Mai-Yee helped carry a few of the empty dishes into the kitchen and left them on the draining board. She walked into the dining room, looking back over her shoulder as she held open the kitchen door. My mother and I were not there to follow her, we had stayed behind to scrape the plates. Mai-Yee blushed and hurried back into the kitchen, picking up a dirty plate. My brother finished cutting up apples and made a pot of oolong tea.

At the table my mother sat down again and had a small bite of apple. "Hong Kong must be very changed," she said to Mai-Yee. "It's been a long time since Su-Jen and I left."

"It's probably even more crowded," said Mai-Yee. "The streets are packed with people."

"You must be disappointed with your new home. The streets here are always empty."

"I didn't expect it to be busy here. I knew I was coming to a small town."

My mother opened her mouth as if she was about to add something, then changed her mind. She smiled politely and mentioned how much she liked the actress and singer Hung Sing Nu.

Mai-Yee looked at her and said, "Yes. She's very good, but she's getting a little old. Not quite so popular any more."

"Is that so?" said my mother, putting her hand to her throat. Then some customers walked in the door and my mother stood up quickly to wait on their table. Lee-Kung excused himself and returned to the kitchen. Mai-Yee finished sipping her tea, then turned to me, "*Moi moi,* little sister, will you come upstairs with me?"

I walked with Mai-Yee into the kitchen, where Lee-Kung had begun preparing for tomorrow's business. They both smiled stiffly, barely making eye contact. Upstairs, she led me into the room that she would be sharing with my brother.

Mai-Yee squatted in front of the sofa, where Lee-Kung had placed her blue suitcase. Without any cushions the sofa looked low and uncomfortable. Mai-Yee opened the case and took out a flat paper bag, which she handed to me. Inside was a pair of Chinese silk pyjamas, a pair of embroidered slippers, and a long-playing record album of the *Flower Drum Song*. I had read about the *Flower Drum Song* and Nancy Kwan, the female lead, in movie magazines. In fact, I bought every magazine I could find that had anything about Nancy Kwan in it. I had read about her being in a movie called *The World of Susie Wong* and about her ballet training. One writer described her walk as so sexy, she made Marilyn Monroe look like a Brownie. Until Nancy Kwan, who was only half-Chinese, I had never read an article about a Chinese woman in a *lo fon* movie magazine. It intrigued me, a film cast with Asians speaking English. The Chinese movies I saw in Chinatown with my mother and Aunt Hai-Lan didn't count. This movie was in English, took place in San Francisco, and was meant for a *lo fon* audience. The only Chinese people I ever saw on television were Hop Sing on *Bonanza* and Peter on *Bachelor Father* and they were servants who could never really be taken seriously. But Nancy Kwan, she was beautiful and desirable.

I was impressed that Mai-Yee knew about the movie. "I hope the movie comes here," I said, gazing at the album cover. I didn't want to tell her that it would be years before the *Flower Drum Song* would come to Irvine, if at all. The Roxy never got new movies. When they arrived they were at least a year old.

"The record is for you," she said softly. "All for you, Su-Jen." Suddenly Mai-Yee seemed sad. She looked tired and said she wanted to have a bath.

I thanked her and went downstairs to show my gifts to my parents and my brother. Lee-Kung nodded when I showed him the lp. Father seemed especially pleased and held the album in his hands, looking at both sides. My mother said, "That's nice . . . Is that all she gave you?" I showed her the silk pyjamas and the embroidered slippers. She glanced at them, then told me to put them away and finish my homework. I later found out that Mai-Yee had brought pyjamas for both Father and Lee-Kung, and that she had brought my mother a length of exquisite turquoise silk. She had also brought a box of high-quality ginseng, packages of medicinal teas, and boxes of preserved sugared plums and dried candied ginger. They were all gifts for us.

Father and Mai-Yee were standing at the back table, where he was showing her how to fill the sugar dispensers. As soon as she saw me walk in the door, her face brightened. "We've been waiting for you to get back from school, *moi moi*," she said. "Will you come with us and help me choose my ring? I want another girl's opinion."

Father poked his head in the kitchen and called Lee-Kung. My mother, who was halfway up the aisle delivering a piece of pie to a customer, looked back at me. "She wants someone modern," she muttered, then went back to her work without waiting for a response.

Mr. Gildner showed Mai-Yee three different rings. She put on each ring and stretched out her hand for me and Lee-Kung to admire. Mr. Gildner winked at me as he invited me to try them on. "Annie, you might as well start looking at engagement rings now. That way, when it's time to get married you'll have one all picked out," he joked. The one that Mai-Yee chose had one diamond in the middle with two smaller diamonds on either side, all in a delicate gold setting. It wasn't the cheapest and it wasn't the most expensive. Still, it cost three hundred dollars. I watched Lee-Kung pull out his wallet and count the money; I thought of the hundreds of hours he must have worked to save that amount. My brother didn't wait for Mr. Gildner to wrap the ring in its box. He left ahead of us, saying that he had to get back to the restaurant to start preparing for the supper hour.

My parents were both in the dining room: my mother reading the newspaper in the back booth, my father across the aisle at the back table looking at another section. Mai-Yee held out her left hand first for Father, then for my mother. They both oohed and aahed. My mother suddenly got up and walked to the cash register to tend to a waiting customer; I saw her aim a dark look at Lee-Kung as he came in from the kitchen. Father said, "In China a bride gets gold jewellery. But in Canada she gets a diamond ring." I wondered if Mai-Yee felt lucky, since she got both. I felt sorry for her, so unsuspecting as she stepped into this family, filled with its secrets, conducting hidden conversations.

Mai-Yee's wedding gown was as beautiful as any I had seen in the bridal magazines at Sniders'. It was floor-length, sewn from a heavy white satin, with a high neck and long, narrow sleeves. Pearly white beads dotted the neckline and the cuffs. Mai-Yee had taken it out of her suitcase when she arrived and placed it on a hanger, hoping to relax the wrinkles. I looked at her dress and remembered how I used to play with my wedding cut-outs. It seemed so long ago when I used to imagine a future of fairy-tale happiness. What had Mai-Yee hoped to find in Canada? Back in Hong Kong had she dreamed about a place where all her wishes would come true?

On Saturday I helped Mai-Yee repack her wedding gown into her suitcase. The next day she and Lee-Kung would be married. I wondered if she was nervous. Mai-Yee, my mother, and I were to take the bus into Toronto that afternoon and spend the night with Uncle Jong and Aunt Hai-Lan. That evening Aunt Hai-Lan would take us to the church for a brief rehearsal. My brother had said since he was unable to attend, he would drive in with Father early on Sunday and talk to the minister before the ceremony.

Aunt Hai-Lan was so excited by the wedding that she didn't seem to notice my mother's sombre mood. She led Mai-Yee up to the second floor and gave her a room that had been empty since mid-August. A new tenant wouldn't be moving in until October. Later I saw Aunt Hai-Lan take the ironing board upstairs.

That night Aunt Hai-Lan made soup with chunks of chicken, dried shrimp, and rice-flour dumplings. Mai-Yee clapped her hands in delight and said she hadn't eaten that dish since she left the village in China. She laughed when Uncle Jong grumbled that it was Aunt Hai-Lan's fault that he was so fat.

Once again my mother and I slept on the fold-out sofa in the sitting room. The next morning she said she felt unwell. I wasn't surprised; she had kept me awake most of the night with her tossing and turning.

Aunt Hai-Lan was up early. For breakfast she had cooked a sweet rice porridge with swirls of beaten egg. My mother ate a small amount, then left the table without warning and ran upstairs. Aunt Hai-Lan stopped eating for a moment; her face became still. Mai-Yee looked up at her from her bowl. Aunt Hai-Lan quickly smiled and offered her some more porridge. When my mother returned to the kitchen, her face was the colour of chalk. She picked up her spoon, but then put it down again. She told Hai-Lan that although the soup was delicious, she wasn't hungry. Aunt Hai-Lan nodded at the compliment, but seemed to be distracted.

After her bath, my mother dried her hair and coiled it into a bun, pinning it with the tortoiseshell clasp from Hong Kong. She ironed her rose-coloured cheongsam she had worn only on a few other occasions. After she stepped into it, she held her slender arms in the air and asked me to fasten the dress up its sides. With her high heels and silky, shimmering dress she was as beautiful as any Hong Kong movie star. The cheongsam showed off her slim, curving figure and her long, elegant neck.

Upstairs Aunt Hai-Lan was fussing over Mai-Yee and her wedding dress. When she came down the stairs in her bridal gown, I thought she looked beautiful, but I knew that just as many people would be looking at my mother.

I was wearing a pale blue bridesmaid dress and white patent leather shoes with low heels. My mother and I had bought the dress at Monroes' Ladies' Clothing at the other end of the block from the Dragon Café. Mrs. Monroe had convinced my mother to buy me a blue dress with a skirt of many layers of chiffon and a matching short jacket, an outfit I would be able to wear to next year's Grade Eight graduation. She said since I was the bride's only attendant, my dress should be extra fancy. I had also wanted satin high heels, dyed to match my dress, but my mother felt I was too young. Mrs. Munroe also sold my mother a pair of white wrist gloves. I told her that she needed them for a wedding and had shown her pictures in my bridal magazines of how a mother of the groom dressed.

Uncle Jong told us to hurry, a taxi was waiting and the meter ticking. My mother, Aunt Hai-Lan, and Mai-Yee crowded into the back seat. I helped Mai-Yee fit the layers of her gown into the car, piling them on her lap, and got in the front with Uncle Jong. I turned around and saw the material of Mai-Yee's skirt bunched so high, I couldn't see her face.

The ceremony was scheduled for three o'clock. Uncle Jong told me that *lo fons* liked Saturdays for weddings, but Chinese people preferred Sundays. Sunday was a quiet day for business, with people more willing to close their shops or restaurants. He winked and said another reason Sunday was considered a good day was because the church already had flowers from the morning service. And again money was saved.

Mai-Yee hooked her arm into Uncle Jong's as she walked up the steps of the Chinese Presbyterian Church on Beverley Street. I held the door open and helped her with her dress. Father was waiting for us in the foyer. Although he looked nervous and uncomfortable in his new grey suit, he seemed eager, a wide smile on his face. My mother wore a tight, close-lipped expression as she nodded at him. Together they walked with Aunt Hai-Lan down the aisle and sat in the front pew. My brother and his friend from Owen Sound were standing in front of the altar, each dressed in a white dinner jacket with a red carnation in his lapel.

As I walked slowly down the aisle a few paces in front of Mai-Yee and Uncle Jong, my hands were rigid around my bouquet, my legs weak and rubbery. People were standing with their heads turned, watching the small procession. My mother was in the front pew between Father and Aunt Hai-Lan; her jaw was clenched, her eyes looked straight ahead. She didn't turn to watch me in my new blue dress. Father's face was surprisingly blank, but as I approached, his eyes caught mine and his lips curled into a smile.

I stood beside Mai-Yee in front of the minister as she and my brother spoke their vows. She had removed the diamond engagement ring that my brother had bought for her. My brother's shaking hand placed the wedding band on her finger. They were now officially married.

At the banquet, the bridal party, my parents, Aunt Hai-Lan, and Uncle Jong sat at a long table on a platform slightly elevated above the floor where the guests sat. Behind us on a red wall were a golden phoenix and dragon dancing over the golden character for double happiness, much like the cover of the wedding invitations. Looking down I counted twelve tables with ten guests per table. I recognized the few *lo fon* guests from Irvine. Mrs. Swackhammer and Mrs. MacDougall had both admired my dress. Many of the Chinese guests look familiar, but I only knew Pock Mark, sitting beside a woman who must have been his wife. I almost didn't recognize him in his suit and tie. I also spotted Uncle Jong and Aunt Hai-Lan's sons, sitting with their families at a table close to the front. I had no idea that Father and Lee-Kung knew so many people. All day it had felt as if my family was playing pretend, that we were performing in a play with our guests as the audience. Except that the audience, the guests who sat in front of us, thought it was real.

It was clear that Father was pleased. Many people gave him little red envelopes that I knew were filled with money for the bride and groom. I had never seen my father smile so easily. For as long as I could remember he had spoken about the importance of *meen,* or face. To *ai meen* was to give face, and to *hoo meen* was to want face. The fact that so many guests came to my brother's wedding meant that they were being *ai meen,* or giving our family face, and Father, by holding such a large banquet, was being *hoo meen,* or wanting face.

Uncle Jong pointed out to me the bottle of Johnny Walker Scotch in the middle of each round table. Chuckling, he told me that Chinese people chose it because they liked the red-and-gold label. There were large oranges on plates with the peel cut so that it uncoiled in a single, unbroken strand. Inside, the flesh was cut in round slices neatly stacked one on top of the other like a child's toy. First the waiters brought plates of roast pork with crispy crackling. In between the courses – of shark's fin soup, whole steamed fish, stir-fried lobster with scallions, crispy-skin chicken, braised duck, scallops and vegetables, fried rice, noodles, and sweet soup – people clanked their chopsticks against their glasses, prodding Lee-Kung and Mai-Yee to stand up and kiss. I watched as Mai-Yee waited anxiously each time for my brother to rise from his seat, but he would continue to eat as if he were deaf. It seemed cruel, how long he made her sit and listen to the growing clamour. By the time they stood up together, any sense of good cheer and fun had vanished. It was painful watching their awkwardness. I don't think their lips ever touched, their cheeks barely grazing.

Partway through the banquet everyone in the wedding party got up and visited with each table to thank the guests for coming. My mother kept my hand in hers the entire time, at certain moments holding it so tightly my fingers hurt. She smiled and nodded when people congratulated her and Father on the addition of their new daughter-in-law. I noticed people looking at my mother and whispering among them how beautiful she was, so elegantly dressed in her knee-length shimmering rose cheongsam.

At one point I caught Lee-Kung staring at my mother while she was accepting good wishes. His face was perfectly still. When we got back to the head table, Lee-Kung took out another cigarette from his package of pale blue Players. By the end of the evening the ashtray was brimming with butts.

THE MORNING AFTER the wedding my mother was sick again. Father was already downstairs in the restaurant. She went back to bed while I stayed home from school to help.

Lee-Kung had left the kitchen in good order. He was reluctant to leave the restaurant for a five-day honeymoon, saying that two or three would be enough. But Father insisted that they stay away until Friday afternoon. He said that with five days they would have enough time to go to Ottawa and maybe even Montreal. Although Father hadn't worked in a kitchen for many years, he said he could manage. He said he knew how to make the different dishes, he just wasn't very fast any more.

My mother rested for a couple of hours before coming down to work. She looked so pale, I asked if I should stay home from school for the rest of the day to help. Father said that Monday was not usually very busy, he could handle everything by himself if he had to, and that I shouldn't miss any more of my classes.

I walked into the yard behind the restaurant and sat down on Lee-Kung's wooden stool, stretching my legs out in front of me. I had stopped at Charlotte's for a short visit on the way home from school. Mrs. Heighington had asked about the wedding as she stacked some dishes from the kitchen table and carried them to the sink. I told her about Mai-Yee's dress, about the church, the food we ate, all the people who were invited. But I didn't tell her how long my brother made Mai-Yee listen to the clamouring of chopsticks on glasses before rising to kiss her and I didn't tell her that when we later arrived home I heard my mother sobbing in the bathroom. Mrs. Heighington said, "Your parents must be very happy." Then she showed me the picture of Mai-Yee in the local paper. "Your sister-in-law looks like a nice girl. Your mum must be so pleased to have another woman in the house. I often think of how lonely it's been for her." I had smiled with difficulty and nodded. I sometimes found myself on the verge of telling Mrs. Heighington. I wanted to tell her that yes, my mother should be pleased about Mai-Yee, instead she appeared to be crumbling before my eyes. But then I would have to tell her why, and I wouldn't know where to stop.

I put my binder and books down beside the stool and picked up my paperback copy of *Gone with the Wind,* not caring that there was a slight chill in the air. Ashley Wilkes was about to leave to fight in the war and Scarlett O'Hara had somehow managed to sneak a private moment to give him her gift of a sash for his uniform. Finding it hard to concentrate, I gave up and sat staring at my mother's garden. Although it was past its peak, there was still much to harvest: bok choy, mustard greens, and snow peas. Hiding under canopies of large green leaves were several fuzzy melons and winter melons. The winter melons, or cold melons as they were called in Chinese, grew well into October and the silvery-green skin had a look of being dusted with frost. They would not be harvested for at least another six weeks. When the nights grew cold my mother would cover them with burlap potato sacks that were slit open. The shape and size of the melons reminded me of the orange pumpkins that the teachers brought to school for Halloween. I gathered my books and opened the back door to the restaurant.

I went upstairs to put my books away and found my mother sitting on the edge of her bed, hunched over something. As I got closer I realized she was ripping the stitches out of a dress she had made just before Mai-Yee's arrival. She was so absorbed in her work that she didn't see or hear me come in. When she looked up and saw me standing there, she quickly put her dress aside and told me to go downstairs and get something to eat.

In the kitchen I found my father at the sink scrubbing pots. I sensed that my parents had said very little to each other all day except to place customer orders. My father looked exhausted. At age seventy he was too old to be operating a busy, hot kitchen. Even on a slow day the work was just too hard. And it was only Monday. How was he going to get through the rest of the week if he was already this tired? I started to prepare the dirty dishes on the draining board for washing.

For dinner my mother had made four-flavour soup, steamed chicken and mushrooms on rice, and wilted Chinese greens. My father sat down beside me as my mother served our bowls of rice. Once he started to talk about the wedding, the tiredness that I had noticed earlier seemed to fall away. He chatted about the people he hadn't seen in many years, the perfection of the food, how beautiful Mai-Yee looked. He was so proud of Lee-Kung and his bride. He would show his son how to keep the books, preparing him eventually to take over the business. I nodded in agreement and added that many people had admired Mai-Yee's dress. But my mother remained silent. She said nothing after my father told her that several guests had said that now she wouldn't have to work as hard, that life would be easier. Her eyes were dull. She picked at her rice for a while longer, then abruptly got up and took her bowl and chopsticks into the kitchen. My father said, "Eat up, Su-Jen. Don't worry. I'll close the restaurant early tonight." I cleared the supper table and washed the glasses before going upstairs.

I had been at my desk for only a short while when I heard my mother coming up the stairs. She stood beside me at my homework table and watched as I used my protractor to measure the different angles that I had made. She put her arms around me and I looked up. "You are all I have," she said to me. I stiffened in her arms. When we went to bed that night, we were both quiet.

My father closed the restaurant at nine-thirty. I heard his footsteps up the stairs, slow and heavy, the tiredness that I had noted earlier in the day seemed to have returned.

On Friday afternoon, Mai-Yee and Lee-Kung came home. When Father saw them in the doorway he rushed over and clasped Mai-Yee's hand. She smiled and called him *Lo Yah*, the proper Chinese title for father-in-law. Father's eyes shone with pride. He told me we must now call Mai-Yee *Sawh*, the title for son's wife. When my mother came out from the kitchen and saw them, she stopped for a moment and smoothed the front of her dress. Then she joined Father and welcomed back the newlyweds, but there was no pleasure in her voice.

Mai-Yee called her *Owon Yeen*, the title for mother-in-law. My mother gave a tight-lipped smile.

Lee-Kung had taken Mai-Yee to Montreal, then Ottawa and Niagara Falls before returning to Irvine. Mai-Yee described the excitement of watching the Falls and I remembered back to when Lee-Kung first arrived and how he promised to take me and my mother there.

&

THE FIRST NEWS STORY from my childhood that I clearly remember was the Cuban Missile Crisis in October. Until then my family had been concerned mainly with news from China and had shown only a passing interest in events that happened in the West. Once again my father voiced his opinion about Kennedy: a man in his forties was too young to lead a country, much less a powerful one like the United States; as far as he was concerned, there wasn't enough experience or wisdom. My brother, though, said that the world was changing, that Kennedy was a smart man and that he admired him for standing up to the Communists. My father scoffed and asked Lee-Kung what good his admiration would be if the Russians set off their bombs. When Pock Mark visited, the talk about the possibility of war continued. He told us if it was going to happen, we would be safer in a small town. My father bought extra dried food and sacks of rice.

Everyone in my family was relieved when the Russians backed down. My brother said that if it weren't for Kennedy, they would have attacked the United States. My father said that if the Americans had had an older leader, the Russians wouldn't have dared to place the missiles there in the first place.

The following weekend my parents, Lee-Kung, Mai-Yee, and I drove into Toronto. The trees along the road were almost bare, with a few brown leaves still clinging tight; fields of ploughed black earth lay ready for next year's planting.

As soon as I saw the Tip Top Tailors building on Lakeshore Boulevard in Toronto, I knew we were close to Chinatown. Aunt Hai-Lan and Uncle Jong were waiting at their house. My mother went up the path to greet Hai-Lan. I watched them walk together, arm in arm toward Elizabeth Street. The way my mother sometimes leaned into her aunt, she seemed more like a girl than a grown woman.

After our dim sum lunch, Aunt Hai-Lan told my mother that some friends were coming over after supper for a game of mahjong and that the two of us should stay overnight in Toronto. She then looked at Lee-Kung and Mai-Yee and joked that it was time they let the older generation take it easy. I didn't want to spend a night in Toronto, a long evening of watching television with Uncle Jong or being bored listening to my mother, Aunt Hai-Lan, and her women friends gossip. I didn't like the way the ladies fussed over me. They treated me as if I were still seven years old. I wanted to go back to Irvine where I could be with my friends.

Aunt Hai-Lan made a simple dinner of chicken with Chinese sausage over rice, and watercress soup. Afterwards my mother and I tidied the kitchen, while Aunt Hai-Lan put some red beans, rock sugar, and dried orange peel in a large pot of water for an evening snack of sweet soup. She opened the mah-jong set that my mother had brought from Hong Kong and placed the ivory tiles on the kitchen table so they were all face down.

The doorbell rang and Aunt Hai-Lan greeted her friends Mrs. Tan, Mrs. Wong, and Mrs. Seto. As I had expected, the moment they saw me, they told me how I had grown and how pretty I was becoming. My mother, of course, protested and said that my looks were only so-so.

Aunt Hai-Lan gave up her spot at the mah-jong table so that my mother could play. She would instead fill in for her friends when they needed a break. When I was younger, I usually played by myself in the kitchen and listened to them gossip and make fun of their husbands. My mother always joined in the laughter, but she never joked about my father, not in the good-natured, affectionate way of the other women. Now that I was older, between watching television shows with Uncle Jong, I poured cups of tea and kept the bowls of peanuts and red melon seeds full.

The ladies mixed the mah-jong pieces. Aunt Hai-Lan was sitting beside my mother, watching. Mrs. Tan appeared to be about the same age as Aunt Hai-Lan, but Mrs. Wong and Mrs. Seto were younger. My mother, her hair in a simple bun, with no makeup, puffy perm, or jewellery, was still the most beautiful of the younger women.

Mrs. Wong had a daughter who was about my age. When my mother and I had visited Toronto during our early years in Canada, I sometimes played with her daughter during the mah-jong games. Mrs. Wong had talked about her Canadian-born children always speaking English. She would sigh and say that she was worried they were losing their Chinese. My mother once said to me Mrs. Wong thought her children were better just because they were *hoo sung,* Canadian-born. It wasn't as if Mrs. Wong was smarter than anybody else, she said; it was just that her husband had brought her to Canada earlier.

Over the sound of the tiles being moved and crashing into each other, I heard Mrs. Tan tell the others that her husband was going into the hospital for a hernia operation. She shook her head with exasperation. "He won't listen to me," she said. "I told him he needs to take lots of quarters with him."

"That's a good idea," said Aunt Hai-Lan. "I've heard that for breakfast you just get half an egg. If you want a whole one, you have to give them money."

"I've heard the same story," said Mrs. Tan. "When I told my husband, he said I was *soay,* soft in the head. Said things aren't like that here. That in Canada you don't go around bribing people like back in China."

"Why don't you just put some coins in an envelope and tuck it in his bag? He'll be thankful later," said Mrs. Wong, smiling and glancing at Mrs. Seto and my mother.

"How long will he be off work?" asked Mrs. Seto, picking up a red melon seed to crack between her teeth.

"He doesn't want to have the operation, just wants to put up with that disgusting thing sticking out from his belly," said Mrs. Tan. "Even with his own son left in charge of the restaurant, he doesn't want to leave."

"Tell him to stop worrying so much about money," laughed Aunt Hai-Lan.

"That's easy for you to say," said Mrs. Tan between sips of tea. "With Jong, even if he's sick at the post office, he still gets paid."

"They say at some of the big *lo fon* factories that if you lose your job, you can apply for unemployment insurance," said Mrs. Seto. She started to divide the tiles between the different players.

"And make money for doing nothing," exclaimed Mrs. Wong as she turned her pieces over.

"But if you really want to be rich, you should work for yourself," said Aunt Hai-Lan.

"Owning a business hasn't made us rich," said my mother.

"Chinese people are like Jews," said Mrs. Seto. "They like to work for themselves. Keep the money in the family."

"If my husband worked for the government," said Mrs. Tan, "they would pay for the hospital insurance."

"But your husband has lots of money," smiled Mrs. Wong, arranging her hand. "Tsk, look what you gave me." She scowled good-naturedly at Mrs. Seto.

"Not enough for him," said Mrs. Tan. "The other day in the doctor's office he complained the whole time about how much everything cost. Li Tung's wife was there and she ignored me, pretended not to see me. She never looked up from her magazine. I don't know if it was because of my husband's loud talking or because she's big belly."

"Who does she think she is?" asked Aunt Hai-Lan. "She doesn't know how lucky she is to be living here and not back in China. If she were in China, she'd either be hanging from a rope or hounded out of the village."

"Not necessarily," cautioned Mrs. Wong. "That only happened if your husband was away, if your belly swelled up while your husband was overseas. Then of course everybody would know. But as long as your husband's around who's going to be able to prove it doesn't belong to him."

"It all had to do with saving face in the village," said Aunt Hai-Lan with a sigh. "No consideration for the woman or the child."

I stood at the stove stirring the sweet soup and thought about Lee-Kung's mother. I'd never been told why she had hanged herself.

"Are you hungry?" called Aunt Hai-Lan from across the room. "Ladle out a couple of bowls for you and Uncle Jong."

"I remember when I was a girl in the village," said Mrs. Tan as she rearranged her tiles. "A woman got a big belly while her husband was in the United States and she ended up killing herself out of shame."

I walked over to the cupboard for the bowls and spoons and went back to the stove.

"Then it was obvious and the family had to save face. But with Li Tung's wife, nobody knows for sure. It's probably better just to carry on," said Aunt Hai-Lan, shaking her head. My mother sat staring at her mah-jong hand and didn't say a word.

"Well, you know why Li Tung's putting up with his wife, don't you?" said Mrs. Seto as she moved a middle tile and placed it at the end.

"It's obvious, isn't it?" said Mrs. Wong with a grin on her face. "She has a good job at the sewing factory, a steady paycheque." The other women cackled.

"Still, it's just a lot of talk," said Aunt Hai-Lan over their laughter. "You can't prove Li Tung isn't the father. And his wife isn't going to say anything."

"That's true, but here he doesn't have the same family pressures, an old mother telling him what to do," added Mrs. Seto, shaking her head as she studied the arrangement in front of her.

"Life here is easier in some ways, isn't it?" said Mrs. Wong, trying out different mah-jong combinations. "No need to have to put up with those old-fashioned ways. In Canada, much better for women."

"You mean easier for playing around," teased Mrs. Seto.

"Don't be *seen geng,* silly," laughed Mrs. Wong. "You know what I mean."

My mother finally spoke. "For you living in the big city, life might be better," she said, "but for me in the small town, it's worse."

"Jing, I keep telling you," said Aunt Hai-Lan with a worried expression, "you should move to the city. Your husband is getting too old to work in the restaurant. And you need to take a break yourself. Buy a house here and rent out rooms. You could probably get a job at one of the sewing factories. And Su-Jen could go to school with other Chinese children, and have Chinese friends." She looked at my mother's arrangement of symbols and smiled.

"But I have lots of friends in Irvine," I interrupted. "I don't need Chinese friends." Aunt Hai-Lan and her friends looked at me, each with an expression of surprise.

"It would be nice for you to have *some* Chinese friends," said my mother, smiling at me. What would it be like to live in Chinatown and go to school with other Chinese kids, where my mother could speak to them and to their parents?

"And Su-Jen would have a Chinese boyfriend," said Mrs. Wong with a grin. I thought of what Darlene and Jonette had said, how they, too, assumed that I would want a Chinese boyfriend.

"Talk to your husband when you go back," said Aunt Hai-Lan. "Now that Lee-Kung is married, he and his wife should be able to manage." Aunt Hai-Lan noticed that I was holding the bowls for Uncle Jong and me, and signalled for me to wait. She reached into her cupboard for a tray.

"Be careful," said my mother, watching me ladle the soup.

"I thought your daughter-in-law seemed like a very nice girl," said Mrs. Tan as I was leaving the room. "What do you think of your *sawh*, Su-Jen?"

"She's very nice," I said. "She's already working in the restaurant."

"That's very important. You don't want somebody who just walks around, doing nothing," said Mrs. Seto as she studied her tiles.

"You mean acting like a big boss?" said Mrs. Wong, laughing.

"Talk about a big boss, guess who's the head chef at the Sai Woo now?" asked Mrs. Tan.

"Who?" asked my mother immediately. I heard the relief in her voice at the change in the topic of conversation. I carefully picked up the tray with the bowls of red bean soup and left the room.

The next day Aunt Hai-Lan convinced my mother to let me go home on my own but to stay herself for the rest of the week. She said my mother looked tired and probably needed some special medicinal soups.

As I got on the bus to Irvine, I was glad to see it was only half full. I sat alone and stared out the window. Whenever I tried to read my book I was unable to get past the first few lines. My mother had been so quiet the night before at the mah-jong table.

ALTHOUGH MAI-YEE WAS able to read some English, she spoke very little and wanted me to go with her to Watsons' Drugstore after I returned from school. We bought a package of pink rollers that looked like bones with elastic fasteners and a kit for a Toni perm. I had seen the boxes in the drugstore and was always struck by the girl on the cover, her head turned to the side, with a wide-mouthed laugh, brown curly tresses flying about from her face.

In her bedroom Mai-Yee laid out her combs, hair clips, a glass ashtray, a toothbrush, rollers, and the perming kit on top of her dressing table. I sat on a wooden chair with an old towel draped over my shoulders. Mai-Yee smiled at me in the mirror as she cut my hair into three-inch lengths, a little shorter along the hairline. Farther back in the reflection I saw the double bed my father and I had ordered from Eaton's. I thought about Mai-Yee and Elder Brother together in that huge bed and winced.

"Who taught you how to do this?" I asked, to distract myself.

"Nobody taught me," Mai-Yee said. "My sisters and I practised on each other."

"I wish I had a sister," I said wistfully

"Now that I'm married to your brother, we're sisters, aren't we?" she answered. She divided my hair in sections, then one by one she wrapped each clump of wet strands with a small square of white tissue paper and curled it around one of the pink bone-shaped rollers, snapping the elastic in place.

"You must miss your family," I said.

"Yes," said Mai-Yee with a sigh. "I have two sisters and two brothers. I'm in the middle. I'm hoping they can come over. My younger sister could come as a mail-order bride like me. My older one, she's already married, she would have to be sponsored, along with her husband and their daughter. Maybe your brother will give her husband a job in the restaurant?"

"My father is getting older," I said, "so my brother will probably need help soon." I had wondered why someone like Mai-Yee was willing to come to a strange country and marry someone she didn't know. I realized now there was more to it than just a belief in arranged marriages.

"I don't know how we'll find sponsors for my brothers. But if my younger sister comes over, maybe she'll be able to help." She reminded me of my father with her thoughts about her family. I wondered if Lee-Kung knew about her plans.

When Mai-Yee finished setting my hair, she opened the bottle of pink perming lotion and poured some into the glass ashtray. She soaked the toothbrush in the liquid, then dabbed each roller. I had to hold a towel over my face to keep the drips from going into my eyes. My scalp tingled and the smell was overpowering. It was stronger than the stench from the tannery on its worst day. After more waiting and rinsing and soaking with more lotions came a final shampoo. When Mai-Yee was finished I put a hand cautiously to my head and my new wet curls. I picked one out and pulled it straight. I let go and it coiled like a spring. Mai-Yee assured me that after my hair came out of the big brush rollers that were used under the dryer, the curls would be large and soft.

When we were finished, I looked in the mirror. The face I saw seemed to belong to someone else. I looked like Aunt Hai-Lan and her friends with their helmets of tight little curls. I thought about the girl on the cover of the perming kit. My hair did not look that like that. Her curls were soft, meant to be lifted by the wind. My curls were so stiff I had a feeling they wouldn't move if I were caught in a tornado.

Mai-Yee set her brush on the bureau and stood back. "Do you like it?" she asked with an eager smile.

"It's okay," I said, trying to smile back.

"Maybe I left the perming lotion on a bit too long," she said, biting her lips. "After you wash your hair a few times, the curls will loosen."

I went downstairs to show Father and Lee-Kung. They both smiled, and my brother told me I looked like a movie star, but I didn't believe him and I covered my face with my hands. My father put his arm around me. Mai-Yee, who had followed me down the stairs, stroked me on the arm and offered to wash my hair again, perhaps rinsing out more of the perming lotion. I pressed my face into my father's shoulder and shook my head, telling her it was too late. I wondered what my mother would say about my hair when she came back.

My friends at school tried to be nice about my new hairstyle, but no one actually said they liked it. Mai-Yee tried in little ways to make it up to me. Upstairs from the restaurant she let me experiment with her cosmetics. I liked it when she shared these things with me, and she never told me to finish my rice, or asked me if I was hungry the moment I came home from school.

Mai-Yee quickly learned the routines in the restaurant. I could tell that Father was pleased with how hard she worked. In the evening after supper while Lee-Kung worked in the kitchen and

Father was perched on his stool behind the cash register, I would sit with my homework in the dining room. Mai-Yee sometimes took a break in the back booth under the gaze of the calendar girl, resting her chin in her hand and sipping her tea. Sometimes she would talk to me across the aisle, asking about my studies and my friends. More often her bright, cheery mask would slip away. One night I walked past the women's washroom and heard Mai-Yee weeping behind the closed door. I knew she was homesick for her family.

Although I missed my own mother, I wasn't looking forward to her return. Things at the restaurant seemed easier and less tense without her. But I thought about her a lot and wondered if she missed us. I worried that she would confide her secrets to Aunt Hai-Lan.

The following Sunday Lee-Kung drove to Toronto to bring my mother home. There was no point in closing the restaurant for two Sundays in a row, so he went on his own. When they arrived back at the Dragon Café, Lee-Kung's face was the colour of ash. He nodded and smiled weakly at me, then rushed into the kitchen.

I walked around the lunch counter from where I was working and gave my mother a hug. Smiling with her lips together, she reached down and patted my new curls. I could tell that she had been crying.

"My goodness, what did you do to your hair?" she asked.

"Mai-Yee did it. She gave me a perm. Do you like it?"

"You look . . . very grown-up," she said with a sad look in her eyes.

My mother seemed different, but I couldn't quite put my finger on it. She was wearing a new dress, loosely tied at the waist with a belt. I later found out that while she was away, she had made two other dresses exactly the same, but from different prints. I thought about the dress she had sewn up the month before, how I caught her ripping out the seams.

The days were getting shorter and shorter; in another few weeks it would be dark not long after the five-o'-clock whistle at the factory. Supper hour had ended early that evening and we were at the back table finishing our meal. Ever since his trip to bring my mother back from Toronto, Lee-Kung had been especially quiet. Mai-Yee seemed to be working even harder lately, often anticipating jobs that needed doing. Over supper my father told Lee-Kung that with Mai-Yee being such a good worker they would soon be able to take over the business. Mai-Yee looked at my brother, as if she expected him to say something, but he never even glanced in her direction. That evening I finished supper quickly so I could go to the library.

Open every Tuesday, Wednesday, and Friday night from seven to nine, the Irvine library was a single room, barely the size of a school classroom, in the town council building. It was a place that smelled of old books, mould, and dust. The shelves reached the ceiling and were so close together, you had to step out to the main aisle for someone to walk past. I made my selection and lined up at a high wooden counter where three old ladies were hunched over a long desk, filling out cards for the books that were returned and again for the ones that were borrowed.

On the way home, I breathed in the autumn air. It was crisp with a faint smell of burning leaves, a smell that I would always come to associate with small towns. I took a shortcut through the alley and came in the restaurant through the back door. As I entered the hall that led to the stairs and to the kitchen, I heard my father shouting at my mother. I froze in the shadow of the door and listened.

"You think I don't know. You think I'm blind. I can tell by the wag of your tail whether it's shit or piss," Father hissed at her. I started to back out of the door. The angry voice followed me. "If it wasn't for the family, for Su-Jen, I'd throw you out on the streets."

"If it wasn't for Su-Jen, I wouldn't be here," my mother cried.

"You stink." Father spoke in a cold, hard voice that I'd never heard before. "You stink like rotten fish."

A pan dropped, making a clanging sound. I heard my mother run up the stairs. My chest felt tight and cramped. I waited in the alley for my heart to stop thumping, then walked around to the front of the building.

My father was perched on his stool behind the cash register. He looked haggard as he tried to smile and asked me if I had found the books I wanted. One of the customers got up and put a coin in the jukebox. The opening bars to "Love Letters in the Sand" floated through the air. During the lull in business, Lee-Kung and Mai-Yee were in the dining room reading the

Chinese newspaper, a cloud of smoke from my brother's cigarette between them.

I could hear my mother filling the bathtub as I went up the stairs. I sat at my homework table and opened my books. At school we were studying the voyages of Marco Polo. Miss Skinner had told us that the Chinese had the longest continuing civilization in the world and that they had invented paper, among other things. She told me that I should be proud of my people, but instead I had felt embarrassed when she singled me out like that. I found it hard to concentrate on my assignment. My father's words repeated themselves in my head. He knew about my mother and Lee-Kung: what else did he know? I worried about what might happen to my mother.

For the next few days a heavy silence hung between my parents. I saw it in their clenched jaws and stiff movements. But one night as I was helping my mother clear the dishes from the supper table, my father touched me on the shoulder. His face was drawn, but his voice was steady. "Su-Jen, you finish that. Let your mother go upstairs and rest." My mother looked at him for a moment, her body seemed to sag, but her face was like stone.

❧

THE TREES WERE BARE and the November sky seemed endlessly grey, casting a gloom over the landscape. I was at my desk with my chin in my hand, watching the rain hit the windows along one side of our classroom. Miss Skinner stood stiffly at the front of the class and waited for everyone's attention. She told us that for Remembrance Day we would memorize "In Flanders Fields" by John McCrae. I glanced at Charlotte, who sat across from me, and saw her stick out her tongue. Miss Skinner saw it too. "And what are your objections, Miss Heighington?"

For a moment Charlotte looked startled. "Well, it's just that we did 'In Flanders Fields' last year."

"So, you think you know all there is to know about it?" said Miss Skinner.

Charlotte blushed, but I knew she wasn't about to back down. "It's not that . . . Couldn't we study another poem as well?"

"And what do you suggest?" From Miss Skinner's tone, I was sure she thought she had put an end to the discussion.

Charlotte was quiet for a moment. Miss Skinner looked surprised and angry to hear her speak again. "What about 'Anthem for Doomed Youth?' My mother says it's the best poem that came out of the First World War."

Miss Skinner glared at Charlotte. "Your mother is not the teacher. In this class I make the decisions."

I was relieved when Charlotte didn't reply.

Until Charlotte and I were placed in her class that September, I had had very little to do with Miss Skinner. She was plain, unremarkable in appearance except for her mouth. When she talked her lips barely moved, when she smiled there was nothing happy about it. Miss Skinner controlled the class with the kind of fear that I hadn't felt since Grade One with Miss Hinckley. But I knew that if I stayed quiet and co-operative I would survive the year. Charlotte had taken an instant dislike to her, and although she was never directly rude, she seemed unable to hide her feelings.

After school Charlotte and I decided to follow Willow Creek to Irvine Lake. Although it was no longer raining, it was windy and the air felt cold and raw. We stopped where the creek widened and became marshy before flowing into the lake.

Charlotte was puffing on one of her mother's cigarettes. She was still upset over her encounter with Miss Skinner. "I hate her," she said. "She's such a bitch."

I shook my head. "Stop making a big deal of it. It's not worth it to make her mad."

"I guess you're right," Charlotte finished her cigarette and ground it out with her foot. "My mum would say she's as homely as a brush fence." I looked at Charlotte and this time we both started laughing. After that we never referred to Miss Skinner by name again. From then on we called her Brush Fence.

By mid-December it was clear that what I had been suspecting and dreading was true. My mother was pregnant. Her breasts were heavy and her stomach was round and swollen, shaped like a gourd. She wore only the three dresses she had brought back from Aunt Hai-Lan's; she loosened the belt little by little to accommodate her new girth.

She became more and more withdrawn. Meals went by without her speaking. She stopped telling me to finish my rice. Gradually she did less in the restaurant. I saw Father hold the kitchen door open for her and take a stack of plates that she was carrying into the kitchen. My mother never protested when Mai-Yee got up during supper and insisted on refilling Lee-Kung's and Father's rice bowls, something that my mother had always done in the past. No one commented when my mother walked up the stairs in the afternoon to nap, often not coming down until I called her for supper. It seemed that the more the baby in my mother's womb grew, the smaller her own presence became. Yet we carried on in silence, pretending that nothing had changed. I sometimes thought about the conversation that night around Aunt Hai-Lan's mah-jong table, what the ladies might say if they knew the truth about our family.

I once caught Lee-Kung staring at my mother's stomach. Another time while Mai-Yee was having a bath, I walked into the kitchen and saw Lee-Kung crouched in front of my mother, his arms wrapped around her waist, his face resting on her swollen stomach. She was looking down, stroking his head. I didn't stay to watch, I turned and went quickly upstairs, suddenly short of breath. In my mind I saw a woman with a bloated belly dangling by a rope from a tree.

AT FIRST THE WINTER had been mild, leading many people in Irvine to expect an early spring. But in February a deep cold settled that was to last well into March. People often came into the restaurant and complained about the frigid temperatures, but I never minded the winter. The sun was far away but bright, its light beautiful and clear. The days were getting longer. The air felt clean and the smell from the tannery seemed distant.

The ice in the shallow part of Irvine Lake had been cleared for skating and hockey. By the middle of February, though, the entire lake was solid enough for children in the town to use it as a shortcut. Mr. Swackhammer said the ice on the lake hadn't been that thick for years.

No one in my family seemed to notice that I rarely came home directly from school. Sometimes Charlotte and I went to her house, but most often we went to play on the ice with groups of kids from school. I had no fear of water demons; they were trapped beneath the surface. Once, I lay down on the ice in the middle of the lake and stared at the thin, blue winter sky. I wondered what it would be like to fade into nothingness.

Charlotte and I walked toward her house from the lake, listening to the snow squeak under our boots. We were going for hot chocolate and to look at some new drawings she wanted to show me.

Once we got inside and had unbundled ourselves, we went up to Charlotte's room. I sat on the side of her bed, with her open sketch pad on my lap. On the page in front of me was a drawing of the creek at school. I recognized the bridge and the trees along the bank. But what caused me to stare were Charlotte's depictions of what lived in the water: creatures with snakelike arms and gaping mouths, exactly like the beings that had haunted me for years. My head was spinning, I knew I had never confided my fears to her. I don't know how long I looked at her drawings, but my hand was trembling as I touched the page. When I asked her if she actually saw these monsters in the creek, she looked at me steadily and told me that sometimes she imagined them in the movement of the water, in the same way that you could see shapes in clouds.

"Do you think things live in the water that we don't know about?" I asked.

"No," she said. "I told you, these are from my head." For a minute I said nothing, then I confessed to her that I saw demons in the water too, that they looked exactly like what she had drawn, but that I believed they were real. I meant to stop there, but I couldn't, and I told her about the fortune teller's prediction, about my water curse. Charlotte stared at me for a long time. She took the book from me and closed it. "It's just superstition, Annie," she said firmly. "I wouldn't think about it if I were you."

MR. SWACKHAMMER CAME into the restaurant for his regular late-morning coffee and congratulated Father, pumping his hand up and down as he said, "You must be very pleased, you and the missus." With a stiff smile, Father nodded in return. Later, a group of men, loud with drink from the Irvine Hotel, joked in the dining room as Father served them. "I didn't think old Hop Sing could still get it up," one drawled, making his friends laugh.

I wanted to go over and scream at them. They had no right talking about him like that. My father told me to ignore them. As long as they paid and didn't break any dishes, he didn't care. I asked him how he could stand it, he became quiet for a moment, then said to me, "I tell myself that this is not my home. They are not my people." He touched my cheek and smiled sadly. I didn't know what to say. I had no memories of China any more. Irvine was all I knew.

My friends began to ask me when my mother was having her baby. I would mutter something about the spring and quickly change the subject.

One evening Charlotte and I were in the town library looking at a book of drawings from the Renaissance. There was a sketch of an unborn baby, nestled inside an open womb that looked like two halves of a walnut shell. "This is what the baby inside your mother's stomach looks like," Charlotte said. I was surprised not by her words, but by the tone of her voice. It was so casual. No one in my family had acknowledged, at least not openly, my mother's pregnancy.

In our all-girl health class at school, the nurse had shown us a cartoonlike diagram of the female reproductive system and one of a fetus inside a uterus, a flat and lifeless representation. But the picture in the library book, which appeared to be done in charcoal or ink, was soft and real. I looked at the drawing again and traced my finger around the curled fetus. "He looks so peaceful," I said. I thought of my father's silly story of the foolish bride who misunderstood her mother's advice to *ngeng hay*, whose pallor turned green from holding in her farts. I began to worry about the baby in my mother's belly, about the air that filled its lungs, the air that was choking everyone in my family.

&

THE TENSION BETWEEN CHARLOTTE and Miss Skinner had been growing steadily worse. She openly picked on Charlotte in class and made her miserable. Charlotte answered her with that steady stare of hers and ever so slightly dragged out the S's in *Yes, Miss Skinner*. Once, in the hallway Charlotte dropped her unzipped pencil case and some of the contents, including a cigarette, spilled onto the floor. As Charlotte rose from bending over to pick up her things, she noticed Miss Skinner was watching her. Charlotte stared defiantly back and walked past her. They were two predators, circling each other, waiting for a weak moment in order to pounce.

It seemed that Charlotte never stopped drawing, in her sketch pads, on the covers of her school notebooks, in the margins on the pages inside. Mostly the drawings were of imaginary creatures, one growing out of the other, a face in the iris of a person's eye, bodies entwined into the shape of lips on a face. Even the tests that Charlotte handed in at school had doodles in the corner.

Most of the teachers didn't say anything. They seemed to recognize that Charlotte was special in her own way and left her alone. Except Miss Skinner. She hated that Charlotte drew on her assignments. One day it seemed she'd decided that enough was enough and she insisted that our tests be clean, with only the answers and the student's name. Everyone knew that the rule was aimed at Charlotte. At first she complied, but a few weeks later, as she walked past my desk to hand in a math test, she flashed her paper at me and I saw she had turned each letter of her name into an imaginary creature. I watched Charlotte place her paper on Miss Skinner's desk, and saw how their eyes met and locked for a fleeting instant. Charlotte returned to her seat looking smug. I don't think anyone else noticed that moment, but I had watched intently, overcome with dread when I saw the line of Miss Skinner's mouth become sharp and lethal, like the edge of a razor.

By mid-March the temperatures finally started to climb. The air was damp and the smell from the tannery began to hang in the air. Our teachers warned us to stay away from the ice on Irvine Lake, that it was getting uneven and dangerous in places. But none of us listened and we continued to go there every day after school. We knew that it would be a while yet before the ice was too thin to walk on.

Miss Skinner was teaching a lesson about perimeter. She had drawn a square, a rectangle, and a triangle on the blackboard. I looked over at Charlotte and noticed she was working on something inside her notebook. From the way she was shielding her paper, I knew she wasn't copying out the shapes on the board. Miss Skinner didn't seem to be aware that Charlotte wasn't paying attention. When the school bell rang, everyone except

Charlotte lined up for dismissal. She was still absorbed in her work. By the time she finished, the classroom had emptied and I had returned to my desk to wait for her. As she started to get up, she smiled and leaned over as if to whisper something to me, accidentally knocking over her books. Everything spilled onto the floor. I gasped when I looked down and saw a drawing of Miss Skinner. Her mouth was a zipper of pointed teeth, and writhing inside her belly were monsters, grotesque and evil. "It's Brush Fence," I whispered under my breath.

I suddenly became aware of Miss Skinner watching us. She rushed over, a suspicious look on her face. Charlotte quickly gathered her books and I picked up the drawing and shoved it inside my binder. "Charlotte," Miss Skinner demanded. "What was that on the floor? Give it to me this minute."

She rifled through Charlotte's books and found nothing. I was almost out the door when I heard her voice slice through the air. "Annie, come back here."

I stood next to Charlotte by her desk. "Give me that piece of paper," Miss Skinner said. My arms were wrapped tight around my binder. I couldn't speak. Miss Skinner eyes glittered. "Give me your binder, Annie. Don't make me force it from you."

Surprising myself, Charlotte, and Miss Skinner, I shook my head. But she reached over and took the binder from my arms.

She found the drawing and stared at it. Her cheeks flushed. Charlotte and I exchanged a frightened glance. "How dare you," Miss Skinner said furiously to Charlotte. "This is filthy and disgusting." She started to tear the drawing into pieces.

"What are you doing?" Charlotte cried.

"What do you think I'm doing?" she said as she tore the picture into even smaller bits. Charlotte seemed helpless, her eyes welling up with tears.

At that moment it seemed that all the teachings from Confucius that my father had taught me – obeying, respecting, and listening to your teacher – vanished. "You bitch." The words were out before I realized what I had said. The three of us stopped and stared, each of us frozen in that moment. I started to shake uncontrollably. Miss Skinner grabbed me by the arm and marched us both to the principal's office. Charlotte and I were given the strap and I was suspended from school for a day. The principal gave me a letter for my parents.

We opened the front doors of the building and stepped outside. My hands were stinging, I was still trembling and close to tears. The air was cold and damp, everything looked grey and the trees were skeletal. The smell from the tannery was so strong I coughed. I didn't want to go home.

"Annie, whatever got into you?" Charlotte said.

"I . . . I don't know," I said, my throat swelling. "I don't know anything. Don't ask."

I started to cry. Charlotte put her arm around my shoulders and suggested we go back to her house, but I didn't want to talk to anyone. How could I tell Father what had happened, that I had shamed my family? I wanted to lie down on the ice at the lake and stare at the sky.

Charlotte and I stood on the shore of Irvine Lake and looked out at the flat, empty expanse of white. For most of the winter the snowy surface on the frozen lake had looked powdery, but today the ice seemed to glisten even though there was little sun. We dropped our books on the shore.

"Let's go out to the middle," I said. Charlotte followed me. We both lay down on our backs and gazed up, the wet seeping into our coats. I reached into the air. The soft grey blanket of clouds seemed so low, if I could only have stretched a little higher, I might have been able to pull it down and wrap it around me, covering myself from head to toe.

Underneath us the ice shifted. We both jumped up and I started carefully toward shore, slipping on the wet surface. I was almost at the edge of the lake when I noticed Charlotte had lagged behind. She was still out in the middle, spinning around and around, her arms flung out to the side. She reminded me of the picture of Barbara Ann Scott, caught in mid-pirouette, which still hung on the wall of Dooleys' Bakery. "Miss Skinner, you bitch," Charlotte cried.

I laughed. "C'mon, Charlotte, let's go." I started walking again, but a sense of foreboding suddenly crept over me. I turned and called out to Charlotte, telling her to hurry up. The ice moaned and heaved beneath my feet. I became paralyzed with panic as I imagined the water demons waking, angered by my disrespect and my disobedience. I could see them with their powerful, slithering arms smashing against the ice. I thought of my father in the river desperately searching for my brother. The demons rose up.

But it was not me they wanted. As I watched in horror, the ice splintered and Charlotte crashed through into the water, screaming. She grabbed frantically at chunks of ice. "Annie! Help!" I started to run toward her, but suddenly she was gone, pulled into the water by the demons below. I stood helpless, mute with shock, staring at the cracked and broken ice. There was nothing left, only a pool of still, dark water in the middle of the lake.

By the time Officer Grisham stopped the police cruiser in front of the Dragon Café, it was well past the restaurant supper hour. I was huddled against the front door of the car. My sobbing had subsided and I was quiet. I kept hearing Mrs. Heighington's moan of pain and seeing her face twisted with fear and panic when I arrived, hysterical at her door. She had called the police and run with me back to the lake. Mrs. Heighington had edged out on the broken ice, making me stay on shore. She had called Charlotte's name over and over. By the time the police had arrived, it had become clear that there was nothing to be done and eventually she allowed herself to be guided gently into the police car with me to go to the station. When Mr. Heighington arrived, she had collapsed in his arms. I was grateful that Officer Grisham was now quiet during the drive, that he left me alone and didn't try to comfort me.

The officer helped me out of the car. He held the restaurant door open and followed me into the dining room. My mother rushed around the lunch counter. Father and Mai-Yee looked up from wiping tables. As soon as they saw me with the policeman in his dark blue uniform their bodies stiffened and their eyes filled with alarm. It made no difference now to my family that he came to the restaurant every day and drank coffee at our counter. My brother ran out from the kitchen.

I saw the terror in my mother's face as she grabbed me by the shoulders. "Su-Jen, Su-Jen," she cried. "*Nay do mutah?* What have you done?" She put her arms around me; her body was trembling.

The dining room was still and empty. There were no customers. My father spoke to the policeman. "No trouble, *offee-sir*? Everything okay?"

"There has been a terrible accident," said Officer Grisham.

"Is Annie in trouble?" interrupted my brother.

Officer Grisham told them about Charlotte's drowning, that we had been playing after school on the ice. At one point his voice broke. I knew he had children of his own. He told me how lucky I was to be alive and touched me gently on the shoulder. Inside, my stomach was churning. In misery, I watched my father's Adam's apple move up and down as he listened. My mother stared up at the policeman, one arm still around me, I could feel her fingers through my winter coat.

"Thank you, thank you," my father said in a quivering voice, then added, "You wanna *gah-fyah*." Officer Grisham said no and shook my father's and then my brother's hand before leaving. Even in this moment of fear, my distressed father remembered to offer the policeman, a man in a position of power, a cup of coffee.

As soon as the policeman left, Lee-Kung explained in detail to my mother and Mai-Yee what had happened. The moment my mother understood that Charlotte had drowned, she gasped and started to whimper. She wrapped both arms around me and held me next to her. I could feel the beating of her heart. My mother released me and held me by my shoulders. The words spilled from her mouth. "*Eiyah!* What were you doing on the lake? You're lucky you're not dead like your poor friend. Su-Jen, you foolish girl! How could you do such a thing?"

"I didn't mean to," I cried. When she tried to draw me back into her arms, I pushed her away. "Leave me alone!" But my mother reached out for me again and led me upstairs.

We sat down together on the bed and she stroked my head. "Poor Charlotte," she murmured. "Her poor mother. Su-Jen, I could not bear to lose you." Her voice was soft and desperate. I leaned on her shoulder and cried as if my heart would break.

That night I lay in bed staring into the dark, seeing images of Charlotte plunging through the ice, of Mrs. Heighington calling for her daughter. I hated Miss Skinner for punishing us the way she did. I told myself that if it weren't for her, none of this would have happened. But deep down I knew that wasn't true, that it was my fault. I was the one who wanted to go to the lake and I was the one with the curse. If it weren't for me, Charlotte would still be alive. When I finally drifted off, my sleep was fitful.

The next morning my eyes were heavy and swollen and I pulled the covers up over my head. My mother didn't say anything when she saw that I wasn't getting ready for school. I eventually went downstairs. My brother had made a sweet dumpling soup for me, but I couldn't eat it. Mai-Yee looked uncertain, then held my hand in hers.

In the dining room, my father was filling the china coffee creamers. I went and stood beside him. The letter from the school principal was folded up and stuffed inside the pocket of my pants. I thought of not telling him about my suspension, I could just rip the letter into pieces and throw it down the toilet. But I couldn't bear the thought of any more lies between us. I took out the letter and told him what had happened. My father's face filled with pain and disappointment. I had brought shame to my family. He said that I had to write to Miss Skinner, asking for her forgiveness, that I must in the future always listen to and obey those who were older and wiser. When I started to cry again, he patted my back and told me that if I did those things I would regain face. He told me not to tell my mother about the suspension.

When my mother came into the dining room my father said that I would spend the day at home and return to school tomorrow. She agreed.

Everything inside me was bruised and tender, nothing felt real. I spent the day trying to do chores in the restaurant, but it was impossible. Impossible not to see Charlotte falling through the ice, calling to me as I stood safely near the shore. Impossible to stop thinking over and over that I had done nothing to save her.

The next morning I willed myself to get ready for school, watching the time so that I would arrive just as the bell rang. As we filed through the school doors, I trailed behind, not wanting to face anyone. Jonette and Darlene saw me and stopped to talk to me outside our classroom, but I kept my eyes lowered and barely muttered a reply before retreating to the safety of my desk. All day the class was quiet in a way that it had never been before. For once Miss Skinner didn't have to tell us to stop talking.

In the afternoon the principal came to our door and asked me to step into the hall. I could feel everyone's eyes following me as I left the room. He told me how sorry he was about Charlotte, that he knew we had been best friends, and that he had spoken to all the students at a special assembly about the accident the day before. It wasn't until he told me that the police had used some equipment from Toronto to search the lake and had found Charlotte's body that I started to cry. He said he wanted me to know first before he gave the news to the rest of the school.

At the end of the day, Miss Skinner asked me to stay behind after class. Her mouth remained thin and pinched, but her eyes were red and she had difficulty speaking when she told me how sorry she was. I had to look at the floor as she spoke; when she finished I said nothing and simply left the room to go home.

I remember very little of the details of Charlotte's funeral, but the experience was so painful that pieces of it remain with me to this day. Her death seemed to have cast a darkness over the town.

The chapel had been full, with many people standing at the back, everyone's faces heavy with grief.

Some students from the school came with their parents. My parents had not come, and no one would have expected them to be there. I was grateful when Mrs. Dooley asked me to sit with her and Jonette. I don't recall speaking to anyone, although I know I must have, nor what Reverend MacDougall said during the service. I only remember keeping my head bowed, trying to breathe through the tightness in my throat. That and the expression on Mrs. Heighington's face when, after the service, she reached for her husband's arm and they walked out of the chapel with Charlotte's grandmother and her younger brothers.

A few days later I was sitting at the back table after supper doing my best to concentrate on my homework when I looked up and saw Mrs. Heighington standing in the doorway, a wet umbrella in her hand. She came over to me and sat down. My father brought over a cup of coffee, set it in front of her, and said, "Everything, too bad." Mrs. Heighington struggled to keep her face composed and nodded. She then turned to me and smiled sadly.

"I'm sorry I couldn't come sooner, Annie. But there is something I'd like to give you," she said, putting a book on the table. It was Charlotte's sketch pad. I reached out and ran my hand over the olive-green cover.

"Charlotte would want you to have it."

"Thank you," I said softly. At that moment my mother came into the dining room, the buttons of her sweater barely closing over her round belly. She walked over to us. She and Mrs. Heighington reached out and clasped each other's hands.

I found it hard to go anywhere, buy anything at Reids' or Sniders' without feeling Charlotte's shadow. Even if people didn't say anything, I knew they were thinking about her when they saw me. Everyone in town was used to seeing us together. They had cleared her desk away from the room at school, yet some mornings when I arrived I still expected to see her in the next row.

Several weeks after the funeral, Jean MacDougall and her mother came into the restaurant to invite me to a spring potluck and cookout at their home. It seemed that the minister wanted to bring everyone together. I explained to my mother what they said and she encouraged me to accept the invitation.

Many families from town came to the potluck, including the Dooleys and the Atkinsons. I looked for the Heighingtons, but I didn't see them there. I was the only child without parents, the town stray.

Reverend MacDougall had set up lawn chairs in the backyard, and placed some stones in a ring for a campfire. We gathered around the warmth, feeling the cold on our backs. Mrs. MacDougall had buttered and wrapped whole potatoes in layers of tinfoil and placed them underneath the logs. Jean showed me how to thread a wiener on a stick for roasting. When her father added prunings from his bushes, the fire roared and I found myself mesmerized by the dance of bright orange flames licking the night air. I looked around and saw everyone watching me. I knew I should be grateful for their kindness to me in these last weeks, but at that moment I didn't want their goodwill. What was wrong with me that I could not accept their generosity with an open heart? I didn't want to talk to anyone, have to answer their questions, or pretend that everything was fine. When people were busy filling their plates with food, I turned and slipped out of the backyard, unnoticed, and began to walk until some time later I found myself at the lake.

The light from the moon shimmered off the black surface of the water. I stood for a long while gazing out at the place where I thought Charlotte had disappeared and found myself wondering if a true friend would have left the ice without her.

When I finally made my way home, I found the restaurant was locked and remembered the early Sunday closing. Father was wiping the counter and I knocked to get his attention. I could see my mother at the back booth and Lee-Kung and Mai-Yee working at the draining board through the open kitchen door.

Father unlocked the door and spoke in a worried voice, "You are home very late. Look how dark it is."

My mother slid out from the booth. "Su-Jen, where have you been?" she called.

"I went to the lake," I mumbled, walking past her.

"*Ei-yah!* Are you mad? What were you doing there?" My mother sounded frightened.

"I don't know why you're worried," I said, turning to face her. "Nothing's going to happen to me now, the water demons have taken my friend. Don't you remember what you said, that the gods had overlooked me? Well, all your predictions have come true. You have nothing more to worry about now." My mother stared back at me, her eyes wide. Even I was struck by how cruel I sounded.

"I know, Su-Jen, how much it hurts losing your friend. But one day when you are a mother yourself, you will understand how a mother feels."

"Annie, you are a spoiled girl," my brother said from the kitchen doorway, "thinking only of yourself. You know how much your mother cares about you."

"You can say that?" I said, unable to hide the anger in my voice. "The only person she cares about is you." I looked at my mother. "Isn't that right? It's all about you and Lee-Kung!" By this time my voice had grown louder, until I was almost shouting. My mother looked stunned and reached out for the table to steady herself. I turned and saw my father glaring at me. All colour had drained from his face.

Mai-Yee looked from Lee-Kung to my mother in shock and dropped the pot she was scrubbing. "*Mo leung sum,*" she hissed at him. "You are heartless." The back door slammed behind her as she ran out into the yard. My brother looked at me for a second longer, then hurried after his wife.

"Su-Jen, many terrible things have happened," my father finally said, his voice steady but barely audible. "Go upstairs. Go rest. Come back down tomorrow." His face was like a mask, his eyes cold.

I had thought that things couldn't possibly be worse, and now they were. By confronting my mother out loud with what I knew I had betrayed her, but I now understood that I had betrayed my father as well.

I still remember Mai-Yee's angry voice through the walls that night, and the occasional low drone of my brother responding. All night I was aware of my mother in the bed, laboriously turning from one side to another. A pall of gloom settled over the household.

The next day at school I didn't want to be there, yet at the end of the afternoon I didn't want to go home. I dragged my feet all the way along Main Street. As I walked into the dining room, my father was perched on a stool behind the lunch counter reading the newspaper. He lifted his head, seeming to look past me, saying only my name. In the kitchen Lee-Kung and Mai-Yee were preparing for the supper business, their movements stiff and mechanical. My brother barely acknowledged me as I walked past, but Mai-Yee gave me a strained smile and asked if I felt hungry. In spite of her effort to smile, her eyes looked unhappy. Upstairs, my mother was sleeping.

That evening was like any other. We sat at the back table and had our supper. Although my mother's stomach was bulging, she seemed diminished. Her shoulders drooped and cheeks sagged. She asked me about school and I told her that the teacher had returned a math test from a few weeks before and had given me an A. Everyone seemed relieved with this news and my father again talked about the importance of education and hard work.

I looked at the dishes on the table and noticed that Lee-Kung had once again made my mother's favourite foods.

On the surface of things we were still the same family, carrying on as if nothing had happened. Below, there was a deep and painful wound. I might have thrown our secret into the open, but nothing had changed. We returned to living in silence.

ONE EVENING IN EARLY May, my mother asked me to go upstairs with her. She had something to tell me. By this time, she was swollen like a watermelon, walking in a laboured, feet-apart way. The vein that bulged and twisted up her shin had congealed just below her knee into a bluish mass that seemed to have a heartbeat of its own. I followed her up the long flight of wooden stairs, watching her shift the weight of her burden from one leg to the other.

She sat down heavily on the bed, gesturing to me to close the door and sit down beside her.

"Su-Jen, on Sunday, *Goh Goh* will take me to Toronto. I will stay there until after the baby is born."

"And then will you come back?"

"We haven't decided that yet."

"But this is where you live."

"Su-Jen, not everything has been decided. You will stay here and finish the school year. And when the summer starts you can come and visit."

I sat quietly, not knowing what to say. My mother gently stroked my hand. After a while I got up, telling her that I had to return some books to the library.

I left the restaurant, but didn't go to the library. Instead I walked around the block to the Heighingtons'. I hadn't seen Mrs. Heighington since the day she came to the restaurant. In spite of the cool night air, the shirt next to my skin was damp.

I saw the light in the kitchen and went around to the side door. The inside of the vestibule was still cluttered with tools and children's toys, and the air smelled familiar and sweet. I hesitated, then took a deep breath and knocked.

Mrs. Heighington opened the door. "Annie! What are you doing here?" she said and invited me in.

I opened my mouth to speak, but nothing came out. Mrs. Heighington put her arms around me and held me close. "Come now, come in and sit down," she said and I followed her into the kitchen, where we sat at the table. I thought she looked so alone in her kitchen with its clutter. I asked her where everyone was and she told me that the children and Grandma were asleep and that Mr. Heighington was at the Legion. Then without any warning I told her that my mother was going to Toronto, that she was going there to have her baby.

I knew from the expression on Mrs. Heighington's face that she had sensed, without knowing the details, that there was something wrong. But there was more, so much more I wanted to tell her.

"Charlotte shouldn't have died," I blurted. "It was always supposed to be me, I was the one who was supposed to drown."

Mrs. Heighington shook her head. "No, Annie, it was an accident. You are not to blame."

"But you don't understand," I said and told her about my book of fortune, about the water demons and what my mother had said about the gods.

Mrs. Heighington took a deep breath and looked at me closely. "Annie, you must listen to me," she said firmly. "There are no demons. If they exist, they exist only in your mind." She lowered her eyes and shook her head again. When she lifted her face, the pain in her eyes was raw. "Charlotte died because of a terrible accident. That is tragedy enough, without you taking this on."

Mrs. Heighington's words stopped me. Was my guilt nothing but selfishness? I left that evening thinking this and wondering whether it's possible to forgive ourselves for the things we do.

For most of the next day my mother remained upstairs. At lunch I took her some soup from the kitchen and in the evening she came down when I called her for supper. She spent her time packing her things or sleeping.

On her last night at the restaurant, I watched her slowly leave the table after supper and return upstairs to resume her preparations. Very little had been said during the meal, although Father asked several times if there was anything she needed. Lee-Kung ate more quickly than usual and left the table as soon as he could.

After supper Mai-Yee and I scraped and stacked the plates and bowls for washing. Several times she asked me if I was all right. Later I went upstairs to help my mother. She had finished packing the large leather suitcase from Hong Kong and was sitting on the bed with the porcelain figurines that Wendy and Rose Jenkins had given me. She held David in her hands, turning him over several times, before putting him down beside her. Next she picked up Venus. Gazing at the porcelain face, I noticed a sadness I had never seen before. "Wendy gave those to me," I said quietly.

"I thought so," she said. Still staring at Venus, she whispered to herself, "Who would want a woman with no arms?"

WHEN I ARRIVED IN this strange country, called *Gun-ah-dye*, China was far away; I spoke only Chinese and I had not met my father. Everything was new, yet I had felt no fear. Now Canada was my home, I spoke English, and my father, I deeply loved. I woke up the morning my mother would leave us and everything about my life felt uncertain, my heart aching and empty. For the first time, I was filled with fear.

Lee-Kung carried my mother's suitcase down the stairs and put it in the trunk of the car. We stood quietly in the alley and waited. My father turned to my mother and took her hand in his. Except for the accidental brushing of shoulders, it was the first time I had ever seen them touch. I looked at Mai-Yee, watching our family, her eyes large, biting the corner of her mouth. My mother nodded at her, then turned to me. We embraced each other, holding on for a long time. My brother held the car door open for my mother, and we stared after the car as it disappeared from sight.

I knew that after my brother drove down the alley, he would go along Main Street, past the school, and onto the two-lane road. In my mind's eye I imagined the water tower loom then disappear as they drove by. I could see farmers' fields ploughed into narrow dark furrows on either side of the road.

I wondered what they would say to each other on that long drive to Toronto. My mother was finally leaving Irvine, her wish had come true. When she used to fight with my father, it always seemed that if only she could leave the Dragon Café, leave Irvine, her life would be so much better, that only then might she have a chance at happiness. But when she had waved at me through the car window, the sadness in her face had felt like a stone in my heart.

There was an unusual sky that morning, bright metallic-grey clouds seemingly lit from behind. The air felt close and heavy with the possibility of a storm later in the day. We went inside the restaurant and unlocked the front door for business.

MY MOTHER'S ABSENCE DID not affect the operation of the restaurant. She had done little over the last few months and Mai-Yee had taken over many of her chores. Since Mai-Yee spoke some English, she was able to help with serving customers.

The temperature began to rise steadily. Plants started to poke through the soil and the trees bloomed with yellow-green flowers. One weekend toward the end of May I rode my bicycle to the cliff. It would be a long time before I would go there again, but for the rest of my life I would find comfort and solace in walking through woods. The air that day smelled of damp soil and decaying leaves from the previous autumn. The forest floor was carpeted with white trilliums. When I reached the cliff face, I lowered myself into the crevice and edged along to our cave, sitting finally on the ledge outside it, where I felt the warmth of the sun on my face.

Several nights before, Aunt Hai-Lan had phoned the restaurant while we were having supper. When my father returned to the table, he said to me, "Your mother has given birth to a son."

"I have a baby brother!" I said. I had wanted to ask about my mother, but then I saw my brother hesitate, his soup spoon over his bowl, the muscles in his face tense, as if waiting for more news.

My father didn't look at my brother right away. After a long moment he said, "Everything is fine."

Lee-Kung nodded, his relief visible.

Mai-Yee put down her chopsticks and turned to my father, then stiffly said, "*Lo Yah,* you must be happy to have a new son." I looked at my sister-in-law and no longer saw the same young woman who had stepped off the plane. There was a new tightness about her mouth and something about her that seemed older. Like everyone else in my family, Mai-Yee had learned *hek fuh,* how to swallow bitterness.

"A new family member is always cause for celebration," my father said. His voice had seemed quiet and tired, without joy.

Afterwards he told me that on Sunday the two of us would take the bus into Toronto to see my mother and the new baby. Lee-Kung and Mai-Yee would stay behind to manage the restaurant.

I gazed down now into the valley below me and watched the gentle movement of treetops. It was a beautiful day, and the woods were green and still, but I took no pleasure in any of it. I was overcome with sadness. Without Charlotte, I felt lost. The gods had taken my best friend, fulfilling a destiny meant for me. I sat for what felt like a long time listening to the sound of the wind and thought about all that had happened.

I left the ledge on the cliff and walked back along the trail to my bicycle. By the time I arrived at the Dragon Café, I had decided to tell my father that I wanted to spend the summer in Toronto with my mother and my baby brother.

AUNT HAI-LAN HAD ARRANGED an offering on an altar made from an orange crate. She had filled a brass urn with sticks of incense and thin red candles. Around the urn she had laid out a boiled chicken, a bowl filled with balls of rice, a plate of dyed-red eggs, and a dish filled with coins.

Father, Lee-Kung, and Mai-Yee arrived late that morning from Irvine. Today we were celebrating the baby's one-month hair-cutting ceremony. I had come on the bus after school on Friday afternoon. Father and I had already been to Toronto several times that month to see my mother and the baby, but for Lee-Kung and Mai-Yee this would be their first visit.

When I greeted them at the door, Lee-Kung nodded and Mai-Yee patted me on the arm. The strain on her face was visible. She appeared tired and pale. Father went into the living room to where my mother was sitting with the baby in her arms. My brother and his wife hovered for a moment at the entrance of the living room. Aunt Hai-Lan told them not to be so formal, to come in and see the baby. My father picked up the bundled child and held him up for Lee-Kung and Mai-Yee. "Look at your brother. My son is a handsome boy, isn't he?"

Lee-Kung pressed his lips together and nodded.

"Not so loud, not so loud," said Aunt Hai-Lan. "Don't let the ancestors hear you. I don't think he's all that good-looking, a little homely, I think." My mother glanced at me as she listened to Aunt Hai-Lan trying to fool the gods.

My father handed the baby to Mai-Yee. "Go ahead, go ahead." She held her arms out and took the baby, rocking him for a few moments, then Lee-Kung lifted the child from his wife and held him close, brushing his cheek against the baby's. As my mother reached out to take back her son, I saw her eyes meet Lee-Kung's. My mother looked away, but in that fleeting moment I saw the anguish in my brother's face. He sat by himself on the sofa and lit a cigarette. Mai-Yee immediately sat next to him. She seemed exhausted, leaning back into the cushions. My brother looked stiff, except for the constant jiggling of his knee.

The doorbell rang and Uncle Jong invited his two sons and their wives and children to come in. Everyone gathered in the living room and stood around Aunt Hai-Lan as she stooped in front of the altar and lit the sticks of incense and the candles. She then took my baby brother from my mother and sat down on a chair, one hand cupping his head. She picked up a pair of scissors and delicately snipped off a small lock of hair above his left ear. He was a month old and this first haircut made him an official member of the family. While Daniel slept, wrapped securely in his soft flannelette blanket, she invoked the spirits of the gods, asking them to ensure that his belly be always filled with rice, that his beauty be as perfect as an egg, and that his life be filled with riches.

When Aunt Hai-Lan finished, she placed him on my back and covered him with a red sling in the shape of a square, with four long straps that tied in a knot beneath my breasts. The borders of the sling were a patchwork of scraps from Aunt Hai-Lan's old dresses, but the red square, she told us, she had made from a length of fabric purchased on Spadina Avenue. She told me to walk three times around the room. The ceremony was complete. My mother untied the knot and Father stretched out his arms to receive the boy. With the sleeping child cradled against his chest, Father walked around the room and held him out for each person to admire. Then he stood in the middle of the room and took a deep breath as if he were preparing for a speech. First he looked at the baby and said, "You are Sek-Hong. This is your Chinese name. And your English name is Daniel, given to you by your sister." Next he turned and pointed to Lee-Kung. Speaking softly to the baby, he said, "This is your *goh goh,* elder brother. This is your *sawh,* brother's wife. This is your *dai dai,* older sister. This is your *yee hoo,* mother's auntie. This is your *yee hoo chang,* mother's auntie's husband. This is your *mah mah*. And I am your *ba ba*." He spoke proudly and with a tenderness that I hadn't expected.

Aunt Hai-Lan raised her voice and called out, "Lai-Jing, put the baby to bed. It's time to eat." She told her grandsons to bring extra chairs into the kitchen. Aunt Hai-Lan had been up since early in the morning, preparing food. On the table now were dishes of chopped white chicken, plump glistening scallops fried with greens and mushrooms, a whole fish steamed with ginger and scallions, and more. But most important were the two soups made especially for my mother: a chicken whisky soup with dried truffles and a pig's feet vinegar soup with peanuts, the first to heal the womb, the second to promote a mother's milk.

Aunt Hai-Lan said what a happy occasion this was for my parents, but the next time we celebrated a birth in the family it should be for Mai-Yee and Lee-Kung. "We will all have to wait and see," replied Mai-Yee.

"Don't worry," said Aunt Hai-Lan. "I will pray for you at church and make an offering to the ancestors." Uncle Jong looked at his sons and laughed.

"But now we should celebrate the birth of this child," said my father. He looked at me. "You and Daniel are lucky. You will be real Canadians. You will go to university, have good jobs. Not like my generation. We knew only hard work."

"Well, you should think about moving to the city," said Uncle Jong. "You're getting too old to work in that restaurant. Buy a house with all the money you have in the bank. You're collecting old-age pension. It's time to take it easy." Uncle Jong turned to

Lee-Kung, "Leave all the hard work for you, eh Kung? You and Mai-Yee should be able to manage."

For a moment no one said anything. "Uncle Jong is right," Lee-Kung finally said. "Mai-Yee and I can operate the restaurant ourselves and if we have to we can hire some part-time help. *Ba,* it's time for you to retire, and spend days in the park with your new son." For the first time in weeks Mai-Yee seemed to relax.

"Maybe," said my father with a slight smile and a glance at Mai-Yee. "We will all have to wait and see."

I looked at my mother to see her reaction, but her face revealed nothing, was empty of expression.

After lunch I followed my mother up the stairs to the room that we shared. We stood beside the crib and watched my sleeping brother. My mother bent over and smoothed his hair. As Daniel began to stir, she picked him up and passed him to me. My brother blinked and looked up at me. I smiled at his funny baby sounds and let him clutch my fingers. I kissed his cheek and felt his warm sweet breath against my face. My mother sat down on a chair and extended her arms toward us. She took Daniel from me and pushed up one side of her blouse to reveal a swollen breast. My baby brother started making suckling sounds with his lips, then clamped his mouth tightly around the dark nipple. I watched my brother curled in my mother's arms and I began to understand how much she loved us and how much she had sacrificed when she arrived in Canada; what she meant when she claimed that her life had been over the moment she stepped off the plane. For my mother the act of living here was in itself an act of love, my mother had given up her own life out of love for me and would do the same for Daniel.

I thought about the spirits of our older brothers, and silently asked them to watch over us.

❧

MY PAST HAS BECOME a distant place. I sometimes choose to go there, turning the pages of a young girl's book of drawings or the pages of the books my mother brought with her from China. But the journeys are usually unexpected. The smell of burning leaves, a particular line from a poem, a certain look about a girl on a streetcar . . . I feel a vague twinge in my heart and once again I am back in Irvine. I am twelve years old. I am with my friend Charlotte on the ice in the middle of the lake under a bright winter sky. We are sliding, falling and laughing. The air is crisp and cold, the ice underneath is thick. We are safe.

ACKNOWLEDGEMENTS

Over the course of writing this book, many people have been most generous in their support.

I would like to give special thanks to my agent, Denise Bukowski, for taking the manuscript under her wing, and to my editors: Ellen Seligman for her nurturing insights that have brought this book to fruition; Dawn Sefarian at Counterpoint Press in New York; Jennifer Lambert, whom I think has grown to love the characters in the novel as much as I; and Heather Sangster for her delicate copy edit.

Last but not least, I would like to thank my family, whose faith has never wavered in this long endeavour.

I would also like to acknowledge the financial assistance of the Toronto Arts Council, the Ontario Arts Council, and the Canada Council.

AVON FREE PUBLIC LIBRARY
3 2529 10066 1529